# UNFORGOTTEN

## Books by Shelley Shepard Gray

### A SEASON IN PINECRAFT

*Her Heart's Desire*

*Her Only Wish*

*Her Secret Hope*

*Unforgiven*

*Unforgotten*

# UNFORGOTTEN

## SHELLEY
## SHEPARD GRAY

Revell

a division of Baker Publishing Group
Grand Rapids, Michigan

Published by Revell
a division of Baker Publishing Group
Grand Rapids, Michigan
RevellBooks.com

Printed in the United States of America

Library of Congress Cataloging-in-Publication Data
Names: Gray, Shelley Shepard, author.
Title: Unforgotten / Shelley Shepard Gray.
Description: Grand Rapids, Michigan : Revell, a division of Baker Publishing
    Group, 2024.
Identifiers: LCCN 2024014222 | ISBN 9780800746032 (paperback) | ISBN
    9780800746506 (cloth) | ISBN 9781493447190 (ebook)
Subjects: LCSH: Amish—Fiction. | LCGFT: Christian fiction. | Novels.
Classification: LCC PS3607.R3966 U55 2024 | DDC 813/.6—dc23/eng/20240408
LC record available at https://lccn.loc.gov/2024014222

Scripture quotations are from the *Holy Bible*, New Living Translation. Copyright © 1996, 2004, 2015 by Tyndale House Foundation. Used by permission of Tyndale House Publishers, Carol Stream, Illinois 60188. All rights reserved.

This book is a work of fiction. Names, characters, places, and incidents are the product of the author's imagination or are used fictitiously. Any resemblance to actual events, locales, or persons, living or dead, is coincidental.

Cover image of woman by Abigail Miles / Arcangel
Cover design by Laura Klynstra

The Author is represented by The Seymour Agency.

Baker Publishing Group publications use paper produced from sustainable forestry practices and postconsumer waste whenever possible.

24  25  26  27  28  29  30      7  6  5  4  3  2  1

For Lesley,
who not only lights up every room
but also my heart.

Lesley, here's a Kentucky book for you.

Though they stumble, they will never fall,
for the LORD holds them by the hand.

*Psalm 37:24*


Find some good in everyone.
Perhaps everyone will find some good in you too.

*Amish proverb*

# 1

## July

**W**onders never ceased. Bethanne Hostetler had seen a lot of things and had even experienced some pretty good surprises. That said, the scene playing out in front of her was like nothing she'd ever imagined.

For sure and for certain.

Right there, up on the fairground amphitheater's stage, stood her cousin Candace. Her dark blond hair hung in curls down her back and shone in the sunlight. Eyeliner and mascara accentuated her hazel eyes, and tinted gloss stained her lips, making her naturally lovely face even more beautiful. As the crowd clapped, Candace stood as still as a department store mannequin, her scoop-necked, emerald-green satin gown hugging her hips before flowing softly around her legs. The toe of one of her silver, high-heeled sandals peeked out whenever a faint breeze caught the dress's hem.

All in all, Candace looked nothing like the little girl who used to follow Bethanne around during holiday get-togethers years ago.

Honestly, some folks might even say that Candace Evans

was the complete opposite of her Amish cousin Bethanne Hostetler.

They might be right too.

"Ladies and gentlemen, let's give these ladies one final round of applause while they exit the stage," the announcer called out on his microphone. "But don't y'all go anywhere. We'll announce this year's Miss Crittenden County in just a few minutes!"

Applause and cheers rang out from all around. In response, all seven women on the stage moved to stand side by side. They held hands and smiled.

Every one of them was pretty and graceful. There was no doubt about that. But as Bethanne gazed at each one, she couldn't help but think that not a one could hold a candle to Candace. Not only was she gorgeous, she was as sweet as spun sugar.

When Candace caught her eye, Bethanne waved and smiled. Her brother, Lott, whistled from his place next to her. Candace's beaming smile widened.

"What do you think her chances are?" Lott asked when the applause started to die down.

Bethanne shrugged. "About as good as anyone else's, I reckon."

He frowned. "Really?"

As the girls exited the stage in preparation for the judge's final vote, Bethanne faced him. "Lott, you know this is the first beauty pageant I've ever been to. I'm still trying to wrap my head around the fact that my English cousin is up on the fairground's stage wearing makeup and high heels. How would I know about her chances?"

"True. Candace sure is pretty, though."

"Jah." Bethanne smiled, though a part of her felt a pinch of melancholy. Once, she, too, had found comfort in the gifts the Lord had given her. Even though her brown hair and matching eyes weren't as eye-catching as her cousin's, she'd always thought they suited her well enough. Now she believed her pleasing appearance hadn't served her very well.

Then again, maybe what had happened seven years ago had more to do with her actions than her appearance. One impulsive decision on her part had changed her life. Everyone might still say she was a victim, but Bethanne refused to believe that anymore.

Hating the dark thoughts that now threatened her happy mood, she rubbed the back of her neck. *Stay in the moment*, she reminded herself. *Stay right here, right now.*

Unfortunately, her counselor's words didn't do the trick. She sighed.

Lott noticed. "Do you have a headache again?"

"Nee, I'm just a little stiff," she fibbed. "I guess I've been sitting for too long."

"Jah. Me too." He glanced around for a few moments. "Hey, are you going to stay here for a little while?"

"Probably. At least until the winner's announced. Why?"

"No reason."

She knew better than that. "Lott."

"Fine. Melonie is here, and I wanted to walk around with her for a bit. You're welcome to join us, of course."

Bethanne smiled. Lott and his fiancée were a good match. He'd really changed his ways so Melonie Zimmerman—and her family—would allow their courtship. Now both families were waiting for them to decide on a wedding day.

Bethanne loved her brother and was very fond of Mel. But did that mean she wanted to walk around the fairgrounds with them, feeling like the third wheel? No. No, she did not. "Go ahead. I'll be fine."

"You sure?" He scanned the crowd again. "Mamm and Daed are around here somewhere. I thought they were going to sit with Candace's parents, but I don't know . . ."

"I'm sure they're around, but I don't need anyone to look after me. I'm fine." Of course, she wasn't exactly fine. She was currently on the verge of another panic attack. In spite of her best intentions, her smile trembled, betraying her emotions.

Holding her gaze, he sighed. "Bethy."

"I'm fine. Really. I was thinking about something else." She hated that her younger brother felt obligated to look after her. She also hated that until recently she would've clung to him like a parasitic vine. One day she was going to act like his older sister again. "Go. I'll see you later."

He didn't move. "You know what? I can take Melonie out—"

"Right now," she finished, her voice firm. Then seeing Melonie walking up the center aisle toward them, she shooed him with her hands. "There she is. Go. We can meet up later."

Lott followed her gaze and waved at Melonie, then turned back to Bethanne. "Do you need me to accompany you home?"

"Nee. It's not a long walk. I'll be fine."

"You sure?"

"More than sure."

Her brother grinned. "I'll see you later, then. Don't forget to tell Candy congratulations for me."

She laughed as he started toward Melonie. "If she wins, I sure will, but I won't be calling her Candy. She hates that nickname."

Feeling like an odd combination of wallflower and doting aunt, Bethanne watched her brother rush to Melonie. He

10

touched his fiancée's hand but refrained from clasping it. Within a minute they were out of sight.

Sitting back down on her chair, Bethanne placed her purse neatly on her lap. If it wouldn't look so odd, she would pull out her book. She always carried one with her, whether it was for pleasure or for her job as a reviewer for a local publishing company. Reading had been a favorite pastime for her, especially after what happened with Peter Miller and Seth.

Then about six months ago, she'd decided that some things about her life needed to change. She had to stop worrying about the past and start thinking about what she wanted to do with the rest of her life. She was only twenty-three. It was past time she got over Peter's death. And the fact that he'd attempted to rape her. And what happened to Seth Zimmerman when he came to her rescue. Why the Lord had allowed Seth to hit Peter hard enough for Peter to fall, hit his head, and die was a mystery. But it had happened, and she'd survived.

Like always, guilt slammed her. If she hadn't been so weak afterward, she would've convinced her parents to allow her to testify on Seth's behalf. She'd witnessed the fight, after all. But she hadn't done a thing to plead for mercy for Seth. So he'd spent two years in prison while she descended into a very dark place.

"If Seth Zimmerman can move forward, you certainly can too," she whispered to herself for not the first time. "You have to." Which meant that she needed to stop dwelling on bad memories. Her counselor had told her more than once that she needed to make peace with the past instead of trying to forget everything that had happened.

"Hey, Bethanne."

As Bethanne looked up, Jay Byler sat down—right next to her. "I thought it was you."

Her whole body tensed even though Peter's best friend had never done anything to harm her. "Why are you sitting here?" she hissed.

He had the nerve to look incredulous. "Do you mean I should be doing something other than waiting to see who's crowned this year's Miss Crittenden County?"

"Come on. You don't care about such things."

"How would you know what I care about? It isn't as if you've given me more than a few minutes of your time these last few years."

Even though his words were true, they still hurt. Everything about Jay made her hurt. Though tempted to stay silent, she wasn't able to. "You know why."

"Of course I know." His voice softened. "But even though I know the reason you ignore me, it doesn't mean it's okay. It hurts."

She shifted uncomfortably and looked away. His tone didn't confirm whether he was being sincere or sarcastic.

"After all, we were once friends."

Were they? She couldn't remember much about their interactions beyond the obvious—that he'd been best friends with Peter and she'd almost been Peter's girlfriend.

Hating that the dark memories threatened to overwhelm her again, she glared at him. "I don't want to talk about you and me. Or our past. Ever."

"Fine. Let's talk about the beauty pageant." He glanced at the mostly empty stage. "I know you're rooting for your cousin, but who else do you think has a chance?"

Jay was as Amish as she was. Yet, here he was, wearing a straw hat over his light brown hair, blue trousers, and a short-sleeved white shirt, acting like he cared one whit about such things. "Why are you so interested? Are you hoping to take one of the girls out?"

"Of course not."

"Then?"

He pulled at the collar of his shirt. "You know putting me on the spot isn't fair." He exhaled. "Why is everything so difficult between us?"

"Because it is."

"That's not a reason."

"Jay, please."

"Nee. Bethanne, I've been trying to talk to you for a year. Longer even." Frustration filled his tone. "But . . . every time I do, you run away like I've got the plague."

"I've hardly been that bad."

"Close, though." Gentling his tone, he said, "Bethanne, please. I just want to be your friend again."

"Why?"

His blue eyes blinked. "Why?"

"Jah. Why do you want to be my friend so badly? Why do you keep trying?" She stared at him, silently willing Jay to speak the truth. To give her something to use as ammunition against him. She needed it so she wouldn't continue to think about how charming he was.

"Because you're worth it."

Her pulse seemed to slow. "Worth what?"

"Everything."

*Everything?* She wanted to fume. To remind herself that she did not want to have anything to do with Jay. But her traitorous body disagreed. A flutter stirred deep inside her, but instead of being scary, it felt warm. Soothing. What did that even mean? In spite of her efforts to remain impervious, her guard fell.

And then, there she was, staring at him. No, gazing into his eyes.

A tiny look of triumph appeared in their depths. "See?" he whispered. "I'm not so—"

"Ladies and gentlemen, the judges have come to a decision!" the announcer called out. "Everyone, get on your feet and welcome these beautiful ladies back on stage!"

Bethanne stood, never so happy for the roar of a crowd.

# 2

Only by sheer force of will did Jay remain where he stood while Bethanne scooted down the aisle of chairs. What he wanted to do was follow her. Maybe press his hand on the small of her back so both she— and anyone around—would know that she was taken. Then he'd stand out of the way while she raced up the metal stairs to the stage to congratulate her cousin.

That was what he *wanted* to do. The reality was that Bethanne would probably slap his face or scream if he put his hand on her without permission. So Jay stayed where he was and watched from a distance.

Candace Evans now had a white satin banner arranged over her gown and a rhinestone tiara sitting on top of her head. She was fetching, there was no denying that. And she looked like the beauty queen she now was.

But he only had eyes for Bethanne.

She stood off to the side of the stage, looking as perfect as she always did. Her skin was smooth and creamy, a touch of pink colored her cheeks, and her dark hair was neatly arranged under a white kapp. Even her light blue dress was spotless, which was a minor miracle considering the dirt, grass, and gravel on the fairground.

But that was Bethanne, at least by his estimation. She'd always managed to seem serene and in control of herself and her surroundings. Most people had thought she always did the right thing. And she did. Until the time she'd agreed to take a walk in the woods with Peter. Jay knew that better than most, he reckoned.

Peter Miller, his best friend growing up, had always been smitten with her. When they were young, Peter would tease and joke around with Bethanne, doing the most outlandish things just to make her smile or laugh. He'd once told Jay that he liked pushing Bethanne out of her comfort zone. Jay hadn't liked that but didn't say anything. Maybe he should've.

After they'd all graduated eighth grade and begun apprenticing or working, Bethanne started showing interest in Peter. He ate it up but never officially made her his girlfriend, even after they turned sixteen. He'd liked the idea of stringing her along.

Watching all that play out hurt. Jay had hoped to eventually court her but then was forced to keep his distance on account of Peter's interest. But he'd known, deep in his heart, that Peter was no good for Bethanne.

Worse, he'd been pretty sure that Peter wasn't good for any girl. His friend had developed a wild streak, though Jay had thought the worst things Peter could do were drinking, smoking, and driving illegally.

He'd been wrong. And when the unthinkable happened, Jay could barely handle the guilt.

"Ain't it something?" the woman behind him called out over the roar of the crowd, bringing him back to the present. "That girl is from right here in Marion. Candace is one of our own!"

Jay swallowed. "Jah. It's something indeed."

When Candace finished a brief speech, he joined in the clapping as the audience headed for the center aisle. He barely had time to watch Bethanne hug her cousin before he had to follow the others in his aisle to leave.

"Never pictured you to be a fan of beauty pageants, Jay."

Jay looked up as he came face-to-face with Walker Burkholder and his wife at the center aisle. With a grin, his boss clapped him on the back.

"I'm not," Jay said. "Not really."

"You just ended up here, then?" Walker's eyes danced with mirth as he grinned. "Not that I blame ya, of course. Nothing wrong with wanting to look at a pretty girl—or seven." He chuckled at his own joke.

That wasn't his reason at all. "I, uh, just wanted to sit with a friend for a while. It's pretty warm out." Except she wasn't a friend, and she hadn't wanted to sit with him.

Something eased in Walker's expression. "Yeah, that is true."

Jay followed them. "What about you? Why are you here?"

"One of the contestants was one of Michelle's students. She wanted to cheer her on." Chuckling again, he added, "And where Michelle goes, I go."

"I knew you were a smart man."

"Of course I am. I hired you, didn't I?"

"I'd say that was a sign of your brilliance, but we both know I didn't give you much of a choice in the matter," he joked. "I begged and pleaded."

"And since then, you've proven yourself to be outstanding. That's what's gotten you your promotions, Jay."

"Yes, sir. I'm thankful."

Walker met his gaze. "Sam treating you all right?"

"Yes, sir."

Walker was the president of Burke Lumber, one of the biggest sawmills and lumber manufacturers in the county. He was as honest as they came and had been good to Jay from the day he'd signed on to work in the mill. But his new manager? Jay didn't have the same esteem for him.

"Walker, are you ready to head to the arena?" Michelle said over her shoulder, now ahead of them. "The boys are about to show their calves."

"Sure thing. I was just catching up with Jay here." Walker clapped Jay on the back again. "He's a good man. He's going to go far at Burke Lumber. I'm sure of it."

Michelle stopped and turned around. "Well, I sure hope you don't spare one more thought about work, Jay. Enjoy the fair and don't forget to go on some of the rides on the midway tonight." She winked as they said goodbye and walked off.

Just in the nick of time too. The last thing he wanted to think about was going on the Ferris wheel alone. Or with anyone other than Bethanne Hostetler.

That wasn't going to happen, though. Not when she despised him.

"Jay, there you are!" his brother Tommy called out, hurrying toward him as he left the amphitheater. "I've been looking for you everywhere."

Tommy had been his parents' surprise baby. Twelve years younger than Jay, he was twelve, had red hair and freckles, and was built like their father's grandfather. Tall for his age, he would've been a great football player if he was English. As it was, he was a good farmhand and one of Jay's best friends.

Jay stepped into pace beside him. "You found me now. What's going on?"

"I'm starving. Want to get something to eat?"

"I could eat. What are you hungry for?" He grinned. The kid was always hungry.

"There's a food truck with tacos."

"Sounds good. Let's go."

The food trucks were off to the side, just before the carnival games and the tent housing all the food and handcraft contest entries. "What have you been doing?"

"Hanging out with the guys."

"Where are they?"

"Able had to go home with his family, and Cade and Zack are hanging out with girls."

Tommy's disparaging tone made Jay chuckle. "You didn't want to hang out with the girls too?"

"Nah. I'm not ready for that. Guess what they're making Cade and Zack do?"

"No idea."

"Pet the baby animals." He grunted. "Like Zack don't have a ton of them on his own farm."

Jay knew that didn't matter. "Sorry, but I'm afraid that kind of thing goes with the territory. Girls like baby animals. Most folks do, come to think of it."

"Whatev. Cade's only doing it because he thinks Mary might kiss him."

"Whoa." Jay looked at him.

Tommy shook his head. "Right?"

"How old is Cade?"

"Thirteen, but he has three older brothers." He lowered his voice. "He knows things."

Good grief. "Ah. That explains it."

"I guess." Tommy kicked a plastic bottle cap that someone had thrown on the ground.

Jay picked it up and tossed it in the nearest trash can.

"Don't be too hard on your buddies. You'll be hanging out with all the pretty girls before you know it."

Tommy shrugged. "Maybe not."

"What does that mean?"

"It means that maybe I'll be like you."

"Still not following, Tom."

"Well . . . I know you don't chase anyone."

"I'm a little old to be chasing women, kid. Besides, it's not good manners. Ladies don't take kindly to being chased."

"You know what I mean." He waved a hand. "Mamm said you're a late bloomer."

Jay's feet slowed to a stop. "Our mother said what?"

"Don't get mad at me. I'm just repeating her words."

"She shouldn't have said that."

"Why? Is it a lie?"

Jay turned to his brother. "Mamm doesn't lie."

"So you're the one who's lying?"

"I am not."

"Something can't be true and false at the same time, Jay."

"It can." How had he even gotten involved in this conversation?

"I don't understand why you're acting upset anyway. Mamm wasn't being mean. And it's not like you've ever had a girlfriend."

"What is that supposed to mean?"

"Pretty much what it sounded like." Tommy folded his arms over his chest. "Have you had a sweetheart before?"

"A sweetheart?"

Ignoring him, Tommy continued. "Was she a secret?" Looking intrigued, he added, "Do you have a secret love life that no one knows about?"

"Where do you come up with such things?"

"You still haven't answered me, bruder."

"I don't intend to. My personal life is none of your business."

"I guess not. But it sure don't seem like it's anyone else's either." He laughed at his own joke before moving toward the food trucks again.

Luckily, it was also before Jay could admit that Tommy might be right. One of these days, he was going to find a way to get Bethanne to finally trust him. He didn't know how, and he didn't know when, but he was going to do it.

And when that happened, everything in his life would be good. No. Fantastic.

Wunderbar.

# 3

Candace's skin began to crawl. Too many eyes focused on her and too many people stood too close. Before long, someone would try to touch her arm or her hair. Or worse, attempt to hug her. She hated that. She really disliked when people—especially ones she didn't know—touched her without permission. Why hadn't she thought more about that when she'd filled out the paperwork?

Feeling her anxiety spike, she pinched the bit of skin between her right thumb and forefinger and counted to five. Concentrating on that made the rest of the world fade away, if only for a couple of seconds. But that was better than nothing.

"You've got this," she whispered to herself. Remembering some of the advice Bethanne had shared with her, she continued, "You are safe and in control of your body." Exhaling in a slow and steady way, she imagined she could feel her heartbeat return to normal.

And . . . maybe it had. Feeling a little bit better, she lifted her chin. It seemed that Bethanne's counselor really did know what she was talking about.

The day was almost over. Just another two or three hours to go. All she had to do was stand still and pretend her feet didn't hurt and that sweat wasn't dripping down her back.

"Candace!"

Her mind registered her sweet cousin's approach just in time. When Bethanne hugged her close, Candace was able to wrap her arms around her. She was even able to inhale the faint scent of Ivory soap on Bethanne's skin.

"You must feel like the luckiest girl in the world," Bethanne said, smiling as they released each other. "Or at least the prettiest."

Only hours of practicing in front of the mirror enabled Candace to keep smiling. She knew her cousin's words came from her heart, and they really were very sweet. Everything about Bethanne was kind and sincere.

It was just too bad that, in this case, Bethanne was completely wrong. Candace didn't feel lucky or pretty. All she really felt was relief, and maybe a little bit sick to her stomach.

Because she'd won, now she would have to do a year's worth of appearances and participate in the Miss Kentucky pageant. All while watching everything she ate, exercising as much as possible, and telling her parents how grateful she was for the money they spent on her dresses, shoes, highlights for her hair, and acrylic nails.

And somehow hoping that the creepy stranger who'd started sending notes to her social media pages would stop. And by now he wasn't exactly a stranger anymore; she didn't know him, but now she recognized him on sight. Until he started appearing—online and in person—she'd never seen him in her life.

The problem was that she didn't know how to get rid of him.

"I'm feeling very blessed," she said instead of any of that. "Thank you for being here."

"I wouldn't have wanted to be anywhere else," Bethanne said. "You know, I didn't think I would find this beauty pageant stuff all that interesting, but I was wrong. I liked all the parts of it, and especially your speech about the importance of children's literacy. That's so very important."

Her cousin's expression and tone were so sincere that tears started to form in Candace's eyes. She blinked. "You really are the best, Bethy."

"Hardly that." Visibly pushing some of her usual apprehension away, Bethanne added, "Would you like to maybe get a Coke or something? My treat."

"You know what? I—"

"Candace, what's keeping you?" Her mother's sharp question startled her. "Oh. Hello, Bethanne."

"Hiya, Aunt Dora," Bethanne said softly. "It's gut to see ya."

After giving Bethanne a quick hug, Candace's mother scanned Bethanne's blue dress, bare ankles, and black tennis shoes before meeting her eyes. "It's lovely to see you too, dear, but I have to admit that I'm surprised you're here."

"I couldn't not be here." Smiling at Candace, Bethanne added, "I wanted to cheer my cousin on."

"That's sweet of you, honey. Even more importantly, I'm glad you're getting out more often. I'm proud of you."

"Me too."

"Before we know it, you'll be back to your old self."

Bethanne averted her eyes, leaving Candace feeling both embarrassed and frustrated. She loved her mother and knew she meant well, but sometimes she mentioned things that didn't need to be mentioned. "Sorry," she mouthed to Bethanne.

Her cousin's cheeks pinked, signifying that she'd read her lips. Loud and clear. In response, Bethanne shrugged, but then, like always, she kept most of her thoughts to herself and was perfectly proper. "How are you, Aunt Dora?" she asked. "I trust you and Uncle Wayne are well."

"We're fine. We're busy as ever. I'm sure your parents feel the same. I am so glad to see you. Tell your parents hello for me. Also, tell your mamm that I'll give her a call soon to make plans for your father's big birthday party."

"Mamm will be grateful for the help. Somehow the guest list keeps getting bigger and bigger," she joked.

Her mother chuckled. "They always do. Well, like I said, tell her that I'll reach out in a day or two. Not only can we plan, but we'll catch up on everything. I miss my sister."

A genuine smile appeared on Bethanne's face. "Jah, I'll do that. Mamm misses you too."

"Thank you, sweetie." She enfolded Bethanne in one more quick hug. "Now, I don't want to be rude, but I'm afraid your cousin has a great many things to do right now."

"Like what?" Candace asked.

"Candy, what's between your ears? Don't you remember that the newspaper is waiting to interview the new Miss Crittenden County?"

She had forgotten. She'd also secretly hoped the reporter had changed his mind about interviewing the new Miss Crittenden County. "I'm sorry, Mom. I'll speak to them now."

"Don't forget to talk about your platform."

"About children's literacy?"

"Yes, and how you want to offer support for victims of violence?"

That was also something she was passionate about. She just hadn't wanted to mention it in front of Bethanne. "I won't forget."

Bethanne had taken a couple of steps away. Not wanting her to ever feel unimportant, Candace closed the distance and reached for her hand. "Bethy, I'd love to see you another day. Maybe we can plan something?"

Bethanne's brown eyes warmed. "Sure. If you'd like that."

"I would—very much."

After squeezing her cousin's hand again, she walked to a long rectangular table set up at the back of the pavilion. Barry Winter, the local reporter who was almost as old as her grandparents, was smiling at her. She smiled back. Mr. Winter was at a lot of their high school's music and athletic events. Everyone knew him. "Hi, Mr. Winter."

"Hi, Candy. Congratulations. Ready to get to our interview?"

"Yes, sir. But I go by Candace."

"Oh. I'll put that in the paper, then. But I thought everyone calls you Candy."

"No, sir. Only my mother. And I only put up with it when I have to. She knows that I prefer Candace."

Mr. Winter raised his eyebrows but nodded. "Understood. Well, now. Let's sit down over here. I even wiped off that dusty chair so it wouldn't dirty your gown."

"That was kind of you," she said as she sat down across from him.

"I raised four daughters. I know all about how important it is for a gal to keep the back of her dress clean."

She giggled. "I bet you do know all about keeping teen-aged girls happy."

"I'd reckon so."

Finally relaxing, Candace sat down. As they began their interview, she thanked him for his congratulations, spoke about how honored she was, and discussed her interest in children's literacy and the many hours she'd volunteered in both the elementary school and the library.

Mr. Winter scanned his notes. "It says here that you've also done some volunteer work for a women's shelter."

"Yes, but not with the victims. I've mainly done some things behind the scenes, like collected garments and such for them or helped address envelopes for a fundraiser."

"That's something to be proud about. I'm sure the judges were impressed with your service."

That made her uncomfortable. She hadn't done any of her volunteer work in order to impress people. "I don't know if they were or they weren't. But both causes are important to me. Everyone needs to learn to read, and I was glad to help out at the shelter. The women there have been through a lot."

"Do you know someone who's been a victim?"

"I think everyone probably does," she sidestepped.

Mr. Winter's easy demeanor turned serious. "Oh yes. Your Amish cousin was assaulted several years ago, if I remember right."

"She was. But that isn't the only reason this cause is important to me."

"No doubt. But I'm sure what happened was hard for you."

Not liking how the reporter was intertwining Bethanne's experience with her pageant win, she gave him a fierce look. "She was the one who was assaulted, not me."

"Oh. Of course."

She was tempted to ask him not to write anything about Bethanne in the article but figured mentioning such a thing would only put her cousin's experience even more on his radar. Not that he would consider the old story something of use for the paper. Besides, they hadn't mentioned any names. Even if he did include what had happened years ago, he couldn't say too much.

As the conversation continued, he switched directions, asking about her dress and where she planned to keep her crown for the next year. Candace answered each question with a bright smile and friendly tone. She figured she probably sounded a little bit ditsy, but that was to be expected, she reckoned. She'd learned early on that people might say they were interested in what she had to say but most folks judged her on her looks.

Finally, Mr. Winter looked up from his notepad. "I think I have everything I need now, dear." He stood up. "Enjoy your crown."

"Thank you so much." Just as Candace was about to stand up too, a prickling sensation spread across the back of her neck. She froze for a moment. Then she looked to her right and left. Searching for an escape route. A place to escape the prying eyes.

Until she remembered that her fear was what he wanted. Gathering her courage and reminding herself that she was in a public place and that he couldn't do anything to her with so many people around—she looked behind her.

And there he was. The man who she'd first started seeing about six months ago but who now seemed to appear in her life more often.

Today he looked almost normal. He wore a T-shirt, jeans, tennis shoes, and a University of Kentucky baseball cap. His light blue eyes seemed to take in every bit of her as he stared intently. For the first time all day, she was aware of how much of her arms and shoulders were exposed. How much of her skin was visible above the neckline of her gown.

When their eyes met, he came closer. Only a few feet. Moving with the crowd around him. He was nothing if not brazen. It had served him well too. He could blend in with anyone and had a knack for looking completely different each time she spied him. One time he was in a suit, another time almost looking Plain. Today's outfit made him a carbon copy of half the men at the fair. The only thing that ever stayed the same were his blue eyes and dark hair.

She knew those eyes well because they leered at her. He always smirked too. The one time she'd tried to report him, the officer had acted like she was a vain woman looking for attention. He'd said something awful about how pretty girls never like to give regular guys the time of day. Then he'd gone and reminded her that nothing had actually happened.

When she'd left the police station that day, she'd felt almost worse than when she'd walked in the door. Chief Foster had been kind but agreed with the other officer that there was nothing they could do for her. Not until the man actually threatened her or attacked her.

So now she was waiting for him to do that.

Afraid that he'd follow her if she left, Candace stayed where she was. She wasn't going to shrink in front of him, though. Looking him in the eye, she silently conveyed her distaste for everything he was.

He moved with the crowd again, this time stopping only two feet from her. "Hello, Candace Evans. You look good with your hair like that. I like it."

She forced herself to respond. "What are you doing here?"

"What do you think?" He smirked as he folded his arms across his chest. "I'm doing the same thing half the county is . . . looking at all the sights."

How could his seemingly innocent words create such a chill inside her? Changing her mind about staying put, she got to her feet.

"Don't go yet," he blurted.

His voice had squeaked. It took her by surprise. It was only then that she looked more closely at his face. He had soft skin, barely the beginnings of a beard. He was a lot younger than she'd imagined.

When he raised his hand, presumably to touch her, she moved out of reach. "Don't," she said in a hard voice.

"Don't what?" He looked almost smug. "What are you going to do? Scream?"

"I could."

"Sure you could." He scoffed. "That would make your mother real happy, wouldn't it? Making a scene with a crown on the top of your head."

She gritted her teeth.

"Just think of me as another one of your fans."

"You are not."

"I know that. I'm special." He lowered his voice. "I promise, all I'm doing is admiring the new Miss Crittenden County. You look so nice in that dress." He inhaled. "And you smell so good."

Her heart rate skyrocketed, and she stepped back farther.

"How does it feel, Candace?"

She felt trapped. She wanted to flee, but there were too many people standing around. If she ran off, everyone would think she was being rude. Or putting on airs. That she was stuck up and too full of herself for her own good. Her parents would be so mad, and the director of the pageant would be upset with her too. "H-how does what feel?"

"Having so many people think you're pretty? Do you need that? Do you need to feel like everyone is watching you? Wanting you?"

A handful of emotions surged through her. Distaste for his words, embarrassment that anyone would think that about her . . . even regret for entering the pageant for scholarship

30

money. "Of course not," she bit out. Hoping that her voice was stronger than she currently felt.

He took a step closer. "Why did you think you needed a crown, anyway? Was I not giving you enough attention?"

"You need to leave."

His eyes widened. "Not until I tell you my big news: I moved."

"You moved?" A slither of hope ran through her. Was her nightmare really about to end?

He grinned. "I did. Now we're practically neighbors."

"No."

"Don't worry, I won't interfere when you're busy being famous. I'll just see you other times."

Her hands began to tremble. She fisted them at her sides. "You can't do that."

"Don't worry, Candy. I'm not going to meddle with your life. I'll stay out of your way." He chuckled and turned to walk away. "Why, I bet sometimes you won't even know I'm there."

The lump that had formed in her throat had somehow moved down to her chest. No, that was her chest aching because at some point she'd stopped breathing. She pressed her hand to it and forced air into her lungs.

He disappeared into the moving crowd. She sat back down and clasped her shaking hands together. Hating that he'd known exactly what to say to put her even more on edge.

She needed to get away from him. But how? At least move out of the county. Maybe even out of the state.

Except that couldn't happen anytime in the next year. Not when she was Miss Crittenden County. Making up her mind, she decided to visit the police station again. Maybe this time they'd take her seriously.

# 4

A box waited on the front porch, just a foot or so from the door, when Bethanne arrived home. Nearby, Lott and Melonie slowly rocked back and forth on matching chairs while snapping beans into stainless steel bowls.

Well, Melonie was. Lott was eating grapes—when he wasn't gazing at her with puppy-dog eyes. The two of them looked like an advertisement for positive relationships.

Or maybe like a beautiful couple on the cover of a romance novel. Their obvious devotion to each other would encourage the most cynical reader to believe that one day she, too, could enjoy such moments of domestic bliss. Bethanne had sure read enough of those books to recognize that.

The sight of them was bittersweet for Bethanne. For a time, she'd been sure Peter would be so devoted. She'd even fooled herself into imagining that one day he would declare his love for her.

That wasn't even the worst of her childish fantasies. She'd dreamed that he would propose early because he didn't want another man to ever think that he had a chance with her. Then, after a year-long engagement, they'd have a big, joyous wedding and settle down into married life with ease. She'd gone to sleep at night wondering how many children they'd have.

The silly, girlish thoughts now embarrassed her. She pushed them away with effort as she climbed the steps. "Hi, you two."

Melonie paused her snapping and smiled at her. "Hiya, Bethy."

"Home already?" Lott asked.

"It was fun but so hot." She stopped by the box. "I might go back tomorrow and look at the food tents. I thought y'all would still be there."

"It's my fault." Melonie lifted a bare foot. "I stepped on a piece of glass."

"Oh no. Are you badly hurt?"

"Only my pride. Lott warned me not to wear flip-flops."

"Several times," he added.

Melonie rolled her eyes. "See what I mean?"

Bethanne smiled. "Lott, perhaps it's not the best time to remind Melonie about your warnings."

He shrugged. "It's not my fault that I was right."

"Bethanne, your brother's unbearable. Help me!"

"Gladly. Bruder, perhaps I should remind you that Melonie was not the only woman who wore flip-flops at the fair. Lots of girls wore them!"

Looking triumphant, Melonie turned to him. "See, Lott? It's too hot to wear tennis shoes."

He huffed. "You aren't helping, Bethy."

Softening her voice, Bethanne returned her gaze to Melonie. "I am sorry about your foot, though. Did you have to get stitches?"

"Jah." Melonie smiled. "I'm thanking the good Lord for the volunteers who were able to drive us to urgent care."

"The doctor did a fine job with the stitches," Lott added.

"He would know, since he held my other hand the entire time." Looking dreamy, she added, "Lott even carried me to the volunteer's car!"

Bethanne reckoned that had been quite the romantic sight. Lott with his muscular build and intense expression, and Melonie blond and delicate-looking in her tangerine-colored dress. "Sounds very heroic." And, dare she say, a little bit over the top?

"She was hurting," he explained. "After she got on her way, I got my bike and met her there."

Looking at Lott fondly, Melonie added, "He even stayed by my side when I got a tetanus shot. It hurt something awful."

"She's supposed to stay off her foot for a couple of days, so I took her home on my bike."

Lott had an electric bike. Two people sharing it wasn't safe, though. "I hope Mamm and Daed don't find out about that."

"I'm more worried about Seth finding out. But I sure wasn't going to let her walk home."

Melonie nodded. "Even though my brother has Tabitha to worry about, Seth still tries to watch my every move." Nibbling on her bottom lip, she added, "He's going to have something to say when he discovers that I got hurt."

"Sounds like a brother. I wouldn't worry about him getting upset with you, though. It was just an accident, plus Seth is even-tempered and kind."

"He is at that."

Lott gestured to the third rocking chair. "You want to join us?"

"Thank you, but I'm in need of a shower and a break from the heat." Bethanne looked down at the box still resting near the door. "Do you know if these are my manuscripts?"

"They sure are," he said. "Paul stopped by about twenty minutes ago. He said there's a note inside for you."

"Danke."

"Are those all for you to review?" Melonie asked.

"Yep. It's become a good job. I read them, write my honest reviews, then type them out on the computer at the library and send them to the book publisher."

"I still can't believe you get paid for doing your favorite hobby."

Sometimes Bethanne couldn't believe it either. "It does seem too good to be true. But the checks still come."

"I'm right proud of ya, Bethy." Lott looked at Melonie. "I happened to see the note that was in with her last paycheck. Her boss said she's a terrific reviewer."

Melonie grinned. "Good for you!"

"He was only being nice. And Lott shouldn't have read the note. It was personal."

"Not that personal. I'm glad I read it, anyway. If I hadn't, no one would ever know how good you are at your job. All you ever tell Mamm, Daed, and me is that you're thankful for the work."

"I am thankful. But you're embarrassing me."

He peered up at her. "There's nothing wrong with being good at something, Bethy."

"I have to agree with him," Melonie said. "Pride might be a fault, but ignoring one's gifts can be a fault too."

Tired of discussing herself, Bethanne squatted down to pick up the box. "I think it's time I got busy. I'd hate to lose my job after garnering all this praise."

Lott stood. "That box has to be heavy. I'll get it for you."

Glad to have her brawny brother carry the box upstairs to her room, she happily straightened and moved to the side. "See you later, Mel."

Melonie again stopped snapping beans. "Hey, want to have lunch or go for a walk sometime next week?"

"Sure." Thinking quickly, she said, "How about Tuesday or Wednesday?"

"That works for me. Let's do lunch on Wednesday. Say eleven?"

"That's perfect. See you then."

Lott grunted. "May I carry this heavy box upstairs now or would you like to make more plans for your social calendar?"

"Oh, hush. Come on before you collapse in pain," she teased.

"They're heavier than they look."

"I appreciate your muscles."

"Hmph." In her room, he faced her. "Where do you want this?"

"Anywhere is fine."

"Nee, tell me, Bethy. Once I put them down, I'm not going to want to pick them back up and you aren't either."

"Fine." She pointed to her desk. "On top of my desk. I'll unpack them there." When he clunked the box down with a loud sigh, she smiled. "Danke, Lott."

"Anytime." He headed for the door but then stopped. "Bethanne?"

"Jah?"

"I . . . I'm real proud of you."

"For what? Reviewing books?"

"To be sure, but I meant for the way you made plans with Melonie just now. You've come a long way."

He was right. Six months ago, she wouldn't have been able to do that. The Lord had really been working with her, she realized. He'd not only opened her eyes but her heart as well. She was slowly accepting more people into her circle and didn't get nearly as frightened as she used to when she was outside the house.

Pleased that he'd noticed, she smiled. "Danke. It feels good. For the longest time, even walking out of this room took a lot of effort."

"You're healing. The Lord hasn't forgotten you and neither have I."

"Danke," she whispered.

He stepped into the hallway before popping his head back into her room. "Hey, I almost forgot. Did Candace win?"

"She did. Our cousin is now Miss Crittenden County."

He whistled low. "Wonders never cease."

"I agree. I think she deserves it, though."

"Jah. It's good to see something nice happen to a good person."

Her brother headed for the stairs, and once again, Bethanne was alone. Surrounded by books and all her favorite things. For so many years, she'd viewed this room as her safe place. Sometimes, it had felt like her only safe place. Thinking back to those awful months surrounding Peter's death and Seth Zimmerman's trial, she shivered.

One time, she'd gotten herself into such a state that her father had taken off the lock on her door. He and her mother had been so afraid that she would harm herself and the lock would prevent them from helping her. She hadn't been thinking about harming herself, though. No, all she'd wanted was to have complete control over her surroundings. She'd twisted things up in her mind, sure that someone was going to come in while she slept.

Eventually, her fears had eased and she'd begun to feel relatively safe in the house. Lott and their parents had been so relieved about that, they had coddled and catered to her. And she'd let them do it. For years.

Now, she realized that both her family and the Lord had given her grace. They'd accepted her as she was and given her time to heal. Eventually, she took back responsibility over her life and started feeling like she could be in charge of who she saw, who she interacted with, and what she did with her time.

It hadn't been easy. She'd had setbacks. Lots of them. But she did the best she could. No matter who had tried to get her to change—the bishop, her parents, the counselor—she'd fought against it. Only after watching Tabitha and Seth Zimmerman overcome their obstacles did she decide that she needed to start leaving the house. Now, she was even able to make future plans with a friend instead of determining what she was capable of each morning.

After picking up a pair of scissors, Bethanne deftly sliced through the seal, opened the flaps, and stared down at the collection of manuscripts packed neatly inside. Out of habit, she looked at the first two and checked to see if any of the authors were ones she'd read before.

But instead of choosing one to begin, she set them back inside. She didn't feel like diving in. Not yet. Curling up in her window seat, she looked outside and thought about Lott and Melonie on the porch.

And then, against her will, she thought about Jay Byler. And realized that she didn't dislike him as much as she used to. Of course, maybe she'd never actually disliked him at all. He'd just reminded her of things she'd preferred not to think about.

That had been a foolish endeavor, for sure and for certain.

"Some things—or maybe some people—are simply unforgettable," she mused. Like the way Jay seemed to stare at her so intently that he could read her mind.

Imagining such a thing, Bethanne almost smiled.

But then she realized that there were many, many things that were unforgettable. Some of which didn't just catch her imagination, they gripped her nightmares. Some nights the images appeared again, playing over and over. Holding her captive.

She wrapped her arms around herself and tried to push back a current of dread and darkness. But it was too late. All the memories had returned. She felt chilled again. Before she could help herself, she walked to her door and closed it tight.

Just for peace of mind.

# 5

Mondays were becoming more and more difficult to take. Sitting in the air-conditioned conference room that was a degree too low for comfort, Jay tried to act as if neither the company's newest line manager's words about safety and productivity nor the frigid temperature bothered him. Revealing his true feelings about either would only get more attention focused on him.

Which, with Sam Kropf, was never a good idea. The man might have been a handful of years older than Jay, but he was also difficult and far less mature. In Jay's opinion, at least.

Sam seemed to view everyone at the sawmill—with the exception of Mr. Burkholder—as competition for his job. He had no problem using his new promotion and managerial duties to his benefit. He also seemed to enjoy making the rest of the workers look bad. Even worse, he used his position to make other people miserable.

Just last week, he'd given Andrew three late-night shifts in a row and then followed them up with a fourth shift early in the morning. Even though that wasn't supposed to be allowed.

When poor Andrew had shown up on the fourth day sluggish and bitter, Sam had used the guy, in a leadership meeting, as an example of some of the staff not working hard. Of course, no one in the room believed Sam. Most everyone knew about Andrew's schedule too.

Except, perhaps, Mr. Burkholder.

Jay allowed his mind to drift as Sam continued to read from the sheet of paper that they all had in front of them. Since it was all about safety protocols that had been put into place years ago, he had no need to pay too much attention.

Instead, he thought about Bethanne and their conversation two days ago. No, it hadn't gone all that well. But at least they'd talked. That was a step in the right direction. Their brief exchange had given him the strength he'd needed to still have hope for a future with Bethy. Despite everything, he wanted the honor of calling her his wife one day.

Sure, it was a pipe dream. As far as he knew, Bethanne hadn't allowed any man to get near her in the last seven years. She barely spoke to men, let alone permitted one to come courting.

But there was always a first time, right?

"What do you think, Jay?" Sam asked loudly.

Feeling the man's almost triumphant gaze settle on him, Jay looked at him. "I'm sorry, could you repeat the question?"

Sam folded his arms over his chest like Jay's inattention was costing the company thousands of dollars. "Why do you need it repeated? Were you not paying attention?"

This was exactly why Sam was not a good manager. He took pride in belittling other people in order to make himself feel more important.

For his part, Jay was proud that he didn't tell Sam that he thought he was boring and long-winded. "I need to have your question repeated because I do."

There was a collective inhale from the table. Sam looked like he was fighting with himself. After a few strained seconds—which felt like minutes—he nodded. "I asked what you thought about the new regulations from the state regarding the machinery."

"I think they make sense and I'll do my best to follow them."

"Your best?" He raised his eyebrows.

"Everyone's best is good enough, ain't so?" Virgil asked. "After all, if someone needs help, all they have to do is ask and help will be given. That's how we've always worked." Virgil was the eldest in the room, and everyone respected him. Even Mr. Burkholder paid attention to what he had to say.

"Yes, of course," Sam said quickly. Color brightened his cheeks as he visibly fought to gain an aura of authority again. "Everyone, please follow the new regulations as best you can."

The rest of the meeting was smooth sailing. Jay did his best to pay attention and listen, which meant pushing his thoughts and worries about Bethanne to one side.

As they walked out, Virgil clapped him on the shoulder. "You all right, then?"

"Jah. Thank you for speaking up for me."

"I didn't mind. But you shouldn't let Sam get to ya. It only makes things worse." He winked. "He'll needle you just like anyone else."

"I know. And as much as it pains me to admit it, Sam was right to call me out. I wasn't paying as close attention as I should have been."

Virgil's expression filled with a new respect. That was the kind of man he was. He admired a person who wasn't afraid to be vulnerable or admit his faults. "Everything all right with your family?"

"Jah. Everyone's gut. I . . . well, I was thinking about something personal."

Understanding filled his expression. "Maybe it has to do with a certain brown-eyed girl?"

"Is it that noticeable?" he asked as they stopped.

"Only to someone who's been around for a spell." He rocked back on his heels. "Care to listen to some advice?"

"From you? Always."

"I know you're a patient man, and that's to be commended. But sometimes a person needs a nudge in the right direction."

A little bit of his hope faded. Virgil's judgment was usually spot-on, but in this case, Jay knew his advice was misguided. The last thing Bethanne needed was to be pushed or prodded into doing something she wasn't ready for. Especially if that push was toward another relationship.

"I hear ya," he said. It wasn't a fib, but it also didn't reveal what he was thinking.

"I'm serious, boy. Sometimes one's desire to be safe interferes with one's desire to be happy. If I've learned anything over the years, it's that feeling safe can also bring a sense of false comfort."

"And maybe even false happiness," Jay whispered.

Looking glad that Jay was at last on the same page, Virgil said, "When my Rachel was eight, she had to get her tonsils out. The doctor said there was no choice in the matter, she had been plagued by sore throats and infections too often. But everyone told Emma and me that her recovery would be hard."

Continuing the story, he waved a hand in the air. "As you probably know, healing from that operation can be painful. Because of that, we were prepared." Chuckling softly, he added, "Emma had more bottles of pain relievers and ice packs than all six of us in the house would ever need!"

"I bet," Jay said with a smile.

"Now listen to this, son. To our surprise, three days after surgery, that little girl was eating ice cream and was all smiles. She hardly complained at all. When Emma asked Rachel how it was possible that she wasn't in terrible pain, my eight-year-old said that her throat had hurt so constantly for so long she had thought everyone's throat felt like that. Her post-surgery pain wasn't any worse than what she was used to."

"So one can learn to accept hurt as something normal."

"Jah. Your girl might have forgotten what it's like to go through life without a heavy heart. But that can change. Love can open doors, jah?"

"Jah," he whispered back. "Danke, Virgil. That was gut advice."

"You're welcome. And keep your chin up here. Sam will settle in. He has to sooner or later."

"I hope so." Somehow, Jay had a feeling that it might be easier to earn Bethanne's love than Sam's respect.

He sure knew which one he was more desperate to have.

# 6

It was embarrassing to admit, but Candace hadn't really thought about what her life would be like as the new Miss Crittenden County. Now that she was almost two weeks in, she was starting to wish that she'd thought a whole lot more about what her duties would entail.

Not that she would've done anything differently. When her mother had suggested she participate, Candace thought it might be a good idea. She'd always liked doing good works and volunteering in the community. In addition, the scholarship money would help pay for some additional college courses. Of course, she'd also wanted to make her mother happy. Oh, it wasn't like her mom had raised her to think that she had to be a winner or pretty or even particularly talented—she wasn't like that. But her mom would've been disappointed if she hadn't given it a try.

Now, though, Candace decided that it didn't really matter what everyone else wanted her to do. She was the one wearing a dress, heels, a tiara, and a sash across her chest. She was the one smiling at a bunch of strangers in ninety-degree heat during the Thursday afternoon ribbon-cutting ceremony for a new auto parts store.

Her feet hurt, sweat was trickling down her back, and some kid had just smeared mustard on the skirt of her dress. Today was almost a carbon copy of the event she'd done two days ago, except that was a mattress store, and a little girl with chocolate on her face had stained her pink lace dress.

The only other difference was this time she was accompanied by Ryan Mulaney, Marion's newest police officer. She'd tried to pretend that she hadn't noticed him when he appeared at the store's entrance, but he was hard to miss. Tall and muscular, with black hair, brown eyes, and a strong jaw, he looked like he'd probably played basketball or football—or both—in school. He strode to her side. "You doing okay there, Candace?"

She couldn't get enough of his northern accent. Rumor had it he was from Connecticut and had moved down to Kentucky because he wanted a change of pace. A slower life. All she knew was that he was gorgeous. "Of course," she said at last. It wasn't exactly the truth, but he didn't need to know that.

Still looking at her with concern, he said slowly, "I'm not sure if you're aware of what my job is today."

"Obviously you're here to help with the grand opening."

Still studying her intently, Ryan shook his head. "Well, I'll help here if I'm needed, though I think we can be honest that there's not many people here to look at new hubcaps or car wash kits. Most everyone is here to see you."

She blushed. She didn't want to display false modesty, but his blunt statement seemed a bit over the top. "Maybe."

"I'm going to be spending the day with you. You're going to the hospital next, yeah?"

She nodded. "And after that, I'll be visiting a nursing home out in Tolu."

He scowled. "I have no idea why they booked you to all

three places in one day, each one forty-five minutes from the other."

She fought a smile. "Well, the 'they' who booked my schedule would be me. And the reason I did it is because I have some things to get done before August."

"Ah."

She appreciated that he didn't give her a hard time. "Thanks for saying hello, but don't worry about me. I'll be fine."

"I didn't come over here to check on you." After a brief pause, he added, "Candace, I wanted to let you know that I'd like to drive you today."

"Why?" Even she knew that the police department didn't have officers to spare for such piddly things.

"You being Miss Crittenden County isn't reason enough?"

"No."

Almost smiling, he said, "To be honest, there are two other reasons I'm coming with you."

"What are they?"

"You're the perfect reason for me to meet more people around here. You know, make connections? If I'm with you, our citizens' first impression of me isn't going to be associated with trouble."

"I guess that makes sense. What's the other?"

"Your recent visit to the police station. The chief thinks my being with you might deter this guy as well."

Relief filled her. They were taking her worries seriously at last.

"Not everyone is too keen on getting friendly with a northerner cop," he added.

Chuck Stark, the owner of the new store, waved as he approached. "Candace, we've got a number of people here to see you. Are you ready to sign some photos and pose for pictures?"

"Yes, sir."

Chuck looked at Ryan. "I didn't recognize you out of uniform. Then I noticed the badge clipped to your belt. You're our new officer, right?"

"Yes, sir." He held out a hand. "Ryan Mulaney."

"Heard you're from up north."

"Connecticut."

"And you're here for the opening?"

"Yes, but I'm here for Candace too."

When Chuck's eyebrows raised, Candace said, "Officer Mulaney very kindly offered to give me a hand. I have three events in different parts of the county today."

Chuck whistled low. "That's a lot of territory."

"By the time I finish, it'll be dark," Candace said.

And just like that, Chuck's expression eased. "Good thinking. No telling what could happen to a young woman on the road by herself."

A chill went through her.

Until Ryan lightly pressed a hand to the middle of her back. "Are you ready to meet everyone?" he asked in a low tone.

Pure relief filled her, which kind of didn't make sense. How could a man she'd just met create such a feeling of security?

Just as quickly, she tamped down her silly thoughts. Of course, she would feel that way about him. He was a cop, and she had a stalker. She was feeling vulnerable, even though she seemed to be the only person in the state who felt she had a right to be.

"Candace?"

"Sorry." She flashed her best smile at him. "I am."

For the next two hours she smiled with little girls, signed glossy photos, and talked about her dress, her shoes, and the tiara on her head. Then, to her dismay—and Ryan's amusement—Chuck asked her to pose for pictures holding spark plugs and car wax. Luckily for her, Ryan had asked her about the time of the next event, factored in time for the drive and a lunch break, and then told Chuck that she was going to need to leave.

When they got to his SUV, he helped her into the passenger seat, stowed her bag in the back, and then headed for the hospital.

It felt almost like a date except it wasn't. Candace didn't know Ryan, he didn't know her, and it seemed they were both benefiting from each other's standing in the community. Or it could be that she had simply grown suspicious thanks to her stalker's presence in her life.

As he sped down the highway, she figured they might as well make conversation. "So, how long have you been in town?"

"Three weeks."

"What do you think of southwestern Kentucky?"

"It's different than what I expected, but I like it."

"Really?" Even though she hadn't been too many other places, she loved her small town and wanted other people to love it too. Even a cop from a big city on the East Coast.

He chuckled. "Yeah, really."

"Well, in that case, I'm glad. It's nice to have another officer on the police force."

"Why do you say that?"

His attention was pointed. Like he was looking for a specific answer. She realized that he had no idea about what had happened with Peter Miller. The right thing to do would be to tell him about it. He was from the big city. Women got assaulted all the time—or at least the news sure made it sound like they were. But here in their area, it had been shocking.

It still was.

But did she want to be the person who relayed it to him? No way. It was too difficult to speak about. Every time she thought about how it had affected her cousin, she wanted to cry.

Selfishly, she realized that she was glad Ryan probably didn't know about what happened to Bethanne. It was kind of nice being around someone who wasn't asking her about the "real" story of what happened. Around Ryan, it was almost as if it had never happened.

Which would be a blessing.

Sure, keeping him in the dark was wrong, but he'd find out about Bethanne before long and connect the dots to her.

That's why she gave the reply that she did. She shrugged and said, "It just is."

Ryan didn't back off. "Sorry, but no one says something like that without a reason."

Not only had his attention sharpened, but his accent became more pronounced. It was disconcerting and reminded her that he wasn't just an attractive man who was offering her a ride. Wariness consumed her. She inhaled and stayed silent. Half waiting for him to pressure her.

When he spoke again, his voice was slow and measured. "You don't have to tell me a thing, but I'm just saying that it's obvious to me that there was a reason you said that."

"You're right," she said at last. "It's personal, though. So I'm going to take you at your word and not talk about it anymore."

"You're serious."

"Deadly," she said.

Sure, that sounded over the top and a bit dramatic, but she couldn't deny her feelings.

Right then and there she realized just how guarded she'd

become. She didn't protect herself the way Bethanne did, but she had built her own walls.

Focusing on the two-lane road, Ryan didn't speak for several moments. Amid the passing trees and hilly, vacant farmland, they'd been the only ones on the road for miles. So much so that when a commercial truck sped past, the sound was jarring.

"Candace Evans, I'm beginning to think you are far more than just a pretty face."

She smiled. "Thank you." He'd never know it, but that was one of the sweetest compliments she'd ever received.

# 7

How's it going, son?" Ryan's dad asked. "You ready to come home yet?"

Leaning against his kitchen counter, nursing his third cup of coffee of the morning, Ryan stifled a laugh.

When he'd decided to take the job with the Marion police, Ryan had every intention of renting a place for a year. Just to be sure the move had been the right decision. This two-bedroom, one-bath Craftsman with a huge front porch had changed his mind. The price had been a refreshing change from the prices back home too. Before long, he was touring it with a real estate agent, falling in love with the small backyard lined with an ancient black iron fence, and dreaming of one day coming home to a wife waiting for him on the front porch. Next thing he knew, he was putting 20 percent down and filling out change of address cards.

None of it was like him. It was shocking, really. His big family still acted like he'd lost his mind.

"I'm good here, Dad."

"Come on. Kentucky can't actually be agreeing with you."

"It *actually* is. You need to come out and see this place for yourself." Frowning at the empty room, he added, "I mean, as soon as I buy some furniture."

"You should've rented a place," he chided. "That's what you said you were going to do."

"I like this house, Dad." After walking to the set of windows that faced his backyard, he grinned at the pair of rabbits sleeping in the middle of the lawn. He'd never been a fan of rabbits until now. "Mom would've liked it too."

"Your mother would've liked anything you liked." He grunted. "But she would've agreed with me. If you're not getting fresh fish from the bay, you're missing out. There's no fresh seafood in Kentucky, son."

"It's got rivers and lakes, Dad."

"Hmph."

"How's everything been going for you?" His father was semiretired and took vacationers out fishing a couple of days a week.

"Good. Going well enough to support my needs. Fish are biting."

"And the tours? Everyone treating you good?"

He cackled. "Well enough there too. Son, stop fussing and worrying."

"I can't help it, Dad. You're on your own."

"I've got two of your nosy brothers and a sister within driving distance. They'll stop by if I call them."

"You know you won't."

"They've got families to tend to. Besides, Wallace and Jeanie have been coming over. I'm not on my own all that much."

His father's neighbors were good people, but friends and neighbors were just that. They weren't family, which meant that neither Wallace nor his wife were going to lose any sleep if Jack Mulaney wasn't seen on a walk for a couple of days. "Why don't you plan on coming down to visit?" Mentally calculating his paychecks, he said, "Maybe at Thanksgiving? I'll have a couch by then."

"I've got a couch here, son."

"The weather's good too. Folks have told me that I won't have to worry about a jacket until October."

"Ryan, you aren't going to be needin' me to wander around on the streets while you're out working. Next thing we know, I'll be picked up for jaywalking and mistaken for a vagrant."

He laughed. "First of all, no one's going to be taking you down to the police station for that. Secondly, I would be the one who picks you up, and I'll let you cross the street wherever you want."

"There's that, I suppose."

"You could try out some of the local fishing holes. We could have supper together."

"I like being home, Ryan. Your mother's things are all right here. You have to understand that."

"I do."

"Good. Now are you sure you can't share anything good with me? You don't have any good stories?"

Like always, his dad enjoyed hearing about his days. He used to light up whenever Ryan was involved in a particularly difficult case. "The only job out of the ordinary is that I've been escorting the current Miss Crittenden County to her various events around the area."

As Ryan hoped, his father chuckled. "Good for you. I bet she's a sweet young thing."

"She is. Emphasis on sweet too. She's a nice girl."

"Does she have a man?"

"A boyfriend? I don't think so. We haven't got that far in our conversations."

"You ought to do that, son. It's time."

During the same six-month span, Ryan's mother had died of cancer and Chloe Anderson, his on-again-off-again girlfriend of three years, had broken up with him for good. Ever since then, he'd been in a fog. He knew it wasn't just because Chloe had ended things, though the breakup had hurt. The fog wasn't even because of his mother dying. She'd been fighting cancer for several years and had overcome a lot of obstacles, living a full two years longer than anticipated. But those two things, along with being passed up for a promotion, had made him eager for a change. He'd certainly gotten that here in Marion.

"I know, Dad. When I meet the right woman, I'll know."

"Maybe, though you might not know if it's the right one at first," he said in a soft tone. "You might even wonder if that person is the wrong one."

Ryan chuckled. "Until she proves you wrong?"

"Or your heart gets involved. That's what happened with your mother and me."

All six of the kids in the family knew the story of their parents' romance well. "Dad, you two were college sweethearts."

"Not at first. At first, she was my French tutor."

Loving the new, warm thread that crept into his father's voice, Ryan felt the knot between his shoulders ease. "I don't remember you telling me that, Dad."

"Yeah. Foreign language was a requirement, and French sounded awesome. I, um, just had no idea how hard it was to speak."

"And Mom knew how to speak French?" How come he'd never heard this? Or was it that he'd only listened with half an ear?

"Of course your mother knew. She was the smartest girl in her sorority. She started tutoring me on Wednesday nights."

Ryan could hear a smile in his father's voice. "And one thing led to another?" he asked as he sat down on the barstool next to the kitchen counter.

"No. One thing led to my roommate taking her to a mixer. That led to me getting jealous enough to ask her out."

"And the rest is history."

"Darn right." He lowered his voice. "That's why, Ryan, when I tell you to keep an open mind, it's good advice. I know what I'm talking about."

"I guess you do. But Candace isn't the one."

"Her name is Candace, hmm? That's a pretty name."

"Like I said, she's young. And she's hiding something too." Then there was the certain feeling he had about her that had nothing to do with his job or her adorableness and everything to do with her secrets.

"Of course she's hiding something."

Again, he was surprised. His father usually talked fish and football. Not love and romance. "Why do you sound like that's not a bad thing?"

"Because everyone hides things, son. Especially with someone new."

"True."

"And if she's not the one, someone else will be."

"Yes, sir."

"Be patient and keep your eyes open. It'll happen."

"Dad, I don't know when you became Dear Abby, but I have to tell you that you're pretty good."

"If you'd listened to me when you were fifteen, it would've saved you a lot of grief."

Ryan had loved pushing boundaries back then. Every other weekend he'd been grounded—and forced to clean his father's fishing boat. "Don't remind me. I'm going to let you go. Love you, Dad."

"Always, son. Always and no matter what."

Ryan hung up with a lump in his throat. He was a lucky man. Blessed to have wonderful parents. True role models. But it wasn't easy hoping to measure up to them. Their bar was set far too high to reach easily.

Moments later when he stepped outside onto his front porch, some of his neighbors were out walking. Others were working on their flower beds. His yard looked pretty spartan in comparison.

Thinking he needed a project to keep him occupied when he wasn't working, he went into the garage and found a shovel, determined to expand the flower bed in front of his bay windows. But when he dug the shovel in, the ground barely gave way; it felt like he was digging into cement.

It seemed he had a lot to learn about his new town—the soil and the people.

After a few more haphazard attempts, he propped the shovel on the side of the house and sat down on the front step. He had big plans for a future in this house and in this town. He just hoped he could make a go of it.

When a woman about his father's age walked by with her dog, she paused. "Hi there, Officer Mulaney. How are you?"

He stood up. "I'm just fine. And you?"

"Me and Trixi are out for our morning constitutional." She chuckled. "Do you need anything? Are you eating?"

His neighbors had all brought him coffee cakes and lasagnas when he'd moved in. "Yes, ma'am. I'm eating plenty. Don't need a thing."

"We're glad you're here. Don't be a stranger, hear?"

"Yes, ma'am."

With a wave of her hand, she started walking again.

Leaving Ryan once again with the feeling that he'd done the right thing by moving to Crittenden County. Somehow, someway, he was going to make a life here.

All he needed to do was pray and give it some time. He could do both.

# 8

*Jennifer ran. The sound of her hard-soled shoes made a clopping sound on the pavement. The noise reverberated in the dark alley, magnifying the sense of danger. Her breaths came hard. So hard that the sound of each one combined with that of her shoes and the pounding of her heart into an awful mix of fear. Creating a rushing in her ears.*

*Disoriented, she turned, knocking into a metal coal bin. It clanged. Loudly. Echoing around her. Tears pricked her eyes as Sir Garrett laughed.*

*He emanated evil. She wasn't going to get free. Not—*

"Bethanne?" Three sharp raps sounded on her door.

She must have jumped a foot. Holding her hand to her heart, Bethanne put the manuscript she'd been reading down on her bed. She was actually out of breath.

Her mother's voice turned more concerned. "Bethy? Are you okay?"

Getting to her feet, she hurried to the door and opened it. "Jah. Sorry, I was reading."

Her mother looked her over, taking in her slightly rumpled

59

plum-colored dress, bare feet, and no doubt breathless expression. "It must be a good one."

"It is. Exciting." She realized that the usual fine lines surrounding her mother's eyes had deepened. Something was bothering her. "Did you need something, Mamm?"

"Well, *I* don't. But there's someone here for you."

"Who?"

"Jay Byler. He's come over to pay you a call."

Now he was at her house? The man had no shame. "I don't want to see him."

Leaning against her bedroom door's frame, Mamm sighed. "Bethy, dear, I think you should reconsider."

"Why? It's my choice, ain't so?"

"Of course it is, but you told me that you've finally forgiven him for his friendship with Peter."

Ignoring the way her mother had said *finally*, she lifted her chin. "I have forgiven Jay."

"Then what's wrong?"

*Everything.* "Just because I've forgiven Jay doesn't mean that I want to see him." She certainly didn't want him calling on her.

"So, you haven't actually forgiven him." Disappointment filled her mother's expression. "That's a shame, daughter."

"Mamm, you're misunderstanding me. I have forgiven Jay. I just . . . on some days it's hard for me to see him and not remember what happened."

"I see." Her pretty mother scanned her face. Pursed her lips. Then she seemed to come to a conclusion. "I promised Jay a cup of coffee. He's no doubt wondering where it is by now. I'd best get that for him."

"I bet you could just ask him to leave." Her cheeks heated as soon as she heard her own words. She knew she sounded snide. Maybe worse. Like a recalcitrant child. She was ashamed, but fear and the need for self-preservation took precedence. Years of counseling had taught her to stick up for herself, and that's what she was doing.

"I'm not going to do that," Mamm said.

"Well, enjoy having coffee with him."

Two lines formed between her mother's brows—a sure sign that she had run out of patience with her. "No, miss. You are going to go downstairs and talk to Jay. And while he is having that cup of coffee, you are going to be pleasant because he is a guest in this house." She took a deep breath. "And then, after he finishes that cup of coffee, if you still don't want him calling on you . . ."

"Yes?"

"You can tell him yourself."

Bethanne felt her cheeks burn. "Mamm, please don't make me do that."

"All I'm making you do is be the woman I raised you to be. Don't disappoint me."

As Bethanne opened her mouth to protest, her mother headed down the hall.

Still in the doorway, thinking over their conversation, Bethanne felt ashamed. Her mother was right. Bethanne hadn't been raised to treat people rudely. She was going to have to go see him.

Bethanne reached for her kapp, intending to take it off and smooth her hair underneath. But that brought back memories of primping for meetings with Peter. As if to make a point to herself, she left her hair and kapp alone. She also bypassed the bathroom. She didn't want to glance at her unkempt appearance and be tempted to improve it.

Walking down the stairs, Bethanne mentally rolled her eyes at her foolishness. *For sure and for certain you're going to show him*, she thought sarcastically. *You're going to look like you just rolled out of bed.*

He'd likely leave their house, glad to never have a reason to step foot inside it again.

"You have much to learn about pride," she whispered to herself.

When she reached the base of the stairs, she squared her shoulders and walked into the living room, where Jay and her mother were sitting across from each other and chatting like old friends. Her mother was speaking, but when Jay noticed Bethanne, he turned his head to watch her approach.

He stood up. "Hey."

Practically feeling her mother's watchful gaze, she looked Jay in the eye. "Hi."

"Bethanne, would you care for a cup of coffee?" Mamm asked.

"Nee. Danke." She needed to stay firm, because a hot cup of fresh coffee did sound pretty good.

"I'll leave you two alone, then."

Bethanne knew her mother was disappointed by her lackluster attitude. Jay's expression was carefully controlled. Revealing nothing. But a new tension lay between them. Or maybe it was the same tension that was always present but now there was the added layer of disappointment.

Jay sat back down, practically daring her to say what she'd come to say.

She wasn't one to go back on her promise to her mother. Sitting down across from him, she said, "How are you today?"

"I'm well. Danke." He sipped his coffee.

She noticed it was only half-drunk. "How is work?"

"It's fine, thank you."

She folded her hands in her lap. Relaxed when he took another sip of coffee.

"I heard rain's in the forecast," he said.

"Jah. Perhaps it will cool things off."

"I suppose.

Looking down at her hands, she wondered how much longer this visit had to last. Another five minutes? Ten?

He cleared his throat. "Bethanne, if you have something on your mind, I'd like to hear it."

"Fine." Taking a fortifying breath, she blurted, "I don't know how to say this without sounding blunt, so I'm sorry for it. But the fact of the matter is that I don't wish you to call on me again."

He looked unfazed by her rudeness. "Why?"

"You know why. There's too much history between us. Too much to get over. Too much to ignore."

He didn't even wait a second before responding. "I disagree."

Of course, he did, she thought sarcastically. "Jay, you are being obtuse on purpose."

"And you are using some of your fancy vocabulary to ignore the fact that you and I actually have no history." He leaned forward. "Bethanne, yes, I was friends with Peter. And yes, you were Peter's girl. But what history do the two of us have?"

"We have lots of history. You know that. We've known each other all our lives."

"I think that's the case with almost everyone in our circle."

He was maddening! "You're oversimplifying this, Jay. You and I both know it."

"Really? I feel like our lives are intertwined but not linked. You weren't my girl, even though I wished you were. I didn't interfere. Peter had made it known that he liked you a lot. Because of that, we really didn't have much interaction."

*Even though I wished you were.* The words were so sweet. Almost hard to ignore. But she did her best. "Still, I'd rather you didn't call again."

He leaned forward and looked her in the eye. "Give me another reason."

She averted her eyes. "I don't need one."

"Instead of giving us a try, of giving your future a try, you're choosing to sit in your room. Yet again."

She hated that Jay was acting as if she hadn't made any progress. She had. Was there room for improvement? Yes. Absolutely.

But would she admit it to him?

No.

If she did, it would be like he knew too much. They wouldn't be on equal terms. No, they'd be even more un-balanced. He had his life together and wanted marriage and family. She was still trying to be comfortable around strang-ers. Sometimes, she even had trouble being around friends for a long period of time. Sometimes she still had panic attacks. What would Jay do when he realized that she was nothing like he thought? More importantly, how would she handle seeing the disappointment in his eyes?

Forcing herself to look at him, she whispered, "You're mistaken. I'm not planning on sitting in my room by myself. I'm just choosing to avoid you."

"All because of what happened years ago."

She hated how he was making so many complicated, com-plex issues into a simple equation. But if that was what he wanted, then that was what she would give him. "Not exactly because of what happened. But if that's how you want to think of it, yes."

Dismay filled his expression before he seemed to come to a conclusion. "All right." He stood up.

"Bethanne, I think you're making a mistake. Maybe not tonight, maybe not tomorrow, but one day soon you're going to realize that I'm really a great guy. And you're going to wish you'd given me a chance."

"Have you finished your coffee?"

He looked down at his cup on the table. It was still about a fourth of the way filled but likely cold. "Jah."

She smiled. "Shall I walk you out, then?"

A muscle in his jaw jumped. "Thank you, but I can see myself out."

As Jay Byler left the living room, she didn't move. The front door opened and then shut.

She could hear her mother washing dishes in the kitchen.

All the while, she thought about how Jay had been wrong. Bethanne wasn't going to need a day or even an afternoon to know that she'd made a mistake. Jay Byler was worth fighting for. Getting to know him was worth a lot of things. He was that kind of man. A good one.

She regretted pushing him away already and wished Jay was still there, that she could change her mind.

But Jay was long gone.

# 9

Standing on the worn dirt path leading from the Hostetlers' house into town, half listening to the cicadas buzzing in the distance, Jay continued to think over his conversation with Bethanne.

He grimaced.

It had gone from bad to worse. Truthfully, it had been a fiasco. Kicking a rock that had the misfortune of being in his path, Jay berated himself. He'd waited so long for Bethanne to finally see him. To realize that he was more than just a friend of Peter's. That he'd grown into a man she could depend on and trust.

Why hadn't he been able to wait a little longer before paying a formal call? He wanted her for the rest of his life. Put that way, why couldn't he have bided his time at least a little while longer? Not pushed so hard?

It was time to do what he should have done from the beginning—rely on the Lord. He just hoped that His timeline didn't involve more years of waiting.

He grimaced. There he went again, wishing and hoping for something to happen quickly. "God, please help me, if You see fit to do so. Please give me the strength to be patient

and put Bethanne's needs before mine." After closing his eyes
and adding a few prayers for his family, he opened them.

And found Seth Zimmerman walking toward him. He
was wearing what Jay had come to think of as his usual at-
tire. Jeans, a white T-shirt, and a pair of tennis shoes. Seth
was also studying him with a concerned expression. And no
wonder, because he'd been standing here with his eyes closed.

The sight of the man—his life intertwined so closely with
Bethanne's—nearly took his breath away. Seth was the one
who'd discovered Peter Miller attempting to rape Bethanne.
When he pulled Peter away, they fought, Seth hit him, and
Peter went down. Hitting his head on a rock when he fell.
When he died, Seth was arrested.

Because Seth had been young, scared to death, and had
only an overworked public defender to speak for him, he was
found guilty of involuntary manslaughter and sentenced to
five years. He was paroled after serving two, but that horrible night's events had divided their community. Some folks
had even gone so far as to doubt that Peter had assaulted
Bethanne.

Jay knew better, of course. He owed so much to Seth.
Without his intervention, Bethanne would have suffered even
more than she had. "Hey," he said as he stepped forward.
"How are ya, Seth?"

"I'm gut." Looking as if he was trying not to grin, he said,
"I've been watching you for the last couple of minutes. I was
kind of worried about you for a spell."

"I was praying."

"Mmm. Gotcha." Stuffing his hands into his pockets, he
nodded. "Well, I'll let you get back to it."

As Seth moved forward, Jay realized his advice would be
welcome. "Hey, do you have a minute?"

Seth stopped and searched Jay's face. "You all right?"

"Jah. Actually, it's not exactly about me."

"Ah. It's Bethanne."

He nodded. "How did you know?"

"A good guess." Looking like he was thinking of more than a couple of secrets, Seth shrugged. "Plus, I've been there a time or two. With Tabitha."

There was no reason to pretend he wasn't in love with Bethanne. "Yeah . . . so I think I just made a big mistake with her."

"Mistakes happen. No one expects us to be perfect. Not even God."

"No, you don't understand. I went calling on Bethanne today."

"That is a right and proper thing for you to do." He paused. "What was the problem? Did her parents get upset at you being there?"

He shook his head. "Nee. Her mother invited me in and then went to get Bethanne." He lowered his voice. "She had to coax her to come down to talk to me, though."

"Why?"

"I . . . I don't even know anymore. I used to think it was all wrapped up in my friendship with Peter, but that can't be the only thing. Plus, I felt something between us. Something important, Seth."

"Ah."

"Bethanne has even said she's forgiven me for not realizing that Peter was capable of such violence."

"That is a blessing." Seth seemed to think about that for a moment. "But forgiving someone isn't the same as accepting a suit, I suppose."

Jay shrugged. "Right now, I'm thinking that they're miles apart. Worlds apart."

Seth laughed. "Maybe not that far."

"Do you have any suggestions for me? I mean, you were able to win over Tabitha."

Seth's amused expression turned serious. "There were a lot of other things going on with Tabitha. She'd been married before and had suffered at the hands of her abusive husband. Then she had to deal with some folks in the community looking down on her because she divorced."

"So, you had to have patience."

"You could say that," he said in a dry tone. "But I had no choice. I knew if I lost her, I'd lose my heart and my future. I had to try."

"That's how I feel. That's why I'm so upset at myself for messing things up. I don't know how to get back in Beth-anne's good graces."

"I brought Tabitha all sorts of food and left it at her doorstep. For months. And when I wasn't delivering food, I chopped her wood."

Jay wasn't sure that would work for him. Bethanne had a whole family to take care of her. But he supposed he could try to find some ways to connect with her. "What did she say each time you stopped by?"

"Nothing." A small, secret smile played on his lips. "She watched me, though."

"How? From the front porch?"

Seth laughed. "Far from that at first. She didn't even want me to see her. She watched me through the sheer curtains in her living room."

Jay couldn't believe all this had gone on and he hadn't even heard a whisper about it. "What did you do?"

A look of satisfaction appeared on his face. "I didn't do anything. One day she got brave."

"That's it?" He felt completely let down. And maybe a little disappointed.

"That's it. But listen to me, Jay Byler. Waiting and being patient isn't a waste of time—it's a blessing. I kept trying and Tabitha kept watching. And I was unaware of it, but every day brought us closer together. The same thing could be happening for you two."

"She said she didn't want me to call on her, though."

"Right." He pursed his lips. "Well, then . . . perhaps she doesn't. It could be Bethanne doesn't want that kind of relationship with anyone. That might be how she feels."

"If that's how she feels, then I'll have to accept her decision, won't I?"

"You will . . . if you want her to be happy. There's something to be said for wanting the woman you love to be happy, ain't so?" Seth talked slowly, as if each word was being pulled reluctantly from somewhere deep within him. "Even if it ain't with you."

*Even if it ain't with you.* There was something poetic and almost tragic about that thought. Or, rather, maybe it only felt that way to Jay.

He allowed that thought to sink in. Settle and stew. Tried it on for size, even though there was no question in his mind how it would affect him.

Simply put, it would hurt. It would hurt so badly that it would feel like someone had stabbed him in the heart.

But even worse than that pain would be knowingly hurting Bethanne on purpose. Forcing her into doing something that she wasn't ready for.

Or not respecting her wishes.

Nee, it would be like he was no better than Peter Miller. He was a great many things, but he wasn't that man. He didn't want to be.

Realizing he'd been staring at Seth, Jay attempted to pull himself together. "Yes," he said.

"Yes?"

"I'm not making sense, am I?" He waved a hand. "I meant to say that you're right. I need to do the right thing by her. Even if it feels wrong for me."

"That's how it is, isn't it? When a man falls in love—really in love. Doing right comes first."

"I guess Tabitha appreciated your patience?"

Seth nodded. "She did. But we still had a couple of obstacles to overcome. Including her ex-husband."

"But you two are married, so that means you're good now. Ain't so?"

"We're better than good. We're happy and she's mine. And . . . she's expecting."

"Congratulations. That's wonderful-gut. Wunderbar."

"It is. Danke." He slapped Jay on the shoulder. "I know it's hard, but try not to give up on Bethanne. God will help the two of you, and when the right time happens for the two of ya, you'll be mighty glad you believed in something greater than yourself."

"God's will?"

"Oh, for sure. But also your lady's happiness. Love is a powerful thing, Jay. It's life-changing. Believe in it, yeah?" And with that, Seth strode on, covering a full yard before Jay mumbled a suitable reply.

As he started walking again, Jay took a slower pace. Thought about not giving up. Decided he would somehow find a way to let Bethanne know that his interest hadn't waned but that he was no longer going to be so pushy.

And maybe, along the way, he'd take a moment to thank Seth Zimmerman for stopping and giving him some much-needed advice.

That would be a good thing too.

# 10

The Marion Police Department was on Main Street, in a rather spacious brick and wood building that had once been a bank in another life. The employees inside were scattered into different divisions, some of which were divided only by partitions made of reclaimed wood. Except for Chief Blake Foster. He got an office. The other room was for holding, and it happened to have the remains of an old vault inside. The officers had a running joke that one day someone they brought in would spend some time in it. Of course they wouldn't actually do that, but every employee there would be lying if he or she said it hadn't crossed their minds. Every once in a while, they brought in someone who simply could not be quiet.

After roll call and a visit to the high school, Ryan Mulaney sat down in his cubicle and glanced at his phone. Again. He had a couple of people he was waiting to hear from about open cases. But what he was really looking for was a text from Candace Evans, aka Miss Crittenden County.

If another officer asked why he was continuing to escort Candace to her various events, Ryan knew he would say all the right things. The first was the excuse he'd given Candace. He needed to get to know the citizens in Marion and the surrounding areas. Meeting them in such a nonconfrontational way wasn't a bad thing.

In addition, he'd remind them she was only twenty-two, petite, and vulnerable. Or how some of the roads in the county flooded easily while others were so remote that obtaining a cell phone signal was about as easy as coaxing a stray cat into one's lap.

Then, of course, was the most obvious reason for him to be at her side—crowds of people surrounded her at these events. Some of them even thought nothing about touching her without her permission, which grated on him like nobody's business. That shook her up—and with good reason. No way should anyone have to put up with a stranger doing that.

Thinking about how, the last time he'd accompanied her, some woman tried to run her hand down Candace's hair, Ryan gritted his teeth. He'd put a stop to that fast. Even the lady's look of hurt outrage hadn't made him regret his decision. Not when he'd caught sight of Candace's face, full of relief.

And . . . that was his secret, he supposed. He might be an experienced cop, six foot four and close to two hundred pounds, but whenever Candace was around, he turned into his goofy younger self. The guy who had a crush on the prettiest girl in town.

But who could blame him?

Yeah, she was pretty as all get-out, but that wasn't what drew him to her. It was the way she didn't take herself seriously—the way she seemed more delighted to visit with people and ask them about their lives than to have anyone fuss or congratulate her on her win. So sweet.

73

It was the way that there was something vulnerable in her hazel eyes that she tried to hide. But it never went away.

And that concerned him.

Though she hadn't spoken anything out loud, Ryan was sure Candace was more afraid of her stalker than she was letting on. She was scared bad enough to accept his company. Scared enough to agree to share her schedule with him and tentatively agree to allow him to drive her to the events.

She relaxed around him too.

So, he spent the next hour working while waiting to hear from her. Doing paperwork. Investigating some of the leads they had on a recent robbery. Helping a lady who came in with concerns about her neighbor's suspicious behavior, and even going so far as to promise to stop by soon.

Just when he was about to reach out to her, Candace texted him.

Hey, Officer Mulaney. It's Candace. Candace Evans.

He couldn't stop the grin as he texted back.

Hi, Candace. I knew it was you. How are you today?

After a few seconds, he spied the telltale line of dots and then her reply.

OK. Busy.

I bet. You got your schedule yet?

I do, but IDK. It's a lot. I feel bad asking you to come.

You don't have to go if you're 2 busy.

Ryan shook his head as he typed his response.

I won't know if I can or can't come with until
you send it to me.

Sure?

I'm sure.

He barely resisted rolling his eyes. Then he remembered
she didn't know him—and that it was in her nature to be
considerate. He'd seen that time and time again.

After a minute passed, he tried again.

Send your schedule my way, okay?

OK. Fine. Screenshot?

That'll do. Send it.

He drummed his fingers on the desk while he waited for
her response. And then, there it was. Scanning it, he noticed that her first event was in two hours. Luckily it was in
Marion, but her last event was out in Sparta. It was right
on the other side of the county line and close to an hour
away.

Realizing that the talk they needed to have couldn't wait,
he rang her up.

"Officer Mulaney?"

"Hey, Candace. Remember what I've told you? You can
call me Ryan."

After a pause, she said, "Um, all right. Is everything okay?"

"Yeah, but I wanted to talk to you about this schedule of
yours. How about you start having me help you set it up?"

"Why?"

"Because if you set up something an hour away at night,
I want to be able to go with you. If I'm busy, you might end
up going alone, and I don't want that."

75

"You don't have to go to every event with me," she added in a rush. "That isn't necessary."

She sounded agitated. "I know it isn't," he soothed. "Obviously there's going to be times when something else comes up. If there's an emergency, I'll have to back out."

"Or you're off. I don't want to mess up your days off."

He wouldn't tell her, but he was going to do his best to escort her even if he was off shift. It wasn't like he had a busy social life anyway. "I'll do my best to accompany you."

"Thanks, but Ryan, I promise, I don't mind doing all this alone."

"I hear you. But still, I'd like to try to be with you. Don't forget, part of the reason I'm going to be there is to get to know the county's citizens."

"But—"

Man, she really was so cute. "Listen, I've got to go. Should I pick you up at your house?"

"You don't mind?"

"I don't mind," he said in a firm, soft tone.

"All right. But I think we should talk about this."

"Okay, we'll talk about it tonight. We'll have a couple of hours together, yeah?"

"Yeah."

There was a smile in her voice now, which made him smile. "Okay then. Text me your address and I'll see you later."

"Okay."

Relieved that he'd gotten his way, he finished up. "Good. See you then."

"Wait!"

He gripped his phone tighter. "Yeah?"

"I . . . well, I just wanted to tell you thanks."

"No problem." He barely stopped himself from adding *honey* to the end of that.

Alex, another officer, stopped at his desk after he'd ended the call. "Everything good?"

"Yeah, why?"

"No reason. Other than I heard you talking about schedules. I'm guessing that was Candace Evans?"

"It was."

"How often do you plan to drive that girl around?"

"She's not exactly a girl. And as often as I'm supposed to."

"You don't seem too put off by that, though." His eyes narrowed. "Is there something going on between you?"

"Definitely not."

"Good, because if there was, that would be a conflict of interest." Alex was in his midforties, a little on the portly side, and a bit of a busybody. "Chief Foster isn't going to be pleased if you overstep yourself."

He knew the other man was trying to be helpful, but his condescending tone was beginning to grate on him. "I came from Connecticut, not the moon. We did things by the book there. I'm not going to do anything inappropriate."

"Good." He exhaled. "Sorry, but I couldn't not say anything."

"Say whatever you want. I'm going to explain myself if I need to, though."

After staring at him hard, Alex lifted his chin. "Understood."

When Alex walked away, Ryan directed his attention back to his paperwork and tried to calm down. He didn't like anyone insinuating that he wasn't acting appropriately. He wasn't that kind of guy.

Still, he knew it probably wasn't a bad idea to keep better tabs on himself. As much as he could say that Candace was nothing more than a citizen of Crittenden County and therefore had every right to police protection, Ryan knew that if things were different, he'd want to ask her out.

An hour later, he pulled up in front of Candace's house. Glad that she wasn't standing on the front lawn waiting for him, he walked to the door and knocked.

Her father answered but didn't move from the doorway. "You must be Officer Mulaney."

"I am, but please call me Ryan." He held out his hand as Mr. Evans stepped onto the stoop.

Mr. Evans shook it, but instead of warming to him, he narrowed his eyes. "Candace told me that you said she could call you by your first name."

"Well, Officer Mulaney is a mouthful." And it was, he supposed, though that wasn't exactly the entire reason. The majority of it had to do with him watching out for her and needing for her to trust him. No way was she going to stick close if she didn't feel comfortable around him.

"I guess it is," her father replied. He sounded grudging, though. After a second's pause, he added, "My name is Wayne."

"It's good to meet you, Wayne."

Wayne stuffed his hands in his pockets. "I didn't tell Dora this, but I'm relieved that you're accompanying Candace as much as you are able. She acts like she's an independent woman, but she's never been on her own. Not really."

"I'm happy to help." He was more than happy, actually.

The door swung farther open. "Dad, who are you talking to? Oh! Hi, Ryan."

"Hey, Candace." It was a true struggle to act as if her beauty didn't affect him. Today she wore a silky-looking, pale green dress and knee-high suede boots with a two- or three-inch heel that made her legs seem even longer. "Are you ready?"

"I think so. Hold on. My stuff is in the duffle bag in the hall."

"I can grab it. If it's anything like last time, it probably weighs a good fifty pounds," he joked.

"It's not that heavy."

Stepping into the entryway, Ryan got a brief glimpse of creamy light gray walls, dark wood, and a blue braided rug covering the floor. It all looked neat and clean. The duffle bag was in the entry, next to the stairs. Sure enough, it was heavy.

When he walked back out, Wayne stared at the duffle as if he was noticing it for the very first time. "What is in there, Candace?"

"A change of clothes. Snacks. And a bunch of stuff from the chamber of commerce."

"How come you have items from the chamber?"

"Because they're my sponsor, Dad," she said in thinly disguised impatience, like it was obvious that she'd told her father that more than once or twice. "They held the contest."

"Oh."

After kissing her father's cheek, she smiled at Ryan. "I'm ready now."

"Let's go, then."

Walking to Ryan's side, Candace lifted a hand. "Bye, Daddy."

"Bye, sweetheart. You have your cell phone?"

She tapped the side of her purse. "It's right here."

"Call if you need anything."

"I will. Bye!" she called out over her shoulder as she headed to Ryan's SUV.

"It's good to meet you, sir. You take care now."

Wayne nodded, but his expression remained serious. "All I care about is you taking care of my daughter."

"I promise I'll do that."

"Good."

Heading to his vehicle, Ryan thought about her father's protective tone. He wondered if he'd always been that way, or if this was something new.

After he joined Candace in the SUV and they punched in her first destination in his GPS, he pulled out and headed down her street. "How are you?" he asked.

"I'm good. Thanks again for taking me around today."

"It's not a problem."

"Well, thanks anyway. I'm really glad I'm not by myself."

Her words were thoughtful, but there was a note of something new in her tone. She sounded apprehensive. "Hey, Candace, is something bothering you?"

"What do you mean?" Her entire posture had changed. She was wary now.

"Oh, you know," he murmured. "You're tired. It's too hot. You've gotten tired of me watching your every move. Or, you're still worried about the stalker?"

"I don't know." She averted her eyes and played with the ends of her hair.

So that was a yes.

"The only way my presence helps is if we're honest with each other."

"I'm being honest."

No, she wasn't. Maybe he should drop the subject, but something was telling him not to do that. Remembering a few women that he'd worked with in the past, he decided to do a little more digging. "I know what happened to Bethanne, Candace. The chief filled me in. You have a very good reason to be a little more wary around men. Maybe my help isn't actually helping you at all?" That was as delicately as he could put it.

Her eyes widened. "This isn't like that. Peter . . . Peter led my cousin to believe he was someone different than she'd believed him to be," she continued in a rush. "What's happening to me? I'm worried that I've begun to look for the worst in people."

"But you've been genuinely worried."

"I have, but maybe I've let my imagination get carried away? It could just be a guy with too much time on his hands."

Warning signals blared in his head. "Hmm."

"Do you not believe me?"

Worry, and maybe even a hint of indignation, laced her voice. He didn't want to cause her more stress, but he also wanted her to trust him. Trust him to help her. He took time to answer her question with care. "If your question is, do I believe that someone is giving you a hard time and might be stalking you, yes, I believe that. Absolutely." That was why he was there, after all.

"Then why do you sound so skeptical?"

"Because I think that, at the very least, you might have an idea of who might do something like this."

Looking increasingly uncomfortable, she mumbled, "I really don't know why a stranger would do this."

"Trust me to keep things confidential."

"I do trust you, and if I see him again, I'll point him out to you. I just don't know who he is."

Unable to keep his frustration with the situation from taking over, he said, "Keeping information to yourself isn't going to help if you're wrong. Remember that."

"I'll remember." She looked away.

Ryan felt the knot in his gut tighten. Call it a sixth sense, but he felt Candace was just giving him words. She'd been living in this community her entire life. No one went twentysomething years without making someone angry or upset.

He was going to have to walk an even narrower line. He needed to reinforce her belief that she was in danger without scaring her half to death. He hoped he was up to the task.

# 11

After her first event at the senior center, Ryan drove Candace north to a recreation center in the little town of Sparta. When the chamber had first mentioned this invitation to her, Candace hadn't been sure she wanted to go. After all, it was on the other side of the county line. But when she learned that a couple of the local organizations who worked with at-risk kids had invited her to visit, she couldn't refuse it. The director had asked her to share her experiences in school and her goals, and, of course, encourage everyone to believe that their dreams were possible with prayer and hard work.

As always, Ryan accompanied her inside. Then, after making sure that she was settled and at ease, he spent some time chatting with the kids. He'd probably be surprised, but everyone really liked the new cop on the Marion police force. Not only was he handsome and had a great smile, but he was so different from the boys she'd known all her life. More mature. More reserved. Candace not only felt safe around him, she felt at ease.

After the director introduced Candace, Ryan joined a group of high school students on the bleachers. She really liked that about him. He had such an unassuming way that seemed to encourage even the shyest of kids to break out of their shell. He also was warm and friendly. Everyone seemed to want to talk to him—even if it was just to talk about his accent.

In the middle of her talk about her junior and senior years of high school, when she shared how many scholarships she'd applied for, she met his eyes. Ryan seemed to be listening to her intently and soaking in every word.

She probably imagined it, but when their eyes met, she was sure his gaze warmed with approval. It made her feel a little tingly and special. Oh, she knew there was no chance of him ever thinking of her in a romantic sense. He acted like she was just a kid. But she was still a romantic at heart. And who couldn't help but have a crush on a guy like him?

After she finished her talk, the director walked up to the microphone. "Everyone, let's give Candace Evans, the beautiful Miss Crittenden County, a big round of applause."

All the kids hooted and hollered as they clapped.

Candace smiled at them, but she took that excessive compliment with a grain of salt. She'd been told all her life that she was pretty, but she wasn't anywhere close to being beautiful. She also really wasn't anything special. It still seemed a little crazy for her to be offering advice to kids who were just a little bit younger than herself.

The director stepped closer. "Candace, would you be willing to stay another fifteen minutes and pose for pictures and autograph the flyers we passed out?"

"Yes, of course." Searching for Ryan, she added, "I don't think that will be a problem at all."

He gave her a thumbs-up sign from across the room.

She smiled back at him.

"All right, everyone. Stand in line if you'd like to get a signed flyer or have your picture taken with Candace."

Candace stood by the table they'd set up and picked up a black Sharpie marker. "Who's first?"

"I am," a little boy said. "I don't want a picture with you. Can you sign the flyer?"

Scrawling her name on it, she handed it to him. "How's that?"

"Good. It's for my mom."

"I want a picture with you," a little girl said next. "My mom's going to take it."

She knelt down, slipped her arm around the girl's slim shoulders, and smiled. "I'm ready."

"Can I touch your crown?"

"Of course. Do you want to try it on too?"

"I can?"

"Absolutely." Carefully removing it from her curls, she set it on the girl's head while her mother took a picture.

And on it continued. She discussed high school and her outfit, signed pictures, and posed with kids. Then she noticed that Ryan had moved to stand by her side.

"Is everything okay?" she asked.

"Yeah, but I think you need to finish up soon."

She almost pointed out that she didn't have any plans except to go home and eat heated-up leftovers, but then remembered that he was probably more than ready to relax—or even go out with his friends or something. "Okay." Looking at the director, she held up five fingers.

The director nodded. "Five more minutes," she called out. "Miss Crittenden County needs to go home, and so do y'all."

When a couple of girls moaned, Candace said, "Maybe I can come another time. Don't forget, I'll be Miss Crittenden County for a full year."

The main door of the gym opened with a sharp click, and a man and two teenagers rushed toward her and Ryan.

"Hey, do you have that navy-blue Chevy Blazer out there?"

"Yeah, it's mine," Ryan replied.

The man stepped forward, his expression grim. "Something happened to the tires. We thought you'd need to know."

After glancing at Candace, obviously double-checking that she was okay, Ryan strode outside with the man.

"What happened?" she asked the boys.

"All four tires are flat."

She raised her eyebrows. "All four?" She'd never heard of such a thing.

"Yeah," the dark-haired boy answered. "Someone did a good job on them too. That truck isn't going anywhere."

That didn't make sense. "I wonder what happened," she said as she began packing up all her stuff.

"My dad thinks someone slashed them."

"Oh no." Grabbing her purse and the heavy duffle bag, she hurried outside.

There was a crowd around Ryan's navy Blazer. The kids hadn't exaggerated. The vehicle wasn't going anywhere except on a tow truck. Since Ryan wasn't in the middle of everything, she scanned the area, looking for his pristine white polo.

She found him standing a little off to the side, his expression serious while he talked on his cell phone. When he met her gaze, he motioned her over.

Even though she knew she had no real reason to feel guilty, she did. If Ryan hadn't come with her, his tires would probably still be intact. She had no idea how much it would cost to get a tow truck and pay for new tires, but it would surely be expensive.

She reached his side just as he finished the call. "Yeah. Thanks. No, I understand. Yes. I'll let you know. Thanks, Chief." After Ryan disconnected, he stashed his phone in his back pocket. "Sorry, Candace, but we obviously have a problem."

"What happened? The kids acted like someone did it on purpose."

"That's because they did." A muscle in his jaw clenched, as if he was trying to hold back his temper.

A chill ran down her spine. "Oh no."

Glaring at his vehicle, he said, "These tires are fairly new. They probably had about another twenty thousand miles before they started showing wear and tear. All four tires going flat means that someone took a knife to them."

"Who would do that?"

"I don't know—not definitively," he replied.

There was something new in his voice. Something that told her that he was more bothered by what happened than the inconvenience of it. "Do you think it was teenagers or something?" she asked.

"I'm not ruling anything out, but it doesn't feel right. Slashing a tire deep enough to cause it to go flat takes a lot of strength. Four would be a workout."

"Unless you had four people."

"Yeah, but even then my gut tells me that something else is going on. I mean, it's pretty easy to mess up someone's day by ruining one tire. To kill four of them on purpose? It's excessive."

He had a good point. "What's going to happen now?"

"I called the station to let them know. They're going to send out a truck and take it to a nearby shop after inspecting the tires." He sighed. "That's probably going to take a while. At least ninety minutes."

She thought more like two hours. "Wow. I'm really sorry."

"I am too. It puts a damper on the rest of your evening."

"These visits were my evening. I'm fine."

"They were mine too. I guess it's good we're both so boring." Concern filled his expression. "Why don't you go wait inside. I'm going to have everyone else go on home."

Because it seemed like he wanted a little space, she headed toward the gymnasium's door but didn't go inside. Now that the sun was low on the horizon, it was pleasant outside. It smelled better too. The gym smelled like every other gym she'd ever been in—like old sneakers and sweat. She stood by the building's front wall as the spectators dispersed. The man who'd told them about the flat tires talked to Ryan for a few minutes before he rounded up his boys and drove out of the parking lot.

Over the next half hour, everyone but the center's director and janitor left. The director had invited them to wait inside, but they'd refused. There was a bench outside, and a mom from one of the high school's booster clubs had already given them a couple of water bottles and a plate of homemade cookies.

After Ryan paced, talked on his phone for a while, and inspected the tires again, he sat down on the bench by her side.

"Here. Have something to drink."

"We've sure been taken care of, haven't we?" he said with a laugh. "Thanks." After gulping down half the bottle, he kicked his legs out. "So, here we are again."

"Not again," she corrected. "I've never been here before."

He grinned, obviously getting her weak attempt at humor. "No offense to the good people of Sparta, but I hope I don't have to return anytime soon."

"I feel the same way." She looked down at her phone again, wracking her brain for something to say. She was drawing a blank. Every topic sounded either too juvenile or too personal.

"What have you been doing?" he asked.

"Nothing. Looking at Instagram." She held up her phone.

"See anything good?"

"Nah, just same old, same old." She could feel his eyes glance at her screen, then sharpen.

"Hey, that's you."

"Yeah. It's a recent post."

Taking the phone from her hand, he said, "It has all of this evening's appearances."

Wondering why he didn't sound happy about that, she nodded. "There's a volunteer at the chamber of commerce. She made all the graphics for me to post."

"Do you have to share these?"

"Yes."

"What about keeping them on your feed? Can we take them off?"

"I guess so, but why would I want to do that?"

"There's a possibility someone could find you at one of these events."

She chuckled. "Officer Mulaney, that's kind of the point. There's no sense in me parading around the county in a tiara if no one is there to see me."

He frowned. "I guess you're right. But it's still not a good idea. And call me Ryan."

Frustrated with the way he was acting, she took her phone back, thumbed through a couple of apps, and then showed him the chamber of commerce Facebook page. "Do you see this?" She held her phone up for him to see. "It doesn't matter if I share the information on my Instagram feed or not. It's posted for everyone to see."

"So it's out of your control."

"It's what I signed on to do. What's the problem?"

"Nothing."

"Sorry, it doesn't sound like nothing."

He crossed his arms over his chest. "I think someone targeted my vehicle on purpose. No one else's vehicles have been tampered with."

"What?" She noticed the plate on his vehicle. "Is it because you have out of state plates?"

"I doubt it. I don't think anyone around here feels that strongly about the state of Connecticut."

Her cheeks burned. She had sounded so stupid.

"I don't know why someone slashed your tires, then. It has to be just bad luck."

"Or someone thinks you're with me."

"You are . . ." She met his gaze. Feeling more self-conscious, Candace whispered, "I mean, you are, but not like *that*."

"Of course not," he said in a rush. "However, a stranger wouldn't know that."

"No . . . and maybe it's not a stranger. I hate to think like this but . . . do you think it's the guy who's been following me?"

He didn't crack a smile. "It's a possibility."

"But . . . why would he think we're together—like a couple?"

"You're twenty-two, right?"

She nodded. "I just had a birthday last month."

"I'm twenty-eight. Six years older."

"Yes."

He shrugged. "I'm not saying that we would ever want to be in a relationship, but someone might think we are."

"Yeah, right." No way was she ever going to admit that she thought he was hot. No way.

Or that she was pretty happy he was escorting her to all her events, because he was a lot more fun to be around than any of the guys her age. They still didn't have a clue, and

90

half of them only wanted to sit around and watch basketball with a beer in their hands.

The approaching tow truck with flashing lights saved her from saying anything more. "Tow truck's here."

"It's about time." As it pulled in, Ryan held up a hand. "I'll be right back. Sit tight."

"Sure." She looked down at her phone screen again.

And noticed that she'd just received a message from an unfamiliar number. She clicked on it.

*You looked pretty today, Candace. I'm glad you wore your hair down around your shoulders.*

No. The evening had just gone from bad to worse.

# 12

Bethanne knew there was no way around it. She owed Jay an apology. There was no reason on earth that she should be blaming him for anything that Peter had done. Especially not after so many years. In a way, he was a victim too. Peter hadn't been the person Jay had assumed he was.

Bethanne sighed. What was wrong with her? She'd said she forgave him. But then she'd hurt Jay's feelings on purpose. She would've given any other man who'd come calling thirty minutes of her time and her kindness. At the very least, she should've thanked him for stopping by. Instead, she'd practically run Jay out of the house.

She was ashamed of herself.

After debating how to best approach him, she decided to combine her visit to him with a stop at the publishing house. She had some manuscript reviews to turn in, and Burke Lumber was just a couple of blocks away. Riding there on her bicycle would be no problem. She could get both important errands done in no time.

Decision made, she readied herself, gathered her materials, and went downstairs to let her mother know she was leaving.

Mamm was sitting at the dining room table writing a letter. Like always, she had a cup of hot tea, a plate full of shortbread, and her box of stationery in front of her. Her mother was a champion letter writer. Bethanne didn't know how many letters she wrote a month, but it was a lot.

"Hi, Bethy," she said when Bethanne appeared at the bottom of the stairs. "Are you going to do some work in here?" She set down her pen and began to clear a spot on the table.

"Nee, I've already reviewed half of the manuscripts they sent. I'm going to go take these to the office."

"Why?"

"It's a pretty day. I thought I'd ride my bike."

"You don't want to hitch up the buggy?"

"Nee." She, like a lot of other people her age in the Amish community, had begun riding her bicycle more and more. Some had even purchased electric bikes. They were expensive but cheaper than the care and feeding of a good horse. Plus, it was so convenient not to have to worry about a horse getting spooked or keeping it comfortable on the hot days of summer and cold days of winter. She didn't have an electric bicycle, but hers was red, had a lovely basket on the front, and made her happy. Plus, it was always good exercise. "I'll be home in a couple of hours."

Frowning, her mother stood. "A couple of hours? Surely they don't need you to stay there all afternoon?"

"They don't. I have somewhere else to go." Knowing that she was going to have to reveal the truth sooner or later, she added, "I'm going to stop by Burke Lumber and talk to Jay."

Worry and confusion filled her gaze. "Why?"

"I owe him an apology."

She sat back down. "For what, child?"

"I was rude to him. I feel terrible and I want to do the right thing."

Her eyebrows lifted. "I see. Well, ah, going into a place like Burke Lumber and asking to speak to Jay is something new for you."

That was an understatement. "I know. But I want to do it."

"I'm glad. That's a blessing."

Bethanne nodded. She was proud of how far she'd come, though until that moment, she hadn't taken the time to reflect on just how far that was.

She'd only been thinking about what to say to Jay. Was she developing different feelings for him, or was she just feeling guilty? She hated that her mind was in such a muddle where he was concerned. It was almost impossible for her to think about Jay, Peter, Seth, or her fears individually. Each felt like part of a grid that created the worst experience in her life. It didn't make sense and it wasn't logical.

"Do you want to talk about it before you leave? I have time."

"Nee, Mamm."

"Are you sure?"

"Yes. I just have a couple of things to discuss with Jay." And those things were private. Not for her mother's ears. Not this time.

"I understand. You have your cell phone?"

"I do." Her parents had received permission from the bishop for Bethanne to carry a cell phone with her at all times. Now if there was an emergency—or if her fears got the best of her—she'd be able to call the police for help.

"I'll listen for the kitchen phone. You know, just in case something goes wrong."

"Nothing's going to go wrong."

94

Standing up again, her mother folded her arms across her chest. "You know, maybe you should call after you get to the publishing house. Just to let me know you're safe."

"I will not." When her mother inhaled, obviously eager to argue her point, Bethanne walked to the back hallway and loaded her books into a canvas tote bag.

Mamm followed. "Child—"

Frustrated with the entire situation, Bethanne turned on her. "Nee, Mamm. I am not a child. I'm a grown woman and it's time I acted like one around here too."

"You might be a grown woman, but you aren't like everyone else."

For too long she'd believed that to be true. But getting to know Seth and Tabitha Zimmerman over the course of the last year had given her a new perspective. They'd learned a lot about forgiveness and taught her about that too— including the fact that she needed to forgive herself.

Now she was realizing that she needed determination to keep one night's tragedy from taking center stage in her mind. That wasn't healthy, and she knew it. Just because something was unforgotten didn't mean it had to be given great importance.

"That's where you're wrong, Mamm," she said at last. "I am like everyone else. Every woman, by the time she reaches her midtwenties, has experienced a hardship of one kind or another. I'm no different than anyone else."

Pain entered her mother's eyes. "But—"

"I need to go. Expect me back by four o'clock."

"It's only eleven."

"I know." Carrying her tote bag with her purse tucked neatly inside, she strode to the barn and got out her bicycle. A few minutes later she was pedaling down the road, feeling warm and free and almost hopeful.

Two hours later, Bethanne was feeling nervous and a bit embarrassed. Her visit to the publishing house had gone very well. Edna, the personal assistant to the editor, was there, and she was so happy to have received so many reviews early that she'd asked Bethanne to lunch.

While they were eating, Edna had mentioned that her roommate had just left and she was looking for a new one. Bethanne couldn't help but ask about the room. Next thing she knew, they were walking through Edna's sparkling-clean home. Bethanne wasn't sure if she actually wanted to live with Edna, but the thought of moving on with her life and getting out from underneath the sheltered existence she'd begun to take for granted was tempting.

Now, after she parked her bicycle in the bike rack in front of Burke's, her nerves returned. She should've used some common sense and realized that Jay was at work. She couldn't just stop by and expect him to be able to take time off to see her.

"Is everything okay, miss?" an older man dressed in slacks and a red shirt emblazoned with "Burke Lumber" on the chest asked.

"Yes. I just realized that I probably made a mistake."

He frowned. "What's wrong? Are you lost?"

"Nee, I . . . well, you see, I'm friends with Jay Byler and decided to stop by. But it just occurred to me that he's likely busy and not able to have visitors. I should've considered that his boss wouldn't be too happy about a friend stopping by on the spur of the moment."

When the man smiled, wrinkles appeared around his eyes. "He likely is hard at work, but I don't think his boss will mind. Everyone deserves a break—especially if it's for a friend. Come on in. I'll find him for ya."

"Are you sure I won't get him in trouble?"

"I'm positive." He winked. "I'm the boss, you see."

"You're Mr. Burkholder?" Boy, she'd just put her foot in her mouth!

"Guilty," he said with a laugh as he opened the glass door and motioned her inside.

Deciding to see the humor in it too, she grinned at him. And then gasped.

They were in a showroom with beautiful wood tables, doors, floor samples, and other woodwork surrounding them, including a variety of rocking chairs. As her eyes adjusted to the dim light, her sense of smell took in the aroma. A luscious combination of pine, hardwood, and lemon furniture oil filled the room.

"It smells so good in here."

Mr. Burkholder laughed. "I've heard a lot of things said about this place, but its smell isn't usually the first thing people mention."

"I bet not. Sorry."

"Don't apologize." He inhaled. "Honestly, I think it smells pretty fabulous myself."

"Do you need any help, Walker?" a man in his midthirties asked.

"I do. I happened to meet this nice young lady on the way inside and we got to talking. Could you please find Jay Byler and send him to the front?"

"Sure thing."

"He'll likely be here in about ten minutes, my dear. If I'm not mistaken, Jay is working at the far back of the campus today."

"Thank you for getting him. I don't mind waiting, and I promise I won't take too long."

Mr. Burkholder shrugged. "Jay's a good employee. Always

a hard worker. And all the employees know what they need to do. As long as they get it done, I don't monitor their every move."

"Yes, sir."

"What's your name, dear?"

"Bethanne Hostetler."

He held out his hand. "Bethanne, it is a pleasure to meet you."

"You too. Thank you again for helping me find Jay."

"Any time." He smiled before walking toward another employee who had a clipboard in her hands.

Now that Bethanne was alone, she took another look around the showroom. Spying a beautiful desk in the corner, she walked over to inspect it more closely. She soon realized there was a sliding compartment in the back. It was a perfect place for receipts or pens and pencils. Or even special trinkets and such.

Deciding that running her hand over the wood wouldn't harm it, she did—and practically sighed in appreciation. It was a gorgeous piece of furniture. She'd love to write her reviews on something so fine.

"I see you found the writing desk."

She turned to see Jay approaching. He, too, wore a Burke Lumber polo shirt, but his was untucked. He also had on Amish-tailored brown pants, a ball cap, and Red Wing boots. He looked perfect.

His blue eyes stared at her intently. "What are you doing here? Do you need a desk?"

"Oh, nee. This desk is a beautiful thing, but I needed to speak to you. I couldn't wait another day."

That obviously took him by surprise. Honestly, the shock on his face probably matched what she was feeling. She decided to go with it.

"I, um, happened to see Mr. Burkholder on my way inside. He said it was okay if I bothered you for a couple of minutes."

"You talked to my boss about talking to me?"

He sounded incredulous. Or, perhaps, surprised? Either way, his reaction made her feel even more nervous. "I didn't seek him out or anything, Jay," she said in a rush. "Mr. Burkholder was walking in the parking lot when I was parking my bike. He asked me if I was okay." Figuring she had nothing to lose, she added, "I told him I was hoping to talk to you."

"Wow, Bethanne."

"I know. Please don't be mad."

As his posture visibly relaxed, a new warmth entered his expression. "I'm not mad," he said in a soft tone. "Now, what did you want to tell me?"

Bethanne clenched her fists and said a prayer for strength. She had a feeling their upcoming conversation was about to change her life.

# 13

Jay looked around the facility's showroom. There were about a dozen people in the vicinity. Mr. Burkholder's office was in the front, as well as the offices of the vice president in charge of finances and Mary, who handled human resources. Everyone was doing their jobs and seemed to give him and Bethanne no more than a curious glance.

He knew better, though. It might be a professional organization that sold millions of dollars of merchandise annually, but rarely did one of their workers get asked to come to the showroom by the boss because a woman had decided to pay him a visit.

As much as he was delighted to see Bethanne, Jay felt awkward. How could he not? And, if he were honest, a little put on the spot. Hopefully nothing was wrong. "Is anything the matter?"

"Jah." When his concern must have shown on his face, her eyes grew bigger. "I mean, nee."

What was going on? Was she playing some sort of game with him? Tamping down his impatience as best he could, he asked, "Is it yes or no?"

She looked down at her feet, then drew a breath and met

his gaze. "I mean, I've been feeling badly about my rudeness when you came calling. I wanted to apologize."

He stuffed his hands in his pockets. "So you decided to come here in the middle of the day?"

Looking even more uncomfortable, she swallowed. "Jah. But I hadn't thought it through. All I was thinking about when I woke up was that I didn't want to wait another day to apologize." She waved a hand. "Jay, I promise. I was about to turn around when Mr. Burkholder got to talking with me. Before I realized who he was, I admitted that I'd come to see you but thought your boss would get mad. Next thing I knew, he was opening the door and ushering me inside."

"Wow." So now Mr. Burkholder was up to date on his social life.

Reaching out, she placed her hand on his forearm. "I hope you're not mad. I didn't know how else to find you easily."

"Except come to mei haus?"

She pulled her hand back, the last of the small bit of confidence that had been shining in her eyes fading. "Well . . . jah. Except that." She tensed and shook her head. "You know what? You're right. Deciding to just come here in the middle of a workday was a mistake. A big one. I'm sorry if I embarrassed you. I'll leave right now."

"Nee."

"See you—" She must not have heard him.

"Nee, Bethanne," he said louder. Stepping to her side, he reached for her hand to lead her through the two glass doors that led outside.

When she didn't fight him, he counted that as a win. And when she curved her fingers around his as they walked into the bright sunlight, he figured it was a miracle.

Burke Lumber not only paid well and had a great staff rec

room, but Mr. Burkholder had also provided a secluded outdoor seating area for employees to eat lunch or take breaks. A privacy fence surrounded the area, and amid the trees and shrubs were tables and chairs and even three rocking chairs.

He led her to a table. "Let's sit for a moment."

Thankfully, she didn't refuse. But she perched on the edge of the chair as if she feared she might need to jump up to put distance between them. With her hands clasped on her lap, she looked prim and proper. And anxious.

No. She looked ready. Ready for him to chastise her and make her cry.

He had no intention of doing that.

But now that they were committed to the conversation, Jay wanted to get to the heart of their problem. No, the heart of *his* problem. Even if it was painful. He wanted to know the answer, even if it would mean that his dream would never be a possibility. That was better than not knowing. "Bethanne, where do you see our relationship going?"

"What do you mean?"

"I think we both know what I mean," he said in as slow and easy of a tone as he could manage. "I haven't been shy about my feelings for you, just as you haven't been shy about your feelings for me."

She nodded.

"So, I'm asking you now, would you like me to leave you alone?"

"You'd do that?"

"Jah."

Was that hope shining in her eyes? And if so, was it hope that he really would leave her alone? Or something else? He wished he could tell without her seeing the hope that was no doubt shining in his own eyes. He wasn't ready to lay himself bare like that.

He didn't have a pair of sunglasses on him, though, so he was going to have to be honest. Even if it killed him. "I'll do whatever you need me to do so you can be happy."

She stared at him. With a shade of wonder in her voice, she whispered, "You mean it, don't you?"

"Yes." The tightness in his throat kept him from saying any more.

She exhaled. Nodded a few times. Then swallowed. "I . . . I don't want you to leave me alone. Jay, I think we could be friends."

Friends. Well, that was . . . something, he guessed. "All right." He smiled tightly, but his insides were a confused ball of hurt. Just what did that mean? Did she want him to call on her again? Wave to her when they passed on the street? Try not to make a nuisance of himself when they sat across the aisle from each other in church?

Maybe it didn't even matter.

He stood. "Thanks for coming by."

"Nee, wait." She scrambled to her feet. "Jay, what I came here to say but somehow lost my nerve . . . was this." She took a deep breath. "If you decide to come calling again, I will come downstairs." Her eyes widened. "Nee. I mean, I'll be glad you are visiting."

"Glad?"

Her cheeks were now a lovely shade of pink. "Yes. Glad."

His expression warmed. "Then I'll pay you a visit soon."

"You will?"

"I'm not interested in making your life more difficult, Bethanne. I just want to be in it." No, he wanted to be so important to her that she couldn't imagine starting a day without him by her side.

She released a ragged sigh. "All right, then."

She looked so lost. Before he thought better of it, he

reached for her hand. It was soft and smooth and surprisingly cool. He ran his thumb along her knuckles. Enjoyed the pattern of the delicate bones underneath the thin barrier of skin.

She watched as he did that, then raised her chin. Met his eyes.

"I appreciate you coming to see me here. I know it wasn't easy for you."

Bethanne nodded. "I'm glad I did."

"I'll see you soon."

Her brown eyes turned languid and soft. Sparking a new wave of desire to know her better. Then, all too soon, she pulled her hand back. He released it.

"I better go now. Bye, Jay."

"Bye, Bethanne."

Needing a moment to come to terms with what had just happened, he stayed where he was as she went back into the building. And remembered all the times when they were younger and he'd wanted to get her attention so badly but knew that wouldn't be welcomed. And he once again wished that Peter Miller hadn't done what he did. Even if it meant Jay would never get a chance with Bethanne, it would be worth it for her not to have been hurt.

He hated what she'd had to endure the last seven years. But now things seemed to be changing for the better—for both of them. Pretty, sweet, shy Bethanne Hostetler had finally consented to him calling on her.

It seemed miracles happened after all.

# 14

"Hey, Irish!"

Ryan's recently acquired nickname echoed through the rat's maze of cubicles in the station, causing more than one officer to chuckle under his breath. He didn't mind it too much. He was from a large Irish family, after all. Nothing he could do about that.

"Irish, you got a minute?" Chief Foster asked again when he appeared at his side.

"Yes." He stood up, glad for the excuse to not start his morning by scanning through police reports of carjackings in nearby jurisdictions. "What's up?"

"I want you to head over to Burke Lumber. Dispatcher just sent out a request for a unit to be on the scene."

"Yes, sir." He reached for his radio and took his pistol from the locked drawer in his desk. "What's going on?"

"There was a fire, but it was small, and the fire department already put it out." He frowned, glancing at his cell. "However, it sounds as if one of the employees might have seen something. I want you to go check it out."

"They don't think it was an accident?"

"I'm not sure what they think. Dispatcher sounded pretty

105

confused about the call. But she did say that she feels it was a legit concern. I don't doubt it. Burke Lumber has a stellar reputation. The owner's name is Walker Burkholder. He should be able to help you talk to whoever you need to."

"Roger that."

After striding out to his cruiser, Ryan pulled out of the station and drove the five miles to the edge of Marion. Thankfully it was the middle of the day, so he didn't connect with much traffic at all. Minutes later, he pulled into Burke Lumber.

A fire engine was in the parking lot. The lights were on, but the crew was obviously cleaning up. Another vehicle, a white SUV with the MFD logo on the side, sat nearby. As soon as Ryan parked and got out of the car, an employee from Burke Lumber walked toward him with a confident demeanor. He looked Amish.

"Hi. May I help ya?"

He nodded. "Good morning. I'm Officer Mulaney. I was sent out here to speak with someone. Do you know who that is?"

"It's me. At least for now."

"All right. How may I help you?"

The man looked him in the eye. "There was a fire, but we think it was a distraction. The door into the main offices was broken into."

"And you are?"

"Sorry. My name's Jay Byler. I've been an employee here for almost ten years."

"Good to meet you."

Jay stuffed his hands in his pockets and nodded.

Ryan hid a smile. The man was all business. He could work with that. "Show me where that is, if you would."

"Jah. I'll be glad to."

Following Jay into the building and then through a vast showroom, Ryan was shocked at how modern everything looked. He had figured with so many Amish working at the business, it might look a bit more homespun. "This place is unexpected," he said. "It's nice."

Jay looked confused, then nodded. "I had forgotten that you're new in town. I reckon you wouldn't have had the occasion to visit before."

"I've been here for over a month now, but you're right. I'm still getting to know all the area businesses."

"Well, welcome to ya. I'm sorry we're not meeting under better circumstances."

"Me too."

Jay stopped in front of the door that led to the main offices. It was black and had a glass insert in the center of it. It was obvious that the door was usually open during the day. However, there was a good dead bolt by the handle. The wood around it was splintered. "This here is how the office was broken into," he explained.

Pulling out his phone, Ryan took several pictures of both the broken lock as well as the marks on the doorframe. "I'm guessing someone used a crowbar."

"Jah. I thought the same thing."

"Do you sell those?"

"Crowbars? For sure. And probably half the workstations in the back have one on hand."

"Any way to tell if one is missing?"

"I can ask, though that might be a long shot. I'm afraid tools get picked up by employees every once in a while." He waved a hand. "You know . . . we're working and we need an extra hand and a crowbar, and someone says, 'Just go grab one from aisle four.' That kind of stuff."

"That makes it difficult to keep track of your inventory."

"I reckon it might. I don't know, though. Mr. Burkholder never seems to be disturbed by it. Plus, most of our customers are commercial. They're hotels, big office buildings, hospitals, etc. We don't exactly cater to folks just wanting one door or desk." He seemed to think about it. "Then there's all the folks who are our suppliers and such. I don't think anyone takes advantage. I've never heard of it."

Ryan figured Jay was probably right. Besides, the real problem wasn't a missing crowbar, it was the fire—and what could have possibly been stolen from the office. "I'm going to need to talk to whoever is in charge."

"That's Mr. Burkholder, but he isn't here at the moment."

"So, you can answer all my questions?"

"I think Peggy Conway might be a better choice." Jay gestured for Ryan to enter first. "She's Mr. Burkholder's PA, so she knows just about everything going on around here."

Ryan's first impression was that the office space looked as efficient as any metropolitan-based corporation. Well, any corporation that was run by someone's cozy grandfather. All of the furniture in the office space was beautiful—expertly built and with a smooth, buttery-looking finish. But it was also a little cramped.

A middle-aged lady in a pair of dark slacks and a white blouse was looking down at her desk when they entered. Her head popped up, then she frowned when she saw Ryan in his uniform. "May I help you?" she asked.

"Peggy, this here is Officer Mulaney," Jay said. "He's here about the break-in."

"I don't recognize you."

"That's because I'm new in town."

Still looking him over, she asked, "Where are you from?"

"Connecticut."

"You're a long way from home."

"I am."

She still hadn't budged from her position at the desk. "Are you finding everything you need okay?"

Ryan's knee-jerk reaction was to remind her that he wasn't there on a social call. But luckily he'd spent enough time in Candace's company that he was learning that easy conversation was just these folks' way.

Even more importantly, this Peggy was likely not simply making small talk. If he mentioned that he was in need of something, she'd likely find a way for him to get it. "Yes, ma'am, I'm finding everything just fine."

"Good to know. We're not the big city, but we have just about anything one could need." She winked. "With a few less cars and a lot less pollution."

He grinned. "You all do have a lot less of that here."

Jay cleared his throat. "Have you found anything to be missing, Peggy?"

"Well, as a matter of fact, yes."

Ryan pulled out his pen and pad of paper. "What's missing?"

"I keep a metal lockbox in the back of this drawer." She pulled open the bottom drawer of a filing cabinet. It was finely crafted, just like every other piece in the showroom. Peering closer, Ryan could see a gap of about eight or nine inches at the back.

"What was inside?"

"Cash, plus a couple of credit cards." She lifted her chin. "Sometimes Mr. Burkholder will ask me to purchase something for the office or for his wife, and I'll use those credit cards."

After getting the description of the box, along with a rough estimate of the cash amount and number of credit cards, he closed the file cabinet again. "Anything else?"

"Yes." For the first time, she looked uncomfortable. Darting a look at Jay, she said, "I feel a little embarrassed about what I did."

Beside him, Jay looked mystified, which sent warning signals through Ryan. Jay hadn't been surprised to learn about the lockbox. Maybe he'd known about it? After making a note to chat with Jay about that later, Ryan scanned the PA's expression. She definitely looked uncomfortable.

"Is this something else a personal matter, Peggy? Would you like to speak in private?"

She glanced Jay's way again and flushed. "No, it's okay."

It wasn't, though. Whatever she had to say, it was obvious that she didn't want Jay to know about it. Turning to the younger man, Ryan said, "If you'll excuse us now."

"Oh. Yeah, sure. I'll, uh, wait out in the main lobby." After darting a look at Peggy, he left the office.

Ryan turned back to her. "What's missing?"

"Some of my index cards."

Huh? "What do they have on them?"

"Well, you see, there are cards on each employee. Basic details, but I also write personal notes on each."

Was she serious? "You keep note cards with personal notes about each employee?"

Peggy stiffened, obviously becoming defensive. "Yes, but this practice is not as bad as it sounds. I promise."

He raised one eyebrow. "How does it sound to you?"

Her cheeks reddened. "Nosy."

She was starting to look like she was going to faint. Or maybe throw up. "Why don't you have a seat, Ms. Conway."

"Am I in trouble?"

"No. I'm just trying to understand. Why don't you show me one?"

"Okay." Opening the desk's right-hand drawer, she pulled out a stack of neatly arranged cards. "Here you go."

He took the stack from her and glanced at the first few in the pile. At the top of each one was a printed name, an email address, a phone number, and a home address. Nothing too out of the ordinary there. Especially since she was the president's personal assistant.

But that was where the usual information ended. Below the basic facts was the employee's birthday, highlighted in color. Then there were several handwritten notes. The employee's spouse and children's ages were listed. Sometimes a pet was noted. On other cards, the days a person had taken off were noted. On others, there were notes about the employee's favorite food or flower. Finally, on about eight or ten of them there were dark check marks at the top.

"What do these mean?" he asked.

Her eyes widened before they squeezed shut. "Oh no."

"Ms. Conway?"

"They . . . well, they're notations I made when they were rude."

"To whom? You?"

She nodded. "Yes. Or to Mr. Burkholder." She winced. "Or they were rude or mean in general."

Pulling over a chair, he sat down next to her. "Did someone ask you to keep these notes?"

"No. I mean, kind of but not really."

"Ms. Conway, I'm here to investigate the break-in. To see if the fire that was set really could have been a diversion. If you think that one of the cards might have been taken, I need to have a good idea about why something like that would happen." Looking at her closely, he added, "Do you understand what I'm saying?"

"I do."

"So?" Honestly, he'd gotten more information out of men questioned for grand theft auto.

"So, to answer your earlier questions, yes and no."

"Explain, please."

"I mean, I started writing note cards on each person in the company as a way to help Mr. Burkholder." She relaxed a bit. "You know, if he has a meeting with a longtime employee, he wanted to make sure he asked after their wife or children. That kind of stuff."

"That makes perfect sense to me."

She smiled. "It worked so well, and Mr. Burkholder was so appreciative of my notes, that I started to add more details." She lowered her voice. "Say if, um, a man's wife was going through cancer treatment. Mr. Burkholder might have known that, but he could've forgotten the exact details of the cancer when he had a meeting with the employee. It wouldn't do if"—her voice drifted off as she flipped through the cards and put one on top—"if he asked Arnie Pyle about Lizbeth but she'd died."

"I see. So, is that where the other notations came from?"

"Yes. I'm afraid I got a little too diligent. It all started on a particularly bad day. See, one of our employees had an upcoming meeting, so I was getting his note card out. And I remembered hearing that he'd gotten a divorce. So I had to see if that was true. It was. So I told Mr. Burkholder, you know, just to be on the safe side."

"Because you didn't want him to put his foot in his mouth."

"Exactly." Her happy smile faded. "Except that man was really mean to Mr. Burkholder and started yelling at him about needing a pay raise. He didn't even care that our boss had taken the time to ask how he was doing after the divorce."

"So you put a check by his name."

"Yes." She sighed. "I was never going to tell anyone about those checks. Honestly, it started to become something of a game to me."

"A game?"

"Well, you might be surprised by the things some people say to me. They aren't always very polite. I started writing little notes just to make myself feel better." Her gaze flicked up to meet his. "And yes, I know I shouldn't have done that."

"Whose cards were stolen, Ms. Conway?"

"Mr. Burkholder's . . . and Jay Byler's."

"But everyone else has a card?"

"Yes. I mean, except for Scott."

"Scott?"

"Yes, he's just recently joined us, but he's going to be a fantastic employee. He's my son. I don't need a card for him, of course." Pride tinged her voice.

"So their personal information and your added notes are in someone's hands now."

"Yes." She lowered her voice. "Mr. Burkholder had no idea that I kept a card on him, but I figured I might as well be fair, right?"

"Right. Can you think of anything off the top of your head that either man might not want getting out into the world? Besides their personal contact information."

"Not really for Mr. Burkholder. All I ever put on his card were his favorite restaurants and his anniversary date. He always forgets."

"And Jay?"

"Nothing to speak of, though I did just add something."

"What is that?"

After a second's pause, she blurted, "That Bethanne Hostetler came for a visit—and a private conversation."

He knew that name. "Say that name again." He was a little rattled. Could it really be Candace's cousin?

"Bethanne Hostetler." Peggy was sounding a bit triumphant.

"Is that significant?" he asked.

"I'd say so." When he simply stared at her, she cleared her throat impatiently. "Oh, come now. You must have heard of her. She's the girl who was almost raped by Peter Miller six or seven years ago. And her cousin is Candace Evans, our current Miss Crittenden County." She winked. "I'm sure you know who she is. Her picture was in the paper."

Peggy was turning out to have a wealth of information. And he was learning that he might have been in Marion, Kentucky, for only a short time, but he was already in the thick of things.

There was no reason to believe that the robbery had anything to do with those cards. It might have all been about the money and the credit cards. Ryan had certainly come across criminals who'd robbed—or even killed—for less.

But there was also something kind of creepy about a company secretary keeping personal notes on every employee. More than a little creepy. It was one thing to have something written down in a personnel file in a human resources department. To know that it was handwritten on a note card, practically available for whomever Peggy decided to share it with? Well, he could imagine that more than one employee would find fault with that.

After pulling out an evidence bag from one of his jacket pockets, he opened it and held it out. "I'm going to need to take these cards."

"Are you sure?"

"I'm positive."

She sighed and dropped them into the bag.

"If you discover anything else missing, please let me know, ma'am."

"You won't share those with anyone, will you?"

"That's none of your concern. It's a police investigation now."

Looking even more deflated, she hung her head. "I made a big mistake, didn't I?"

Ryan wasn't sure if she was referring to her personal stash of cards or telling him about her habit. Maybe a bit of both. After all, he would've never searched through her desk for personal information if she hadn't brought it up.

Which posed one more concern.

What had been on those cards that had made her so worried that she'd tell him about them? He was going to need to find that out.

# 15

Sitting beside Officer Mulaney in his Blazer, Candace felt uncomfortable. He'd been polite as ever when he'd picked her up to take her to the shopping mall out near Johnson City, but he was acting distant. His responses to her comments and questions had been almost curt. Had she done something to upset him? Or was he feeling like she was a big pain in his backside because of all her appearances?

If that was the case, she didn't know what to do about that. Escorting her around the county and the surrounding areas had been the police department's idea, not hers. But maybe he was having second thoughts?

When she glanced at him for about the fifth time and noticed that his jaw was clenched, she knew she was going to have to say something. Give him a way out of his responsibilities. "Ryan, if you have other things to do today, you can just drop me off at the mall. I'll get someone else to take me home. It's no big deal."

Stopped at a traffic light, he eyed her curiously. "Who would you call?"

"I don't know. My mom or dad. Maybe a girlfriend," she

added, though she wasn't exactly sure who would be available. Most of her girlfriends had jobs that kept them busy.

He shook his head. "Candace, don't worry about it. I told you I would take you and stay by your side. And I will."

The light turned to green, and he drove through the intersection.

"I just wanted you to know that I don't expect you to continue doing this," she said in a rush. "I mean, you've probably got other things to do."

"I do. But one of my jobs is to escort you to appearances."

"But maybe there's an intern or something?" She vaguely remembered a kid in one of her classes her junior year who had received some credit for shadowing a police officer. She hadn't thought much about it at the time, but if it was someone brawny with half a clue, that would be enough to deter most people.

Though he didn't smile, the lines around his eyes crinkled. "You're gonna give me a complex, Candace. Do you really think I'm no better than an intern?"

"No. I mean, of course not." When she saw a dimple appear in his cheek, she flushed. "You're messing with me."

"Only a little bit. It's hard not to, the way you are always trying to lose me."

"I'm not. It just seems like you're bothered today, and I'm afraid it's because of me."

Stopped at another light, he stared at her for a long moment. "I just have some things on my mind."

"Anything I can help you with?"

"What, are you starting to think you want to be a police intern too?"

Easing a bit, she chuckled. "No. But, ah, I'm a good listener." Liking the idea that she could help him with something, she added, "I could be your sounding board."

As they reached a stop sign, he glanced her way again. "If I do ask you something, can we keep it between us?"

"Sure."

"I'm serious." After a pause, he added, "It doesn't really have anything to do with a case, but I'm feeling at a disadvantage because I'm new in town."

"If I can help, I will. But I haven't paid a ton of attention to city things. I've never kept up too much with politics in Marion."

"It's nothing like that. It has to do with Bethanne."

"My cousin? What about her?"

"I want to know what she's like."

Candace went into protection mode. "What do you mean, what she's like? Bethanne is Amish, Ryan."

"That doesn't tell me anything. There are a lot of Amish around here."

Figuring he had a point, she said, "Well, let's see. She's kind and thoughtful. She likes to read a lot too."

He glanced her way. "That's it?"

"Well, no. Bethanne is a lot more than that. But most people are fairly complex, don't you think?"

"Yeah."

Ryan said nothing more, and Candace had to wonder why he would want to know about Bethanne. Surely he could look up the police reports from seven years ago if he wanted the whole story. But maybe he'd wanted to hear from someone who knew her well. Candace considered asking him why he wanted to know, but she really didn't feel like talking about Bethanne.

When he eventually pulled into the shopping mall parking lot, he spoke again. "It's 1:30. What time to do you need to be inside?"

"The meet and greet is at two. We've probably got ten

minutes or so." She liked to get there a little early, but not too much.

"All right." After parking, he unbuckled his seat belt but didn't turn off the ignition. "Beyond Bethanne being sweet and Amish, what's her story?"

"Well, as you know, she's my cousin."

"Are you close?"

"Yes. We were born less than a year apart, and our mothers are sisters."

"But you must have very different lives."

"Or course. She's Amish and I'm not." She drew a breath and sighed. "You already know about Peter Miller. She's had a real tough time since what happened with him, although she's been doing better lately."

"How so?"

Ryan's digging made her uncomfortable. There was no way any cop's curiosity was more important than Bethanne's privacy. She might feel like Ryan was becoming a friend, but they had a long way to go before she was willing to share everything she knew about Bethy. "Well, she's leaving the house more often. She works from home as a book reviewer for a publishing company in Marion."

"What does she do for fun?"

Indignation boiled through her. "Fun?"

"Yeah." He now sounded a bit impatient. "Who is she dating?"

Candace's mom had said that an Amish guy named Jay had visited Bethanne at home earlier that week, but Candace hadn't heard anything more about that. "She's not dating anyone."

"You're sure?"

She resented how he was acting like she didn't even know Bethanne. Resented that he seemed to be playing her. Here she was, trying to help him out, but instead he'd turned the tables and wanted gossip about her cousin.

She opened her car door. "Look, time's up. I need to get inside."

"Hold up. I'll walk with you." Ryan got out and shut his door, then walked around the SUV to her. As if by habit, he slowed his stride as they headed for the mall doors, enabling Candace, in her three-inch heels and a form-fitting dress, to walk at a comfortable pace.

Memories of senior prom, when Candace's date seemed oblivious to the challenge of doing much at all in four-inch sandals, tumbled into her mind. By the end of the evening, she'd had two blisters and a cranky attitude from being on her feet all night. Her date had been annoyed with her too. He'd asked her to take the shoes off, but she'd been too afraid of them getting stolen or ruined. She'd worked three overtime shifts at the ice cream parlor to pay for them.

"Thanks," she said as he opened the door for her.

He met her gaze. "I appreciate how polite you are, but there's no need to keep thanking me."

"No, not for being here. I know it's part of your job. I'm just . . . feeling gratitude for you not making me walk any faster."

He chuckled once they were inside. "First, I'd never make a woman run in high heels. I do have some manners. And secondly, *feeling gratitude*?"

"What's wrong with that phrase?"

"Not a thing. It's just a new one for me."

"Well, it's how I feel."

"I'm aware. And . . . here we are."

As they turned the corner, she gasped. A crowd of easily fifty people stood around a podium with a big banner proclaiming "CANDACE EVANS, MISS CRITTENDEN

COUNTY." Would she ever get used to people being so interested in meeting her? "Wow."

He chuckled.

As the woman who organized the event approached them with a big smile on her face, Candace pressed her lips together. She hoped that would give them a little color, because she'd been so focused on her conversation with Ryan that she'd forgotten to look in the visor mirror to check her hair and lipstick.

"Do I look okay?" she whispered as she kind of bared her teeth. "Please tell me I don't have anything in my teeth."

"You have nothing in your teeth." Leaning closer, Ryan added, "You look as gorgeous as you always do. Go get 'em, tiger."

"Thanks."

"Hi, Candace, I'm Jennifer Martin," the woman introduced herself. "Community Relations Director for the mall."

Candace held out her hand. "It's nice to meet you, Ms. Martin. Thank you for having me."

"We're planning for you to speak for fifteen minutes. We'd like you to lightly discuss your platform about literacy and supporting victims of violence." Lowering her voice, she added, "Please keep in mind the wide age range of the crowd. Don't say anything too intense or alarming."

There were lots of little girls aged ten and under in the crowd. "Yes, ma'am."

"Oh, and if you wouldn't mind, please share a couple of beauty tips."

"Of course."

Jennifer pointedly looked at the top of her head. "Where's your crown?"

"Oh." She hadn't put that on either. "My escort has it. Ryan, could you get something for me?"

121

He'd been looking at his phone, but his head popped up. "What do you need?"

"I need my crown."

"Oh, sorry." He opened the tote bag he'd carried in for her, pulled out the container holding the crown, and opened it for her.

Wishing she had a mirror, she smoothed back her hair, then placed the crown on her head, situating it so the two small combs at its base held it securely. "Does this look all right?" she asked Jennifer.

Jennifer stepped closer, adjusted the crown to the right, then arranged two of her curls. "I think you look great. What do you think, Ryan?"

"Perfect."

She chuckled. "He's a keeper, dear."

"I agree," Candace said with a smile. Yep, she could tell herself that they were only friends, but she felt something more for him than mere friendship.

"Are you ready, Candace?"

"Yes, ma'am."

"Okay, I'll step up and introduce you. Then, of course, after you speak, you'll need to pose for pictures and sign photographs."

"Yes, ma'am."

"Very good."

As Jennifer walked toward the podium, Candace assumed what she'd begun to think of as her beauty pageant pose. Straight back, stomach in, chin up, hands to her side, one leg slightly in front of the other. While Jennifer spoke about the pageant and Candace, some of the little girls smiled and waved in her direction. Just as Candace waved back, she caught sight of her stalker sitting at a table in the food court. He was glaring at Ryan as he held a worn paper bag in front of him.

Imagining all sorts of awful things, she looked Ryan's way. When their eyes met, she gave a brief nod of her head toward the food court.

Ryan turned his head, caught sight of her stalker, and then stood up.

"Please welcome Miss Crittenden County!" Jennifer called out.

As Candace stepped forward, her heel wobbled, but she quickly regained her balance. *Please don't let him have a gun,* she thought.

Just as she reached the microphone, a crash came from the food court. Her stalker was gone, but his chair had been overturned and the paper bag lay on the ground.

She sucked in her breath, reminding herself to keep calm. All these people were watching her.

Ryan, who'd been scanning the area, focused on her. He clearly hadn't understood what she was trying to convey. "You okay?" he mouthed.

She nodded even though she wasn't. But what else could she do with all these people looking at her? Panicking would only make the situation worse. She needed to give her speech like nothing had happened. So she forced herself to focus and did just that.

Afterward, she invited questions from the audience. A bunch of little girls' hands went up, and she pointed to one girl. "Yes?"

"Where does your crown sleep at night?"

In spite of the way her nerves were strung tight, Candace smiled. "When I'm not wearing this pretty crown, it sleeps in a wooden box on my dresser."

Up went five more small hands. "How about you?" she asked a dark-haired girl sitting with her father near the back.

As the child asked her question and then Candace answered

in as cheerful of a tone as she could manage, she watched Ryan out of the corner of her eye. He was moving toward her. By the time she called on the next child, he was slipping through the small crowd, apologizing to a couple of the mothers holding their little girls' hands.

"Excuse me, please," he said to a teenage girl with glasses.

When Ryan finally reached her side, she sighed in relief. He was strong and solid and familiar. Unable to help herself, she leaned a little closer to him. His aftershave—a woodsy, dark scent—further calmed her nerves. Centered her.

"Candace, what's going on?" he whispered to her.

"I think that was my stalker."

His posture changed. "Yeah, I thought that guy might be him." He grimaced. "Unfortunately, after seeing him, I scanned the area to make sure he was alone. By the time I started toward him, he was gone."

"I have no idea where he went. One minute he was there, the next minute, all I saw was that chair clattering on the ground."

"Did you see him when we walked in?"

"No." Or had she? She was feeling flustered now. "I mean, I don't think so."

The look Ryan gave her let her know that they were going to be having a long conversation on the way back to town. She deserved it too. She shouldn't have told Ryan she was okay. "He was at the nearest table in the food court. See the sack on the floor? He was holding it."

His eyes searched the food court. "I see it. Five minutes."

Five more minutes. She could do that. "Sorry about that, everyone. Are there any more questions?"

Up went a few hands. Choosing an older girl who looked nervous, Candace tried to smile as naturally as possible. "How about you in the red T-shirt?"

124

"You said you got a lot of scholarships. How did you do that?"

"First, I studied hard in school and made the best grades I could. Then, I asked the counselor at the high school about applying. She helped a lot. The scholarship was the main reason I entered the Miss Crittenden County pageant. It's a good one."

After another two questions about her dress, Ryan signaled that it was time for them to go. He was holding the bag in his hands and texting on his phone.

"Last question," she said brightly. Choosing a girl who looked to be about twelve who wore glasses, she said, "How about you, honey?"

"Is he your boyfriend?" The girl smirked mischievously.

When the crowd turned to look at Ryan, she gave the answer that would end the moment as quickly as possible. If she hesitated, or tried to describe their burgeoning relationship, Candace knew she'd become flustered. All she wanted to do was get out of there. "Yes, he is." She smiled at him, hoping he wouldn't tell the whole group that she was lying through her teeth.

A crowd of girls clapped, making Ryan's eyes widen.

"I knew it!" the smirking girl said.

Jennifer stepped up to the microphone. "Everyone, let's thank Miss Crittenden County for visiting us today."

Dutifully, they clapped. And then, obviously ready to do some shopping, the crowd dissipated.

"You did such a nice job, Candace," Jennifer said. "In addition to being lovely, you're a fantastic speaker."

"Thank you, ma'am."

Shaking her hand, Jennifer added, "I wish you the best of luck this year. And with your future endeavors. And now I'll let your guy have you back." She winked. "He's very devoted. I swear, I thought he was going to stand by your side the whole time."

"Yes," she said weakly.

"You two have a good day now."

"Thank you," she whispered.

Ryan moved to her side, holding the paper bag in one hand and her duffle bag in the other. "Let's go."

Oh no. He was mad at her—probably for saying he was her boyfriend. And who could blame him? She reached for her crown. "All right. I'll just—"

"You can take that off in my vehicle," he interrupted. "We're leaving now."

This was even worse than she'd imagined. He was angry and was probably going to tell her in no uncertain terms that he had no desire to accompany her ever again. She was going to have to do all her future appearances by herself.

Feeling like a recalcitrant child, she walked by his side, looking straight ahead in her struggle to keep up. He seemed to have forgotten about her heels and dress.

When they got outside, Ryan took hold of her arm. "Stay with me," he bit out.

In her effort to keep up, she almost tripped.

Muttering something under his breath, he slowed down. "My apologies. I . . ." He shook his head. "Here I just told you I would take care walking with you and now I'm practically making you run. Are you okay?"

"I'm fine. I'm just—"

"Trying to keep up?" he asked in a far gentler tone. "I'm sorry for acting like a jerk."

When they got to his vehicle, he helped her inside. She buckled up as he got into the driver's side.

Moments later, as Ryan pulled out of the parking lot,

Candace couldn't hold back what she needed to say. "You're in a big hurry—what has you looking so rattled?"

"That paper bag was filled with gifts for you." He sounded serious. Deadly serious.

"What kind of gifts?" She almost didn't want to know.

"The kind no man should be leaving on a table in the mall. We're making a police report, Candace."

Her mind was going toward crazy ideas. She needed more information, not what he was giving her—which was close to nothing at all. "Why?"

He looked away as if he didn't want to say anything, then pursed his lips. "The bag is full. Clothing. And pictures of you—lots of pictures. Most clearly taken without your knowledge. This man . . . he's obsessed, Candace."

Pictures of her. He'd been spying on her. "I just don't understand. I'm not anything special. Why me?"

Ryan's voice softened. "I don't know, but we'll figure it out. I promise you that."

Candace paused. "I'm so sorry I told that girl we were a couple. I was rattled and I didn't want to tell everyone you were a cop. It would bring up too many questions."

"It's fine. I understood."

"I promise, I won't get weird on you. I won't—"

"Candace, I'm not mad." As he stopped at a left-hand turn signal, he scanned her face. "Honestly, I think it might be a good idea if we kept up the ruse. If you don't mind. Until we find this guy, let's just say I'm your new boyfriend. It's a good reason to keep us close."

"I understand." But she didn't understand. Didn't understand this man's obsession or the reason he'd left pictures of her in a paper sack.

What she did understand was she wasn't the least bit

sorry about everyone thinking that she and the newest cop in Marion were a couple.

What was it about him that she found so different than any other man she'd met before? Was it because he made her feel safe? Or because there seemed to be a pull between them that couldn't be denied—one that she was beginning to think she didn't want to deny at all?

# 16

Why, Bethanne, what a nice surprise, dear," Aunt Dora said as she ushered Bethanne inside her sprawling ranch house. "I didn't know you were planning to stop by. Usually Martha lets me know."

Her aunt was looking at her curiously. And perhaps with more than a little bit of worry? She hated that. She hated that everyone assumed she was mere seconds from having a panic attack.

"I didn't tell my mamm I was coming by."

"No?"

"I . . . well, I went out for a walk and then realized I was close by and thought I'd visit with Candace for a spell." She peeked down the hall. Hopefully she would appear any second.

"She'd like that, but I'm afraid she's not home," Aunt Dora said as she led the way into the kitchen. "She's out at yet another Miss Crittenden County event."

Feeling foolish, Bethanne paused near the kitchen table. "I guess I should have guessed that. I'm sorry to bother you. I'll go on home."

"No, no. Please stay." She chuckled, holding up her hand to indicate the countertop. "Look what I've been doing."

Bethanne smiled. Several dozen jelly jars and assorted caps waited there, along with containers of strawberries, a cutting board, and a knife. A glass bowl held a few hulled strawberries. "Are you going to make strawberry preserves?"

"I am and I'm already overwhelmed." Picking up the recipe card lying there, she moaned. "When I looked over the directions, it sounded so simple. Why, I thought it would take no time at all. I was so wrong."

Bethanne pressed her lips together to keep from bursting out laughing. Canning two or three dozen jars of anything never took "no time at all."

Frowning at the counter, Aunt Dora said, "If I made you a snack, would you consider helping me for a while? You've made preserves before, right?"

"I have. I guess you haven't?"

She chuckled. "Obviously not. Your mother was the domestic one. It was no wonder that she married an Amish man and I went in the opposite direction. I . . . well, I was always anxious to get out of the house."

Aunt Dora and her mother had grown up in a conservative Mennonite household in southern Ohio, and they'd been close but like night and day. While Bethanne's mamm had fallen in love with an Amish man and moved to Crittenden County, Aunt Dora had gone on to college and fallen in love with Uncle Wayne, who happened to be from Marion. He worked in town while Bethanne's father managed his family's farm.

To everyone's surprise, the two families got along well despite their differences. They didn't see each other all that often, but when they did, her mamm and Aunt Dora chatted and laughed together.

So, they still had plenty in common . . . except in the kitchen. She couldn't remember Aunt Dora making too many

things that weren't in her "fast and five ingredients" cook-
book.

"I'll be happy to help you. No snacks are even needed."

Pure relief filled her eyes. "Thank you, honey. Now let
me call your mother and let her know where you are." She
paused. "She still has a phone in the kitchen, right?"

"Jah."

"Okay. You wash up and grab an apron." She pointed
to an assortment of bright printed aprons, each one more
festooned with ruffles and piping than the next.

Hiding a smile, Bethanne picked out one with cartoon
smiling bananas and oranges all over it. She couldn't wait
to tell her mother about her sister's cooking project.

Holding a hand over her cell phone, Aunt Dora said,
"Bethanne, I just told your mamm I'd bring you home
later." She frowned. "Probably close to suppertime. Okay
with you?"

"That's gut. Danke."

Flashing a smile her way, Aunt Dora finished the call.
"I'll see you later. Yes, we'll catch up soon. I'll bring you
some jam!" Hanging up, she giggled. "Your mother sounded
alarmed about my undertaking."

Bethanne reckoned she had good reason to be. "I'm surprised Mamm didn't offer to come over to help."

"Oh, she did. But I told her you and I would do just
fine."

That made her happy. It was nice to be treated like she
was capable. "I reckon we will."

Aunt Dora looked around the kitchen. "What do you
think we should do first?"

That was easy. "Finish hulling the strawberries."

Looking like she was about to go into battle, she picked
up a knife. "Are you sure you don't want a sandwich?"

Her stomach chose that moment to growl. "Actually, that sounds good."

Aunt Dora grinned, looking like she'd just escaped the most horrible of chores, then went to the refrigerator. "I'll make us lunch. Would you mind working on the berries?"

"Not at all." Bethanne grinned as she took her aunt's place and began quickly hulling berries.

"I know. I'm hopeless."

"It is a big task." Considering her aunt seemed to plan on making enough jam for the entire town.

"Things like this have always been my problem, I'm afraid," she said as she pulled a variety of lunch meats, as well as lettuce, cheese, and brown mustard from the refrigerator. "I start a project, lose interest or get overwhelmed, and then have no idea what to do about the mess." After fetching the bread from her bread box, she asked, "Do you like your bread toasted, Bethy?"

"It doesn't matter." When her aunt continued to wait for a real answer, she shrugged. "Toasted, please."

"All right." She placed four pieces of bread in the toaster, then pushed the lever and got two plates out of a cabinet. "Now, you, dear, have the right idea."

Bethanne picked up the next container of strawberries. "About what?"

"Oh. I was talking about your lovely job reviewing books. Your mamm is mighty proud of you, dear. She's told me all about the boxes of manuscripts that arrive on your doorstep like clockwork."

"I'm glad she's proud."

"And it sounds like you love it. That's what matters the most, I think."

"I do."

Aunt Dora nodded. "I hope Candy gets a job she likes as much as you like yours."

"Me too. She's got time yet, though. Now that's she's our family's beauty queen."

As she finished making the sandwiches, Aunt Dora smiled at her, though it then dimmed a bit. "Come sit down and let's eat. What do you want to drink? I have water, milk, or Diet Coke."

"Diet Coke."

"I'm going to have that too," she said with a pleased smile.

After they both said their prayers in silence, Bethanne asked, "Is Candace enjoying all the appearances?"

"I think so, though she doesn't share too much about them. Other than that Officer Mulaney is accompanying her."

"Why is that?"

Aunt Dora paused before shrugging. "Security reasons, I suppose. I'm thankful she doesn't have to go anywhere alone. Some of her appearances are at the opposite end of the county. Some of them even farther out than that. And a number take place at night."

"I never thought about the dangers of her traveling by herself."

"I'm afraid her father and I didn't think too much about it either. I was only thinking about the scholarship money. And the fact that she might enjoy the experience, of course."

Bethanne sipped her drink and nodded. Just as she was about to take a bite of her sandwich, the back door opened.

"Mom?"

"We're in here, Candy!" Aunt Dora called.

"Who's we?"

Aunt Dora winked. "Come see."

"Oh. Hey, Bethy," Candace said in a quiet voice.

"Hiya, Candace."

Candace smiled, but her expression didn't match the

cheeriness of her voice. "It's good to see you. I didn't know you were coming over this afternoon."

"No one did. It was kind of a spur-of-the-moment thing."

As Bethanne's words penetrated, her cousin's grin turned more genuine. "Bethy, I'm so proud of you!"

"It's nothing much." Glancing at her aunt, she added, "We're having a good time."

"I feel certain that the Lord brought her to me today," Aunt Dora said as she pointed to the cluttered countertops. "I was on my way to making a mess in here."

Candace's lips twitched. "I reckon so."

"We're having lunch and then Bethy's going to help me make strawberry jam. You can help if you'd like."

"I'd like that." But then tears glinted in Candace's eyes.

Aunt Dora stood up and went to her. "Honey, what's wrong?"

"Oh, Mom. I've been keeping something from you. But Ryan told me that I need to tell you."

She frowned. "You mean Officer Mulaney?"

"Yes."

"Well, what's the news?" She gasped. "Are you two seeing each other?"

Bethanne almost smiled. Aunt Dora did try to find romance in almost any situation. But to her surprise, Candace blushed.

"No . . . but we have become good friends."

"How good? Isn't he older than you?"

"Ryan is older, but not by that much. He's twenty-eight."

"So, six years." Frowning, Aunt Dora sat back down. "Has he been taking advantage of you?"

"Mom! Of course not."

Aunt Dora continued to stew. "You know, I don't know what your father is going to say about this."

"Dad doesn't need to get involved."

"Of course he does. And why didn't Ryan come and ask our permission to court you?"

She rolled her eyes. "Probably because he isn't Amish and neither am I."

"That's not just for the Amish, dear. It's good manners."

"No, Mom. It's old-fashioned. Plus, it's not the point."

"Candace—"

"Mother, listen to me!" Candace drew a deep breath and blew it out. "Ryan isn't the issue."

Aunt Dora exchanged a look with Bethanne before looking back to her daughter. "What is going on, then?"

Candace bit her lip for a second. "I still have a stalker."

"Who is it?" Bethanne asked.

"I'm not sure."

"You don't know his name?"

"No. He's contacted me online. And sometimes he shows up when I'm at various places. Sometimes he speaks to me. Other times he just watches me."

Aunt Dora pressed a hand to her mouth. "This is my fault," she whispered.

Candace started toward her. "Mother, it is not."

"But I encouraged you to enter the pageant. I wanted you to have that scholarship, and I also thought you would be so perfect." Standing up again, she wrapped her arms around her midsection. "The truth is, I guess I wanted to live a little bit through you. Growing up the way I did, being in a beauty pageant was the farthest thing from anyone's mind. And I knew I shouldn't care about such things, but I did." Turning to Bethanne, she looked even more pained. "I'm sorry, dear. That's probably a shock."

"Nee, but, um, maybe you two don't need me here? I could go home."

"Stay," Candace said.

She loved her cousin, but she also respected Aunt Dora. "Are you sure you don't mind me being here?"

"Darling, when I said that the Lord brought you here to help me make jam, it was said half in jest. But now, seeing how distraught Candace is, I think she's going to need us both. Please stay."

Well, that was decided. "All right." She met Candace's gaze. "So, um, how does Ryan fit into all of this?"

"He's been my escort in case things escalated."

"Do you think they will?" her aunt asked.

"I think they have." Taking a deep breath, she added, "The man was at my appearance today, and he left a paper bag of photos. They were all of me." Suddenly looking a little pale, she added, "There were even pictures from years ago too. All taken when I had no idea someone was watching me. It's so creepy."

"Oh, Candace," Bethanne whispered.

"Does Officer Mulaney have these pictures now?" Aunt Dora asked.

"Yes. They're going to check them and the bag for fingerprints."

Aunt Dora closed her eyes for a few moments. "Maybe you need to quit all these appearances."

Candace stared at her. "Quit being Miss Crittenden County? I can't."

"But, Candy, your safety needs to come first."

"Mom, he was stalking me before I even competed in the pageant. He's going to continue following me around no matter what."

"I don't like this."

"I don't either," Candace said.

"I think your father and I need to speak with the police,"

Aunt Dora said. "And I'm just warning you, your dad might insist that you stop the appearances for a while."

Candace's chin lifted. "I'm not going to stop, Mom," she said in a firm tone. "Ryan's accompanying me. He said he's going to watch out for me, and I believe him."

But her mother kept talking. Just as if she hadn't said a word. "Best intentions are all well and good, but things can happen," her mom said with a nod. "The more I think about it, the more I believe you'll be safest here at home."

"Nee," Bethanne said.

Candace turned to her, a look of surprise on her face.

"Don't make her do that," she continued. "It's . . . it's miserable being a captive in your own home."

Dora's expression softened. "Honey, I understand where you're coming from, but Candace's situation is very different than yours."

"I know. But not living your life is an awful existence. I wouldn't wish it on anyone."

Candace reached for her hands and clasped them tightly. "You're right, Bethy. If I stay home, all I'm going to do is let fear get the best of me."

"And fear is a terrible thing to live with," Bethanne said.

It was almost as bad as the memories.

# 17

Deciding to take Bethanne at her word, when Jay got off work, he went home, showered, and then headed over to the Hostetlers' house. As he drove the horse and buggy down the back streets, he gave himself a pep talk. He wanted to expect the best from Bethanne, but experience had shown him that even her best intentions for moving forward had to battle with the old insecurities that seemed to always take over.

He'd wanted her to be his girl for most of his life. He was pretty sure he was in love with her. But he also realized that he was just a man who wanted a wife and a family. If Bethanne pulled away from him again, he didn't know how much longer he could wait.

Seth Zimmerman's words of wisdom about being patient had merit. But his experience with Tabitha had been different. Tabitha had been abused. But despite all of that, she'd slowly gotten to know Seth and wanted to overcome her fears and be with him. Bethanne, on the other hand, might want to move forward but not with Jay.

After he parked the buggy in the front drive, he climbed out, settled the horse's leads around the hitching post, and then turned toward the front door. It was time to come calling again. He hoped and prayed it went well.

"Wilkum, Jay," Martha Hostetler said as she ushered him into the house. "How are you this evening?"

"I'm well, danke. And you?"

"We're the same." She gave him a tired smile. "I don't know why this weather always seems to bring out the worst in me. Even though the trees in the yard keep most of the house nice and cool, it never feels cool enough."

"Mei mamm says the same."

"I'm glad I'm not the only one hoping for a short summer."

He smiled. "You're not the only one, I'm certain of that. It's so hot at the lumber mill. Between the heat and humidity, I sometimes go through several shirts a day."

"In any case, we're glad you stopped by. As soon as Bethanne spied your buggy on the drive, she ran up to her room to change."

He took that as a good sign. "She didn't have to do that."

"I think she wanted to. She was gone all day and only came home a while ago."

"Really?"

"I know. It's hard to get used to, ain't so? I'm ashamed to say that I've gotten so used to her always being here, I sometimes don't know what to do when she lets me know that she won't be home for hours."

Maybe all of his worries had been for nothing. Maybe Bethanne really was ready to move on with her life—and if she was up in her room primping, maybe she hadn't changed her mind about him.

"Bethanne's going to keep us on our toes," he said. Feeling optimistic, he added, "Perhaps that will serve me well."

She smiled. "Indeed." Directing him into the parlor, she

said, "Bethanne put out a puzzle and I brought out large glasses of half and half—tea and lemonade. Would you care for anything else at the moment?"

"I'm good."

"Well, then, I'll, uh, go let Bethanne know you're waiting."

"She knows, Mamm," Lott said as he came into the room. "Jay, Bethy wanted you to know that she'll be down shortly."

"Danke."

As his mother headed for the kitchen, Lott sat down at the card table. "I sure hope things work out between the two of you. It's nice having another man around the house."

That made two of them. "How's work?"

"Good. I got hired on, and the boss has me working with just about everybody. Every morning, I'm going somewhere new."

"Do you like that?" Jay wouldn't. He thrived on things staying the same as much as possible.

"I do. It keeps things interesting."

Jay sat down on the couch. "Seth Zimmerman works there too, doesn't he?"

"Jah."

"Is he . . . difficult to work with?"

"Nope. He's far more patient than some of the other guys. I would've thought he'd be the opposite. But he says that prison taught him the value of perspective. He doesn't get too upset about much, which I'm glad about since I'm engaged to his little sister."

"I haven't talked to Melonie in a spell. Is she doing well?"

"She is." Lott laughed. "For some reason, she still puts up with me."

Bethanne entered the room wearing a dark pink dress and pink flip-flops. She looked so fresh and pretty—like she was ready for a day in Pinecraft. And she seemed *happy*. "I'm sorry you had to wait, Jay," she said.

Jay stood. "It was no problem. Lott and I were catching up. Plus, your mother walked me in and made me feel welcome."

Bethanne glanced at the table. "And she already got us drinks. Would you like some cookies? I made molasses drops yesterday."

"Not yet." Jay's gaze drifted to her brother.

Catching the unspoken signal, Lott stood up. "I'll, uh, go see what Daed is doing. See ya, Jay."

"See ya." Finally alone with Bethanne, he stepped closer to her side. "Hi."

Her cheeks pinkened. "Hi." Looking a little more self-conscious, she added, "I'm glad you came over this evening."

"I'm glad you wanted me to return." And very glad that she hadn't changed her mind since then. "So, where were you today? Your mother said you only recently got home."

"I was at my aunt's house," she said as she sat down on the couch.

Right next to where he'd been sitting.

He was so pleased by that choice, he felt like a foolish boy. "And how was your aunt?" he asked as he sat down beside her.

"Overwhelmed." Looking like she was trying not to laugh, she added, "Aunt Dora was attempting to make jam. I don't know how many containers of strawberries were on her counters. When I got there, she looked like she was about to box up everything and take it all to my mother to deal with."

"Uh-oh."

"We put up forty jam jars of strawberry preserves."

"Forty? That's a lot."

She blew out a burst of air. "You don't know the half of it. You'd have to know Aunt Dora to get the full effect, but

141

imagine a woman completely unsuited to the kitchen always imagining being an Amish cook."

He laughed, appreciating her humor. "That bad?"

"Jah. She's a good sport, though. Honestly, her awkwardness makes every cooking chore more fun. I never know what she's going to do."

"Her daughter is Candace, right?"

She nodded. "Our county's own beauty queen. She came home soon after I got there and ended up helping us."

"Sounds like a fun afternoon."

"It really was. Except that she told us she's been having some trouble."

"With what?"

She swallowed as worry lines marred her brow. "She thinks a man is stalking her. It's bad enough that she told Officer Mulaney, the new officer who's been escorting her to her appearances."

"Wow. I just saw him. He was at the lumber mill."

She looked even more concerned. "He was? Why?"

"There was a fire near one of our dumpsters. People are saying that someone set it on purpose."

"Why would someone do that?"

"Keep this to yourself, but I'm pretty sure the cops think that it was to cover up a theft." He waved a hand. "That maybe something was taken from the office. I'm not privy to a lot of information."

"Oh my stars. I hope they find out who did it, and soon."

"Me too." Not eager to focus on the craziness at work anymore, he tapped the top of the jigsaw box. "I heard you put this out for us."

"I did. Um, I thought maybe it would give us something to do while we talk. And if you did decide to come back." She looked away. "But maybe that was a silly idea."

He opened the box and scooped a handful of pieces onto the table. "I think it was a good idea. How do you start a puzzle?"

"The same way as anyone else. I put together the edges."

She sounded so prim and sure. He thought it was adorable. Just to tease her a bit, Jay said, "That's not how I begin. I collect pieces of the same color. See?" He picked up two burnt orange–colored pieces and showed her that they had to both be pieces of part of the sunset in the picture.

She wrinkled her nose. "You do one part of the picture at a time?"

"What's wrong with that? It works for me."

"Only you."

"Maybe we should see who's more successful at piecing together a thousand-piece jigsaw puzzle."

Her gaze was warm when she glanced his way. "Obviously, it will be me."

"Bethanne, I had no idea you were the competitive sort."

"Only at certain things," she retorted. "Such as puzzles."

His heart swelled. At long last, he and Bethanne were sitting together. Just enjoying each other's company. Talking about nothing of worth but making the kind of connection he'd dreamed about. "I hope I won't hurt your feelings with my puzzle prowess."

To his amusement, Bethanne didn't look cowed by his ridiculous bragging. Instead, she lifted her chin. "I guess we'll see, won't we?"

"Does this mean I can come over again soon?"

"You're going to have to. I mean, mei mamm is going to want her game table back eventually."

"Tomorrow night, then?" he murmured. "I don't want to upset your mother."

She smiled. "Is that the only reason?"

"You know I don't want to spend my evenings doing anything else, Bethy."

She stared at him, seemed to try his words on for size, and then nodded. "I'm glad."

He was too. At long last, he was courting Bethanne. As he collected another orange piece, he allowed the feeling of satisfaction to seep in.

It felt good.

# 18

"Mulaney, any thoughts on those cards you pulled from Burke Lumber?" Chief Foster asked after the morning's roll call.

Still standing in the station's all-purpose room, Ryan shook his head as he gathered his notes and half-drunk cup of coffee. "Not really, sir. Most of the cards Peggy collected have little information. It all seems pretty run of the mill too. You know, the employees' birthdays, addresses, spouses' and kids' names. It's the kind of stuff that would usually be in an HR file. There's only about ten that have more notations."

His expression sharpened. "And what do those notes say? Do they have anything in common?"

As much as Ryan wanted to have something useful to report, he had to be honest. "I'm not sure. At first, I thought the cards with more notations were the longtime employees." He shrugged. "You know, like maybe the more Peggy Conway knew about them, the more she wrote. But then I realized that two of the employees have only been working at Burke for less than a year."

"What do those cards say?"

Ryan barely refrained from rolling his eyes. "They all

145

sounded like personal problems Peggy had with folks. You know, like someone didn't listen to her advice or looked at her—or her son—strangely."

"Her son?"

Ryan rubbed the back of his neck. "I need to dig a little deeper into that, though I hate to waste time following a lead that has nothing to do with anything." He shrugged again. "It could be that those notecards are nothing more than a personal assistant on a power trip with an ax to grind." Thinking of some of the cases he'd worked on in the past, he added, "It wouldn't be the first time."

The chief nodded. "Good point. How private were these cards? Do you think Walker Burkholder knows about them?"

"I don't know. My gut says no, but I could be wrong. Again, it could simply be Peggy's way of recordkeeping. Maybe Mr. Burkholder likes to send birthday cards to employees or something."

"Yeah, or he wants to have a way to remember someone's wife or kids without digging into the personnel file." Chief Foster nodded as if he liked the sound of that. "Sounds like it's time for a private conversation with him, then, Mulaney."

"Yes, sir. But if you don't mind, I want to check one more thing. Peggy told us about the two cards that were missing, but I'm starting to wonder if more are missing and she didn't want me to know."

"What possible reason could she have for that?"

"There's no telling. But it's not like she has a good reason for using her time at work to write down gossip and snarky comments either."

"Point taken."

"Has the fire inspector told you anything more?"

"Yeah. It was set on purpose. They found the accelerant. A bottle of bourbon."

"Whoa."

"Right? Whoever set it could've chosen any number of things that would be hard to trace. This bottle of bourbon might be a good clue."

"Well, we are in Kentucky." There seemed to be at least one distillery in every county in the state.

The chief grinned. "This is the bourbon capital of the world, but it's not like there are a lot of drinkers working at Burke's. Over a third of the workers are Amish and they don't drink." He tapped the clipboard in his hand. "I think I'll visit Walker Burkholder myself. We've got a good relationship."

Relieved that he wasn't tasked with asking one of the most prominent citizens in the area about his personal business, Ryan said, "I'll continue working on those cards and visit with a couple of the employees."

"Sounds good. Thanks." He paused before turning away. "Are you still escorting Candace Evans around this afternoon?"

"Yes, sir." He lifted his chin. He understood the importance of the fire and robbery at Burke's, but he was emotionally invested in Candace. He didn't want to be told to stop escorting her.

The chief frowned. "Those photos that were left at the food court were no joke. I'm surprised she didn't want to cancel her appearances."

"I was too, but I think she's afraid if she doesn't make herself available in public, he's going to start seeking her out otherwise."

"Maybe. But I wouldn't be surprised if he's already doing both."

"I agree."

The chief nodded. "We need to figure out who this guy is. Are you sure she has no idea who he could be?"

147

"She says she doesn't. Candace says he changes his appearance each time she's seen him. She might not have ever gotten a real good look at him."

"Let's keep digging. If he's taken pictures of her for years, he's not a stranger to this town. Someone knows him."

"I agree." Figuring he needed to be honest about their plan he added, "I told Candace that I'd like to give the appearance of there being something between us."

"Of you two being in a relationship?"

Ryan could tell the chief was wondering just how emotionally involved he was with Candace, but he chose not to address it. "Sometimes that's all it takes for a stalker to lose interest."

After a slight pause, he nodded. "Or it might set him off, Ryan. Be careful."

"Yes, sir."

"You know I'm not just talking about the stalker here, right?"

It felt as if the chief was reading his mind. The truth was that as much as he wanted to keep things strictly professional between the two of them, his feelings were getting involved. "Yes, sir."

"All right then."

Finally dismissed, Ryan went to his cubicle and pulled out the cards again. Then, he pulled out two lists—one of all current employees, the other of employees who'd left within the last two years.

After an hour he'd gone through every current employee. This time he realized that another card was missing—Wayne Evans's.

It took him a minute, then he realized this was Candace's father. Why would his card have been removed?

He wrote that down to check, then moved on to the listing of ex-employees. He'd just settled in, prepared to spend hours researching the names, when his phone dinged.

It was Candace.

Hey. Are you still good with taking me today?

> Yep. We'll leave at 2. OK?

The coordinator of the first appearance asked if I could arrive 30 to 40 minutes early. There's a little girl in the hospital who wants to meet me and try on the crown.

He glanced at the time.

> So we need to leave within the hour.

Yeah. Sorry. I couldn't say no.

> Of course you couldn't. I'll be there in 30.

You sure?

> Yep. Don't worry. I'll be there.

Thanks.

Ryan didn't bother replying because he didn't need her thanks. He was simply glad she was reaching out to him. He didn't want anyone else looking out for her or keeping her safe. As far as he was concerned, he wanted to take on that job.

He knew his heart was in danger, but what could he do?

It was yet another thing in his life that seemed out of his control.

# 19

It was so late. Candace was exhausted, and she was pretty sure that Ryan felt the same way. After visiting the sweet little girl in the hospital, she'd gone to a retirement home and then two libraries and talked about literacy. Each appearance had been fulfilling and once again surpassed her expectations of what she'd imagined her life would be as Miss Crittenden County.

To her shame, she originally hadn't thought she'd have to do much but wear her crown for a couple of hours during the fair and enter the Miss Kentucky pageant—which she was sure she wouldn't have a chance at winning. She'd only thought about the scholarship and maybe using the experience to secure a future internship in social work, but never had she imagined that she'd find so much joy in serving others and meeting the people who came to the events.

So, the afternoon's and evening's visits had gone well. It was too bad that everything seemed to go downhill after that. From practically the moment Ryan had pulled out of the library parking lot, they'd encountered one problem after the other. First had been a traffic jam on 91. Then, just when they got through that, a couple had been in trouble at the convenience store they'd stopped at. They'd had a blowout and didn't have a spare tire. While Candace had stood to the side, Ryan had helped them find a tow truck service for their vehicle. And when they got back into his Blazer, a storm rushed in, bringing with it a freak smattering of hail.

They reached Marion two hours after they'd planned. When she'd called home for the third time to fill in her parents on the latest, her father had been so grateful, he'd called the diner where they were eating and asked to cover their bill. Ryan had hemmed and hawed, but in the end agreed to accept the free meal, especially after he'd admitted that he wasn't going to count most of their time together on the clock.

Candace had been surprised but also more than a little giddy about what his words had signified. She was no longer just a job to him. If that was the case, Candace was grateful for that. Her crush on Ryan had moved into something deeper and far more meaningful.

Even better, she knew he felt something for her too. They wouldn't have so much to talk about, so much of a connection, if her feelings for him were completely one-sided.

"I think we need to do something to commemorate this occasion," Candace said as they left the diner.

Walking to the passenger side of his Blazer to open her door, he didn't even try to hide his amusement. "And what occasion is that?"

"This, Officer Mulaney, marks the twelfth place we've visited together."

He looked amused. "You've been counting?"

She waited until he walked around to the driver's side, got in, and buckled his seat belt. "Maybe."

"Hmm. Well, I guess this moment should be noted. Accompanying you around this whole county has been a lot of work."

His tone was light enough for her to realize that he was teasing. There was a thread of truth to his words, though. She had taken up a lot of his time, especially since only about half of the appearances went off without a hitch. "What do you think we should do to mark the occasion?" she asked. And yes, she was kind of, sort of flirting.

Maybe more than that.

He pulled out of the parking spot. "I have no idea. Besides, you're the one who decided that we needed to do something."

"So it's my choice." She smiled.

"Yes, but within reason." He looked wary.

"Well, we did just go out to eat together."

"That's true, but your parents bought the meal." He frowned. "Which was unnecessary, by the way."

"Don't try to pretend you weren't hungry."

"I won't, but I would've felt better if I paid."

"But—"

"If I'm taking you out, I'd like to pay," he said in a tone that proved he didn't want to debate the topic. "Besides, taking you around hasn't been a chore."

She felt like it had been something much more pleasant than a chore. Against her better judgment, she blurted, "I've loved being with you, Ryan."

He swallowed. "Candace."

The cab of his Blazer was dark except for the dim light coming from the dashboard. It was both a blessing and a curse. It hid her reactions, but it also shadowed his thoughts. All she had to go by was the strain in his tone.

There were two ways she could play this. She could pretend that she had no idea what was giving him discomfort, or she could confront it and try to speak openly and honestly. One might ease the discomfort, but it would only be a temporary thing. She now knew that she wanted something more between them. A real relationship. That meant she needed to go the other route and simply let Ryan know what she was thinking. If he didn't feel the same way, at least she'd know.

"I think we need to talk," she said.

"There isn't anything to say," he said as he drove out of the diner's parking lot.

"So, you're saying that I've completely misread what's been going on between us?" She hated how insecure and worried she sounded.

Ryan darted a look her way. Again, his face was shadowed. She had no idea if there was a flicker of weakness in his expression or not. "I just don't know if any good will come out of this conversation—at least right now. It's late. I'm going to take you home. We can talk about this another time."

"It's not that late." Seeing the park on the right ahead of them, she said, "Can you pull into the park up here?"

He glanced at her again. "Why?"

"So we can talk."

In the glow of a streetlight passing, she saw his jaw tighten. "You're serious."

"Yes."

Muttering under his breath, he put on his turn signal, turned right into the parking lot, and then headed toward the back parking space. It was next to a stand of trees and partially obscured from the road by the corner of the park's pavilion. "Ten minutes," he said. "I need to get you home."

She had a feeling he was giving himself that time limit. "Fine."

He turned to face her. "Candace, I'm not going to lie. You're a great woman. If our situations were different, I could see something happening between us."

Warmth filled her. She hadn't been misreading him this whole time. But as the rest of his statement sank in, she felt off-kilter again. Treading carefully, she said, "What's wrong with our situations?"

"First? Our ages. We're six years apart."

"I can do the math. Six years is nothing. The difference doesn't matter to me."

"How about this, then? Our spending time together has been part of my job. It's supposed to be, anyway."

"Maybe so, but that doesn't mean we can't have feelings for each other, does it?"

He grimaced.

"Or is there some kind of police department policy that doesn't allow for a relationship between an officer and someone he's spending time with while on duty?"

"Probably."

"But you don't know for sure?"

"Candace, it's not like I've been combing the employee handbook about the possibility of dating a woman I'm supposed to be keeping safe." Before she could comment on that, he lifted both hands. "What would I tell Chief Foster?"

"I don't know . . . that you like me?" Then realizing he hadn't actually come out and said such a thing, she blurted, "Wait. Did I just imagine that—"

"Candace."

She faced him. "Ryan Mulaney, do you like me?"

His jaw clenched. "Come on."

"Do you?"

He looked back at her, his brown eyes somehow looking even darker. "Candace, we're not kids."

"You're right, we're adults."

When his expression didn't ease, she added, "Ryan, don't you start throwing my age at me."

"I meant that you're young and sheltered."

It was obvious he was grasping at straws. "And you're a cop from a big city up north," she said with a touch of sarcasm. "I get it."

"Good." He moved to put the vehicle into gear.

Oh no. No way was she letting him end the conversation yet. She grabbed his hand. "Wait. Just because I get what you're saying doesn't mean that I agree with everything you're insinuating. I've got plans. I'm almost through college. I entered the pageant to help pay for the last of it."

When he started to interrupt, she cut him off. "Haven't you noticed what I've been doing? I've been working with people of all ages. I've given speeches. I've volunteered. I haven't been standing still and just waving and posing for strangers."

His throat worked. "You're right. I . . . it was wrong of me to suggest you aren't everything you are."

"That means I deserve to know how you feel."

"There's no point."

"Ryan, this isn't just your job we're talking about. This is us. This is my heart. This is yours too. Don't you see that means something?"

After a few moments he nodded. "Yes." He turned to face her and reached for her hands. Clasped them both, enveloping them in warmth and security. "Fine. I like you, Candace. I like you a lot. I think about you when we're not together. I intentionally set my schedule around yours because the idea of you going on your own to one of these places drives me crazy. Almost as much as sending you with another cop on staff does." Averting his eyes, he added, "But that doesn't mean we can act on our feelings."

"Why not? What would be the worst that could happen?"

"I get fired. Your reputation gets damaged."

"Or you break my heart?"

155

His hands holding hers flinched slightly. "Don't be dramatic." Averting his eyes, he said, "Really, it would be best if we—"

"Can't we just take things slow?"

He met her gaze. "How slow?"

"As slow as we need to go." She waved a hand. "Like I said, I've got to finish college."

He nodded slowly. "There's something else. The chief can decide he doesn't need another officer. I'm here on a grant. To see if a bigger force makes a difference for the town. If the chief can't justify to the powers that be that my position is warranted, then I'll be out of a job. I'd have to find another job and move."

"I see."

He ran his thumb along her knuckles. "I don't think you do. The timing just isn't right. Right now I need to focus on my career."

"What do you want me to do while you wait until the timing is right?"

"What are you talking about?"

"Do you expect me to just wait until you decide we can have a relationship?"

"I don't expect you to wait."

"Do you expect me to date?" She squeezed his hands. "It wouldn't bother you if you saw me with another man?"

He scowled. "It would. Of course it would."

"Are you sure?" She leaned forward a few inches.

He inhaled sharply. "Candace, please don't. I just want to—" He stopped.

"No. Say it. Say what you're thinking."

"This." He released her hands, slipped a hand around to the nape of her neck, and pulled her close. And when her lips parted with a gasp, he kissed her.

And it was as far from the gentle, considerate, oh-so-proper Officer Mulaney as it could get. Ryan kissed her like they were out of time, out of breath, and unable to do anything but feel. It was everything she'd been dreaming about.

No, it was better.

Candace leaned into him, grasped his bicep, and felt the muscle bunch under her fingertips.

It was like she'd finally been kissed for the first time in her life. No peck good night or clumsy make-out session halfway through her senior prom or at a college party could come close.

It was everything.

Moving away, he pulled in a breath. It was obvious their kiss had affected him too. "Candace—" he began, but then flinched as his gaze followed something outside of the vehicle.

"What's wrong?"

"I'm pretty sure I saw a camera flash. Or something. We were seen." He turned on the ignition. "I need to get you home. Buckle up."

She fastened her seat belt as he reversed out of the parking space, then he pulled his seat belt on over his torso and clipped it into place as he pulled onto the road.

Her mind was mush. She didn't know if she should be looking for someone wandering in the woods, apologizing for pushing him, or crying since it now seemed that he felt nothing but regret. Figuring she'd said enough for one evening, she crossed her arms and looked straight ahead.

Beside her, Ryan looked just as agitated. Which wasn't a surprise. Clearly he wished he hadn't pulled over. Maybe he was sorry that he'd kissed her senseless.

Five minutes later, he pulled into her driveway.

She unbuckled her seat belt. "Thanks for the ride."

"I'll come around."

"I can get myself out of a car, Ryan."

"Let. Me. Do. This." After he got out and opened the door, he took her hand like always, then reached into the back seat and pulled out her duffle.

To her surprise, he didn't release her hand. She wondered if he was simply unaware that her palm was still nestled in his.

When they stopped at the front door, she pulled out her keys.

"Are your parents asleep?"

"It's a quarter to eleven. Probably. Since I was out with you, they knew I was in good hands." And there was the image of his hand pulling her close. "I mean—"

"I know what you mean."

"Good night." She forced herself to meet his gaze.

He was staring at her lips. "I'm not going to kiss you good night. I . . . the way I'm feeling right now, I don't think it would be a good idea."

"Okay—well, bye."

He stopped her, curved a hand around her jaw. Ran his thumb along her bottom lip. "It was foolish of me to kiss you like that. But I don't regret it."

Hope surged. "You don't?"

"How could I? It was the best kiss I've ever had, Candace."

"Yeah?" She couldn't have stopped the silly, pleased smile that spread across her face if she tried.

"Yeah." Leaning toward her, he pressed his lips to her forehead. "Sleep well. Lock the door after you get inside."

"You sleep well too." She opened the door, stepped inside, closed it, and locked it. As she watched through the door's sidelight, he walked back to his SUV.

She sighed with contentment.

"Candy?"

Glancing to her right, she realized that her mother had been sitting in the living room. "Hey, Mom. I didn't know you were awake."

"I was just making sure you were okay."

"I'm fine."

She lowered her voice. "When you didn't come inside immediately, I looked out the window. Candace, did he just kiss you on the forehead?"

"Yes." She steeled herself. Waited to hear a lecture that she didn't intend to actually listen to.

Her mother studied her a moment, then nodded. "That's what I thought. Good night, dear."

"Night, Mom." She climbed the stairs to her bedroom, her mind a muddle. She wondered what her mother had seen in her face that had eased her enough to not ask another question. Thought about the conversation she and Ryan had shared. How fierce he'd looked. How intense he'd sounded.

The way his lips had felt against hers. The way her heart had felt like it was about to explode because the moment had been so special.

Thirty minutes later, after she took a long, hot shower and crawled into bed, she checked her phone. She had a text. Her heart danced a bit and her face heated as she wondered what Ryan would be telling her now.

She clicked on the app.

And felt her insides crumble.

Next to an unknown number were the words *"I saw you. You're going to pay."*

# 20

can't believe I ever thought throwing a party for your father was a good idea," Mamm said as she scanned their backyard. "I must have lost my mind."

Bethanne bit her lip so she didn't start laughing. "It'll be okay, Mamm."

By her side, her brother, Lott, didn't seem to agree. Looking at her mother's neatly written guest list, he frowned. "We have nearly half the county coming over. Daed doesn't even know what to think about it."

"All he needs to think about is being happy."

Lott looked up at the sky. "Mamm, really?"

"Jah, really. Turning fifty is a big deal."

"So was turning forty, but we didn't throw him a party then. Or when he turned forty-five." Folding his arms over his chest, her brother scowled at the five tables they'd rented since even the wagon that held all the furniture for church didn't contain enough. "We haven't had a party like this in years. I'm just saying I don't understand why you're throwing one now."

"That's enough, Lott," she said in a sharp tone.

"What did I say wrong?" Glancing at Bethanne, he sighed. "Oh."

And there it was. Yet another consequence of her being unable to cope with life for several years. They'd all put their lives on hold while she got her bearings.

To be honest, she still wasn't very comfortable with a crowd around her. But she would handle it for her father. After all, she'd gone to the county fair to see Candace. She could help her mother host a birthday party too. Especially since she had her bedroom here. If she needed to, she could always go there and escape for a moment.

"You doing okay, Bethy?" Lott said in a low tone.

That right there was what broke her heart. Lott was her little brother. Memories of when she had taken care of him for almost a year flooded through her. Bethanne had been nine and Lott six when their mother had had a miscarriage and had been so sad. Bethanne had made their breakfasts and lunches and got them both to school every morning. One particularly bad night, he'd crawled in bed next to her and she'd rubbed his back, promising that one day everything would be happy in their home again.

And it had been for a while too.

Adopting a light tone, she said, "I'm gut. Don't worry about me." Winking at their mother, she added, "You should be taking notes anyway, Lott."

"Why is that?"

"Chances are good that Melonie is going to be thinking about her wedding day. You'll have to glean what kind of gathering she's going to want."

He frowned. "You think Mel is going to be thinking about that?"

"Jah."

"How do you know?"

He looked so suspicious, she giggled. "Because that's what women do. Women of a certain age who are engaged, that is."

"Hmm."

"Don't worry, son," Mamm said as she patted his back. "You might not be the only person in the backyard thinking of future celebrations."

"Who else would be?"

"I'm not going to say, but it might surprise you." Their mother had adopted a singsong tone.

"Mamm!" she exclaimed.

"No worries, Bethanne. Now let's get to work. Will you greet all the ladies who are bringing dishes?"

"Of course."

"There's going to be a lot of dishes to organize," her mamm warned.

"I know, which is why I asked Candace to help me."

Her mother brightened. "That was a good idea, dear. Between the two of you, everything will be organized."

"Does that mean you don't need me?" Lott asked, sounding hopeful.

"No, it does not. You're going to need to help me decorate, set out chairs, and prepare the firepit."

"I'm on it."

Four hours later, Bethanne was staring at the massive amount of bowls, platters, and covered containers lining the dining room table. Beside her, Candace was writing notes.

"What do you think? Should we call people to the buffet by tables or let them go up whenever they feel like it?" her cousin asked.

"Mamm said almost a hundred people will be coming."

"I know. If we call each table up and have me, Melonie,

and one other girl serve, we can move everyone in an organized fashion."

Bethanne was stunned. "How in the world do you know how to organize such things?"

"I'm not even sure. I just do." She winked. "I guess I have a gift for telling people what to do."

"Should we ask our moms what they think?" Bethanne asked as they headed outside.

"No way. If we involve them, it will be an hour's discussion."

Candace did have a good point. "Our mothers do like to discuss things to death."

Standing up, Candace walked along the rows of tables. "Next thing we know, they'll start tackling seating charts and decide we need napkins rings."

Looking at her cousin fondly, Bethanne chuckled. "I'd forgotten all about that." When she and Candace were kids, their families had hosted Thanksgiving, and at nine in the morning, their moms had decided everyone should have ribbons with fake leaves wrapped around each napkin. She and Candace had to stop playing school and start folding napkins. It had taken them hours. Then Candace had cried when most of the people just tossed the ribbons to one side.

After walking toward the back of the yard, she returned to Bethanne's side. "Okay, decision made. When everyone arrives, they can put gifts on the back table your mother set up and get something to drink, and then your mom can tell everyone to sit down. After we say prayers, you will be in charge of calling each table to the buffet."

"I can do that. You better not ever move away, Candace. I couldn't do this extended family stuff without ya."

"Since I'm not planning on it, you don't have to worry about it."

"Yeah, right."

"No, I'm serious." Wrapping one of her hands around her forearm, Candace lowered her voice. "I think I'm here to stay."

"What about all your big plans?"

"I'm beginning to think that I can achieve all my dreams by staying here."

Bethanne was shocked. For years now, Candace had talked about earning multiple degrees. "What changed?"

"I think I've fallen in love," she whispered.

Her face was dreamy and sweet and showed everything Bethanne would ever want for her cousin. It was still confusing, though. "Who?"

"Ryan."

"I don't know . . ." She wracked her brain. "Is he one of your second cousins over in Indiana?"

She scowled. "Absolutely not. I would never fall in love with a cousin."

"Then what Ryan is it?"

After peeking over her shoulder, she lowered her voice. "He's the police officer who's been escorting me to my Crittenden County events."

"Candace, you've fallen in love with your policeman?"

She nodded happily. "I think so. At the very least, I know I'm on my way to falling in love."

Bethanne didn't know whether she should hug her cousin or give her a good shake. Or maybe burst into tears. Candace's proclamation was outlandish. "I hope you haven't told your parents."

"I haven't. But that's okay, because I think my mom already knows. She saw me when I came inside the other night. I know I was flushed."

"Why?"

"Well, he kissed me on my forehead." Grinning, she added, "And he might have kissed me when we stopped at the park to talk too."

"Candace!"

"I know!" Grinning wildly, Candace reached out her hands.

"So . . . it was good?"

"Bethy, it was better than good." Looking dreamy, she added, "Ryan's kisses were life-changing."

Bethanne couldn't resist grabbing her hands and jumping up and down with her. No doubt they looked like they were kids again, but some moments didn't call for reason. Only big emotions.

"Girls, what in the world?" Mamm called out.

"Sorry, Mamm. We, um, just got excited."

She chuckled. "Candace, if your mamm was here, she'd be thinking the same thing that I am. It's nice to see you girls do that again."

Candace smiled. "I was just thinking the same thing." As they walked upstairs to retrieve the boxes of tea lights that were going to line the centers of the long tables, she asked, "What about you, Bethanne? Have you received any kisses lately?"

"Not hardly."

"Nothing from Jay?"

She almost stumbled. "Nee."

"What would you do if he did try to kiss you?"

"What do you think?" she asked as she opened a closet door and pulled out the first package of tea lights. "I'd kiss him back."

"Really?"

She stopped at the top of the stairs. "What is that sup-posed to mean?"

"It means that Jay might be worried about how you might react."

"Candace. It's a kiss. That's all." Bethanne knew she sounded far more blasé than she ever actually would be, but she was tired of everyone assuming that any little thing was going to set her off. She was a lot stronger than she'd been in years. Even more than she was a year ago.

"Think of it from his point of view. Come on, Bethanne, you hardly left the house for years."

"Peter tried to rape me. And then he died. That's a little bit different than a kiss, cousin."

"It's still intimate. It still means something."

She had something there. "Do you think he's waiting to make sure he doesn't spook me?"

"I don't know his mind, but maybe. Is he going to be here tonight?"

"For sure. I'll ask him."

Candace smiled. "I hope you do. And I hope he replies by finally kissing you."

"That would be nice, but if it doesn't happen yet, I'll know that the time isn't right. I'm okay with that." All this talk of kissing made her realize that Candace was going to be alone at the party. "You should ask Ryan to come tonight."

"No way. And don't say something like it being no different than Jay Byler. Ryan is older than me and a cop. It would create quite the talk, and tonight is all about your father."

"I guess you're right. It would've been fun to have the chance to see the two of you together, though."

"If I have my way, one day we'll be together all the time."

Bethanne smiled. "I like that."

"Me too."

"Girls, those tea lights aren't going to take care of themselves!" her mother called from downstairs.

"We're heading down now, Mamm."

"Come on. The party is going to start before we know it."

Jah. Bethanne whispered a silent prayer as she headed outside. That's what she was counting on.

# 21

The evening weather was perfect. Not too hot, not too humid, thanks to a hint of a northern breeze coming down from the Ohio River Valley. Jay gave thanks to the Lord for providing such a perfect backdrop for John Hostetler's fiftieth birthday party.

After getting home from work, he'd spent some time with Tommy, then helped his father with chores in the barn. Then he took a long, hot shower. By the time he was finally ready, he'd somehow ended up walking to the Hostetlers' party with his father. That wasn't a bad thing, it was just unexpected. It was also rather unexpected to see his father carrying two large stoneware jugs of cider. They were his gift for John.

"You sure you don't need me to carry one of them, Daed?" Jay asked.

"Certainly not. I haven't gotten so old that I can't carry a bunch of apple juice, son."

"It was just an offer, not a judgment."

"Good to know." Looking up at the sky, he breathed deep. "It's a gut evening out, ain't so? Not too hot or buggy."

"You're right. It's a perfect night for a gathering."

"And what a gathering it is. You woulda thought a young'un was getting married, there's so many people coming."

"John Hostetler is a good man. He's well liked."

"Jah, he is." Sobering a bit, he added, "He's had his share of hardships too."

"Like what?"

His daed cast him a sideways glance. "Like the obvious. His daughter's trauma."

"I never thought of him being affected. I mean, I know he loves Bethanne and worries about her, but I didn't think it had affected his life." Of course, now that he'd said the words out loud, Jay realized he'd been naïve.

"One day you'll understand just how much a child's hurts can affect a father, son. It's the lot of a parent, I reckon. You kinner might be experiencing something, but mothers and fathers feel the hurt almost as much. In some ways, I think it feels almost harder because there's nothing we can do but sit and watch."

Jay nodded slowly. "I can see why you'd say that. I felt that way a bit."

"Of course you did. You not only lost Peter, but you realized that your buddy was not the man you believed him to be."

"That's exactly how it felt. It was a long time ago, though."

"Indeed it was." He brightened. "And now, here we all are. About to celebrate a birthday together. Seems like a perfect time for all of us to move forward, don't you think?"

"Is that your not-very-sneaky-way to hint about me courting Bethanne?"

"I don't think it needs to be sneaky, son. She's had your attention for years."

"She has."

"And . . . ?"

"And I think we're doing good."

He coughed. "But are ya serious?"

"You know I am. I'm visiting her house as often as I can."

"You're certain that she's the one for you?"

"Mighty certain. I know I'm the one for her too. I can be the man she needs. I know it. I love her."

"One last thing. Your courtship is your business, but time is a funny thing. One minute it feels like it won't ever pass, then the next, too much has passed in the blink of an eye. If you are sure of your love, don't be afraid to tell her."

"I don't want to scare her off."

"Being honest shouldn't scare her. I reckon there's a lot of other things to scare a person in life."

A sense of foreboding filled Jay, though he couldn't exactly say why.

When Bethanne looked at the clock and discovered it was already after ten, she deemed her father's birthday party a success. About half of the guests had gone home, but the house was still filled with the remaining adults, while about thirty of her and Lott's friends were gathered in groups around the firepit.

Lott and Melonie were laughing at something his friend Anson had said. Jay, who'd spent most of the evening by Bethanne's side, was standing with a couple of guys from work near the last of the drinks. When his eyes met Bethanne's, he smiled at her. All was good.

Until she noticed that Candace looked out of sorts. She was sitting on a bench and staring off into the distance.

"What are you looking at?" Bethanne asked as she sat down next to her.

"Hmm? Oh, nothing. I was just thinking how I've been

surrounded by tons of people tonight, but I still felt a little lonely. I wish Ryan was here."

"Next year, right?"

Instead of looking relieved, she frowned. "Bethanne, Ryan's not a part of my group of friends. He's not only a cop, but he's from out of town and six years older."

"I know all that. But if it's meant to be, then you'll be together."

"Do you really think getting my parents to accept him will be that easy? It's not going to be like that for you and Jay."

"I don't think it will, either. Jay and I have a past that was intertwined with a lot of hurt and brokenness. Learning to overcome those things hasn't been easy. I could be wrong, but I don't think you're looking for easy either."

Looking sheepish, she muttered, "I guess you have a point."

"Candace, you've done hard things before. You've had big dreams that other girls in your high school didn't want to think about. You've wanted to go to college, and you entered a beauty pageant to make completing your degree possible. If this man is worthy, then everyone you know will think he's perfect for you."

She sniffed. "Great. Now you're going to make me cry."

"I didn't mean to do that. I just want you to realize that I believe in you."

"I believe in you too, Bethy," she said as she gave her a hug. When she pulled away, she added, "Now, I'm getting tired, so I think I'm going to take off."

"How will you get home?"

"In my car. I parked down the road. I wanted to leave some space close to your house for older people when they arrived."

Clouds had started forming about an hour ago. They hid

some of the brightest stars and the moon. She hated the idea of Candace driving home alone in the dark. "Should we tell your parents that you're going to go?"

Her eyes widened. "No way. If I leave, they're going to ask why I don't want to stay later, or they'll try to leave too."

"Or, worse, try to guilt you into staying and cleaning up." She winked.

"I didn't want to say it, but I was thinking the same thing."

"If you're tired, you should go." Standing up, Bethanne held out her hand. "Come on. I'll walk down with you."

"Thanks for the offer, but there's no need to walk me to my car. I'll be fine."

"I don't mind. The smoke from the firepit is bothering my eyes anyway."

Candace hesitated for a second before nodding with obvious reluctance. "Okay, but let's compromise. You can walk me halfway. Then neither of us will be by ourselves the whole time."

"That's a plan. Now, do you have your keys?"

She patted her jeans pocket. "Yes, Mom."

Without announcing that Candace was leaving, they headed for the road. If they stopped to let everyone know, Candace would never get to leave—and Bethanne was exhausted. It had been a long day between the preparations and the party.

When they reached the front yard, Bethanne was struck by how quiet it was in comparison to the backyard. The few streetlights cast shadows on the road.

When a burst of laughter erupted from the woods to their right, they both jumped.

Candace stopped and looked in the direction it had come from.

"It's probably some Amish kids who just entered their running around time," Bethanne said. "When I started going to singings, me and my friends would hike through the woods instead of walking down the road."

"Why?"

"Well, either to sneak a kiss . . . or just be a little daring." She shrugged. "It probably sounds pretty tame to an Englischer, but it was what we did. Even Lott used to run around in the woods when he turned fifteen."

Candace smiled. "In that case, I hope they're having fun." She started walking again but took only two steps. "This is close enough. Thanks, Bethy. Have a good—"

"Nope. I said I'd walk with you halfway and I'm going to."

"Fine." As they continued on, Candace pointed to two couples their parents' age walking in the distance. "I'm kind of glad to see those folks. We're not as alone as I thought we were."

"I was just thinking the same thing."

She pointed up the street, maybe fifty feet. "Look, my car's right there."

Bethanne breathed a sigh of relief. Her car wasn't too far off at all. "I'll stay with you to the Browns' mailbox." Remembering the way they used to hold hands, Bethanne linked her fingers with Candace's. "You don't have to be Miss Crittenden County tomorrow, do you?"

She laughed. "No. I don't have any more appearances until the end of the month."

"You'll have to think of a way to see Ryan—"

"Bethanne!" Candace screamed.

Before Bethanne could process what was going on, a man dressed in black grabbed Candace. With a jerk, he pulled her out of Bethanne's grip and back to his chest. One arm held her securely against him while the other held a knife to her neck.

"Candace!" Bethanne shrieked.

"Scream again and I'll cut her," he said.

Bethanne froze.

He glared at her. "Will you stay quiet?" When she nodded, he pulled out a thick rope and tied it around Candace's hands. She cried out in pain.

Bethanne gasped. It was as if her mind couldn't come to grips with what was happening. "I . . . I . . . ."

"Bethanne, I'm so sorry," Candace whispered. Fear had widened her tear-filled eyes.

"Nee!" Before she realized what she was doing, she'd reached for her cousin.

But the man slammed his hand against Candace's ribs. As she fell down with a cry, he wrapped a hand around Bethanne's arm. "You're both coming with me."

"No, please!" Candace protested. "Leave her alone. You don't need her."

"She'll talk," the man muttered. Then, with a low curse, he slapped Bethanne.

She tasted blood on her lips as her entire body began to shake. To her dismay, he'd used her shock to quickly tie a rope around her wrist.

"No, please." Candace struggled even more. "She won't. You won't say a thing, will you, Bethy?"

The man jerked Bethanne's wrist painfully, but there was no need. Even if she hadn't been tied, she would've gone with her cousin without any force. "I . . . I'm not leaving you, Candace."

"Oh, good. A sweet Amish girl who knows how to listen," the man said as he began to tie a knot so they were attached. "She might be just the person you need to have around you for a while. Maybe you can learn from her." When he yanked harder, Candace cried out again.

"What do you want?" Bethanne asked.

"You know what I want." He put the tip of the knife against Candace's neck. When she pulled away, Bethanne's anxiety rose.

"I don't," Candace protested. "I don't know a thing."

"Quiet." After pulling off Bethanne's kapp, the man grabbed a chunk of hair at the base of her neck and pulled hard.

Gasping in pain, she stumbled forward.

"Please," Candace begged. "Leave us alone."

He pulled them into the woods. "Do you even remember my name?"

"How could I? We've never met!"

Her answer seemed to infuriate him further as he dragged them toward an empty gully. "Of course we have." Within seconds, they were surrounded by darkness. "We know each other. All this time I've been following you. You've seen me everywhere. I know it. But you don't remember me?" A new thread of emphasis filled his tone. "I'm Scott, Candace. Don't you remember me? We knew each other in high school!" He jerked the knife.

Candace cried out as the blade pierced her skin.

"Candace!"

He turned on Bethanne. "Don't say a word. Keep quiet or I'll kill you and leave you here."

"Where are we going?" Candace asked.

"Someplace safe. Someplace no one will find you." Scott lowered his voice as he pulled them deeper into the woods. "Someplace where you're going to learn to forget about that cop."

Bethanne's dress kept getting caught on brambles and twigs. Each time the fabric snagged and released, a loud snap reverberated through the air. As they journeyed deeper and deeper into the holler, the back of her head became damp. The man's fingers had obviously pulled portions of her hair by the root and made her skin bleed.

She said nothing, though. She didn't think he was bluffing about killing her. Worse, she feared he would eventually realize that she was Candace's weak link. Candace had always been protective, and Bethanne feared her cousin would do just about anything to keep her safe from harm. And that, Bethanne realized, was the crux of it all. Here she'd spent years attempting to get past what Peter did, but now she might be the one who would inadvertently betray Candace.

Worse, she could only imagine what this man intended to do to her cousin. She wished her imagination wasn't as vivid as it was.

# 22

Jay had spent the last thirty minutes helping Lott and Seth Zimmerman stack chairs and take down the long rectangular tables. As they'd worked, the tea lights that had been illuminating the space slowly ran out of wax. One by one, each of them extinguished. In addition, the fire in the pit had now ebbed to low flames.

When the last of the chairs had been stacked, Lott stretched his arms out in front of him. "I don't think we need to do any more tonight. This is clean enough for now."

Seth looked relieved. "All right then, I'm going to head home. I bet Tabitha's wondering what's taking us so long. I took her home almost an hour ago."

"I appreciate you coming back," Lott said as they clasped hands.

"You need a ride, Jay?" Seth asked.

"Sure, but I want to say good night to Bethanne first." He looked at Lott. "Do you know where she is?"

Lott shrugged. "Inside with the women?"

After asking Seth to give him a couple of minutes, Jay went inside to the kitchen. But only three women—two Amish and one English—were sitting at the kitchen table drinking ice water.

Martha smiled at him. "Are you heading home, Jay?"

"Jah. Seth is going to give me a ride, but I wanted to say good night to Bethanne first. Have you seen her?"

"Nee. I thought she was outside."

Another lady at the table, this one dressed English, frowned. "She was with Candace. Look for an English girl with long blond hair and you'll probably find Bethy."

"I know Candace. I haven't seen her for a while either." Thinking back, he murmured, "Last I saw, they were walking together holding hands."

Martha and the English woman looked at each other and smiled. "They used to do that when they were little girls. I would call them my paper dolls," Martha said. "You know how paper dolls have linked hands when you cut them out of paper?"

Jay had no idea what Bethanne's mother was talking about. "Nee. I can't say that I have much experience with them," he teased.

"I reckon not," Candace's mother said. "Anyways, if they're together, I'm sure they're fine."

Martha suddenly looked more serious. "You know, they weren't in here when we all washed dishes. I didn't think anything of it at the time, but it isn't like Bethanne not to offer to help. Jay, when did you see the two of them together?"

"A while ago." Trying to give a better estimation of the time, he shrugged. "It had to have been an hour ago at the least. I was talking with Bishop Wood when I spied them."

The third woman in the kitchen tapped her finger on the edge of her glass. "The bishop left over an hour ago."

Candace's mother stood. "Maybe they're up in Bethanne's room. I'll go check." She started toward the hallway. "If they went up there and lost track of time, it wouldn't be the first time."

"Danke, Dora."

The back door opened, and Seth poked his head inside. "Jay, you ready now?"

Jay shook his head. "Sorry, I'm not. You go on ahead."

Seth stepped into the kitchen. "What's going on?"

"We're looking for Bethanne and Candace."

Seth frowned. "What do you mean?"

"We just realized none of us have seen them in over an hour now."

"Dora went to see if they're upstairs," Martha said. "I'm sure they're—"

"They're not upstairs." Dora's concerned voice preceded her into the kitchen.

Martha stood and headed for the living room. "John? Come here, would'ja?"

"Ach, I know it's late. We're almost done."

"Nee, it's about Bethanne."

Low murmuring was followed by movement, as all the men who were with John walked into the kitchen.

"I don't know what John is going to do if something happened to her," Martha whispered.

Jay didn't know what he would do either. "Let's not go borrowing trouble yet." It was in his nature to reassure, but the truth was that he had a bad feeling in the pit of his stomach. "Bethy's probably fine."

"Bethy? What's wrong with Bethy?" John asked as he looked around the room. "Did she get sick? Where is she?"

"That's the problem," Martha answered. "We don't know where she is."

John's expression gentled as he squeezed his wife's shoulder. "Come now, Martha. You know better than to get yourself into such a state. She's fine. There are a lot of people here."

It was obvious that she was now barely holding it together and that her temper was about to fly. Jay stepped forward. "Sorry, but there aren't many people left outside. Lott, Seth, and I have been stacking chairs and folding tables. I don't think she's out there."

When it looked like John was about to protest again, Jay quickly explained what he and the others had done during the last ten or fifteen minutes. Bethanne's father listened, his expression slowly transforming from relaxed to confused to concerned.

Candace's father cleared his throat. "Okay, everyone. Let's not get too spun up. If she's with Candace, then we can reach them on her cell phone. That girl never takes a step without it." Pulling out his own phone, he made a call.

They all waited with bated breath. Jay figured each one of them was doing the same thing he was—hoping and praying that a sleepy Candace was about to pick up.

After four rings, he disconnected. "She didn't answer. If she was sleeping, though, she might not pick up. I'll try her again."

While Wayne made the call again, Jay considered other options. "How did she get here? Did she ride over with you?" he asked Dora.

"No, she drove separately in case we wanted to leave before she did." She looked at her husband, who lowered his phone from his ear and shook his head. "Wayne, go see if her car is still here."

"On it." He went out the back door.

John placed a hand on his wife's shoulder. "Maybe they went for a ride together and lost track of time."

"Maybe," Martha replied, but she looked as doubtful as

180

Jay felt. He couldn't imagine Bethanne leaving her father's party without telling her mother—or someone.

"We canna jump to conclusions," John said. Lowering his voice, he added, "Thinking the worst doesn't do anyone any good."

"He's right," Seth agreed.

"I just . . . I just wish we knew where she was."

Lott moved toward his mother. "I'm sure she's somewhere obvious, Mamm. We're just getting each other riled up and thinking the worst."

Jay felt a little responsible for that. "I'm sorry. I was just concerned."

Lott shook his head. "Nee. You're only looking out for them."

When the front door opened ten minutes later, everyone in the kitchen turned toward the hallway. Wayne soon appeared, his footsteps quick and his eyes wide. "Candace's car is still out there. And worse"—he paused, visibly attempting to control himself—"her purse was on the ground." He swallowed. "And a kapp."

Martha swayed for a moment, and Lott rushed to her side and helped her sit down. With everyone seemingly stunned speechless, Jay decided to take the lead. After all, he'd been the one to notice Bethanne's absence and start searching for her.

And—he loved her. He loved her enough to risk everyone's fear and doubt in order to do the right thing, and that was to call Ryan Mulaney. "I'm going to call the police station."

"Jay, I fear you're jumping to conclusions," John said.

Jay felt sorry for Bethanne's father. The man was so afraid to learn something bad about his daughter that he was willing to fool himself.

"I hope I'm wrong, John," he said quietly. "I would like

nothing more than for Bethanne and Candace to walk in the house and tease me for imagining that something awful happened." He took a deep breath. "But if they don't, I'm never going to forgive myself if I wait."

"The police may think we're worried for nothing."

"I don't care what they think. I've loved Bethanne for years now. I stood aside when it seemed she wanted my best friend. I patiently laid low as she recovered and then barely left the house. But I'm finally in her life now. There's no way I'm going to let her go—let go of my dream of having Bethanne as my wife. I need to do something now."

"Here," Wayne said as he handed Jay the phone. "We know Ryan. When he first started escorting her to events, he gave her his cell number. She passed it on to me."

Ryan's contact information was on the phone screen. All Jay had to do was tap Call.

So he did. And held his breath until the police officer answered.

# 23

Ryan wouldn't have answered the phone if Wayne Evans's name wasn't on the screen. He'd been sound asleep, exhausted from having driven all around the county with another officer to locate a lowlife who'd been seen peddling drugs to a group of kids at the middle school. By the time the teacher had told the principal, who'd called the station, the guy was gone. The next five hours of Ryan's life had been spent interviewing students, cross-checking the man's appearance with other jurisdictions, and then trying to track the guy down.

But they'd done it. The guy was now behind bars.

"Wayne? Or . . . Candace, is this you?" She'd been on his mind as he'd drifted to sleep.

"Nee. This is Jay Byler."

Why did he recognize that name? And why was someone else calling from Wayne's phone? "Who?"

"Jay Byler. We met when you came to Burke's about the break-in and the fire."

"Oh, right." He sat up, now fully awake. Something had to be wrong. "What's going on?"

"I'm sorry for waking you up, but it's urgent."

His body tensed. "What's going on, Jay?"

"Well, um, Wayne handed his phone to me. You see, we were all together for a birthday party tonight. It's John Hostetler's fiftieth, you see."

No, he absolutely did not see. "Why are you calling?" His voice was harder now, but he didn't care. He wanted some answers.

"Well, um, it's like this. We were going to call the police station, but figured you might be interested—"

"Jay, what is going on?" he practically yelled.

"Candace and her cousin Bethanne are missing."

Ryan's whole body turned cold. "Tell me what happened." After climbing out of bed, he pulled on the pair of jeans that lay on the floor.

"We had a birthday party for Bethanne's father here at the Hostetlers' place. I was getting ready to leave and started looking for Bethanne but couldn't find her. So I started asking folks if they'd seen her, and eventually we figured out that she was with Candace. When Candace's dad went looking for her car—it was parked out on the road—he found Candace's purse and Bethanne's kapp on the ground." Jay inhaled, clearly trying to keep his composure. Other upset voices spoke in the background.

Ryan felt like someone had knocked the wind out of him. He honestly couldn't breathe. But he had to. He had to keep it together.

Grabbing his keys and his wallet, he slipped his feet into the tennis shoes that he'd kicked off the moment he'd entered his house. "You did the right thing by calling me. Give me the address. I'm going to call the station while I head your way."

"Okay, but every minute is wasting time."

"I hear you, but stay put," he added as he opened the locked cabinet he'd installed in the kitchen that contained

184

SHELLEY SHEPARD GRAY

his weapon. Finally, he grabbed his badge and attached it to his belt. "Everyone there needs to stay put, okay? I'm getting in my vehicle now. Tell me the address."

A new voice came on the line. "Ryan, this is John, Beth-anne's daed. Here's our address."

After grabbing a pen out of the bin on the side of his car door, he found a scrap piece of paper and wrote the address down. "Thank you, sir. I'm going to get off the phone and call the station," he added as he started typing the address in his GPS. "I should be there in ten minutes."

"Ten?"

It was obvious that John needed him there an hour ago. "I promise, ten minutes is doable," he said as firmly as he possibly could. "Understand me? Keep everyone as calm as possible. I am on my way."

Once he'd entered the address into his phone, he called the station while heading for the Hostetlers'. The overnight supervisor answered, and Ryan relayed everything he knew as he sped toward his destination. When he ended that call, he took a deep breath and started praying.

And when he finished, he started praying again.

Two hours later, Ryan was still praying. After speaking with the families and going out to the area where the kapp and purse had been found, more law enforcement profes-sionals had been called in.

He'd put on gloves and inspected the items and bagged them, finding nothing significant on Candace's phone. His stomach dropped a bit as he checked her texts. Most were between Candace and her friends, but there were also many he'd exchanged with her. Though he'd been professional in his correspondence, he hoped that Chief Foster wouldn't

185

have concerns about their communication, especially after the conversation he'd had with him the other day. However, when the chief arrived and also checked her phone, the only thing he'd done was squeeze Ryan's shoulder sympathetically. Clearly, he realized that Ryan's relationship with Candace had become close.

Still, his concerns couldn't be compared to what the families were experiencing. They looked completely beside themselves with worry. Even the presence of Audrey, a good friend of the chief's who was a counselor at the hospital, didn't seem to help much.

Now they were waiting for Bowling Green's K-9 team of two beagles. Chief Foster had suggested Ryan take a few moments, eat some of the offered leftover food from the birthday party, and pull himself together. Ryan wanted to go back out into the woods but had to follow his boss's directions. No good would come of making a mess of any paths the girls and the person who'd abducted them had taken.

It was hard, though. He was sure Candace's stalker was involved, but he had nothing on the guy other than a vague description.

When Jay Byler joined him, he mentally tensed, preparing for the man to let him have it. Ryan wouldn't blame Jay for giving him a hard time either. He had been supposed to take care of Candace. Watch her. Be a decent cop and do his job.

Instead, the worst had happened, and he wasn't even good enough to lead the search for the women.

Pushing aside his own feelings, he stood up. "The trackers should be here within the hour."

Jay looked weary but not angry. Maybe more resigned than anything?

He gestured for Ryan to sit back down. "I know they're

on their way. Chief Foster told me." Pulling over a chair next to him, he said, "I came over to see if you need anything."

"Me?" He didn't even try to hide his surprise. "Don't worry about me. I'm fine, Jay."

"You sure about that? Because judging by the way you look, you don't seem fine at all. Truly, you look like you've been through the wringer."

"I've been through no more than you. I know you're worried about Bethanne."

"Of course. I can't help but keep thinking about her—and Candace—being scared and hurt."

"I know, and I'm sorry."

Jay shook his head. "I know you're a policeman and all, but you canna read minds. Plus, you weren't even here. Them missing isn't your fault. I was here. I should've looked out for Bethanne and Candace. I should've."

"Don't. You can't take responsibility for the girls getting abducted. It's obvious that whoever was waiting for them suspected that Candace might walk to the car by herself. It's not your fault that she did, and that Bethanne was with her."

Jay stared at him intently. "Do you hear yourself?"

He hung his head. "I do. My situation is different, though. I knew someone was watching Candace."

"That's a heavy burden. Maybe too heavy, yes?" When Ryan didn't answer, Jay sighed. "I . . . well, I just wanted to tell ya that no one here is blaming you."

"I appreciate that, but protecting Candace was my responsibility." At least, that's where his heart was. He wanted to protect her and keep her safe.

"Forgive me, but you weren't hired as a bodyguard, were ya? I thought it was more of an escort so a young woman like Candace wouldn't be traveling the backroads of our county alone all the time."

"You're right, but I did know about the stalker. I could never find enough information about him to make a difference."

"Hopefully the Lord will see us through from here on out."

"I've been praying too." The problem, unfortunately, was that he didn't know if his prayers were going to be enough to save the girls. The Lord had placed him near Candace and given him the skills to do detective work and solve crimes. In this case, he'd failed in every regard.

Walking a few feet away, he murmured, "Lord, I know I've been weak and unworthy, but please help me. I surely need You right now."

Then, taking a deep breath, he turned. No matter what, he was going to push forward. He wasn't going to give up.

# 24

Dawn was breaking. Bethanne could see the first glimmer of sunlight through the small gaps between the newspaper covering the window and the frame surrounding it. The light was dim, but it allowed her to see Candace's sleeping form next to her. And that the floor of the building wasn't dirt like she'd first thought. Underneath the dirt and grime was worn wood.

When they'd arrived, the man had pushed them onto the floor. Of course, they'd fallen in a jumbled mess. It was dark, they were scared to death, and each pair of their hands had been tied together by a scratchy, frayed rope. Then the man had picked up two pieces of old rope from the corner of the shack and tied their hands together so neither could move without the other having to do the same. The skin on her wrists was already rubbed raw and probably bleeding in spots. She wondered if they'd bear scars from this ordeal for the rest of their lives.

It was also so painful. For the first few hours, her arms and shoulders had protested the position. Now everything felt numb. In some ways, that was even more worrisome.

"Bethy, you awake?" Candace whispered.

"Jah."

"Did you fall asleep too?"

"I guess."

"I know I did." She inhaled, her breathing sounding ragged.

"We've been in here for hours, Candace. It doesn't matter if you were awake or asleep."

"You're right." She moved a bit. Since they were so close together, Bethanne could feel her cousin attempt to move her hands. It was obvious that Candace was hoping not to hurt Bethanne as she repositioned.

Bethanne's heart went out to her. "How are you feeling? Are you hurting worse?" Candace had tried to fight Scott when he'd clawed at the soft skin above her collarbone. His jagged fingernails had broken the skin, and his harsh grip had made Candace cry out. Tears had run down her face as Bethanne had attempted to break free.

"It's not too bad." Scooting closer to her side, Candace whispered, "I'm so sorry, Bethanne. I never, ever would've wanted anything to happen to you again. This is all my fault."

"Being taken from my yard, dragged through the woods, and tossed in here is not your fault."

She sniffed. "Well, it's sure not yours."

"It's neither of our faults. It's his." When her cousin sniffed again, Bethanne knew the tears were falling again. "You mustn't cry. There's no way to wipe your tears."

"Sure there is." A few seconds later, she added, "I'll just wipe my eyes and nose on your clothes."

"Thanks a lot."

"Anytime."

"We'll get through this, Candace. I know it."

"I hope so."

Snuggling as best she could next to Candace, Bethanne closed her eyes. If she breathed deep, she could catch a whiff of her cousin's perfume. Or maybe it was her lotion or shampoo? "What makes you always smell so good?"

"What?"

"You've always got a good scent surrounding you. It's . . . I don't know. Like flowers and vanilla and maybe honey?"

"I can't believe you're asking about my perfume right now."

"It seems like the perfect time, especially since you smell good."

"I guess I should be glad I don't stink."

"Jah. We should both be glad of that," Bethanne teased. "Anyway, I'd rather think about your perfume than imagine how gross this floor is. So, what is it?"

"I went to some party with my mother years ago where they make up a scent just for you."

"Fancy."

She chuckled. "I thought it was silly and a waste of time. But maybe not, because I've always liked the perfume I was given. It's got jasmine and gardenias and is supposed to have vanilla undertones."

"I'm not even sure what that means."

Sounding a tad bit calmer, Candace said, "I don't know if I do either. I guess the perfume maker added a touch of vanilla. I think the rest of what you smell is my lotion." She exhaled. "You're so funny, Bethanne. I can't believe you brought it up."

"I've always wondered what it was. I was just too embarrassed to ask."

"Why would you be embarrassed?"

"Come on. You're Candace and I'm me."

"I don't know what you're getting at. And for the record, you don't smell either. You just smell like Bethanne."

"You know what I mean. Jah, I'm Amish and you're not, but there's more that's different. You've always been so pretty. But more importantly, you've always had goals and been confident. I've always wished I was more like you."

"You're perfect the way you are."

"Oh, please. I could hardly leave my room for years."

"Bethanne, stop. What I'm trying to say is that you're pretty too. But the more important thing is your character. You're sweet. You always take time to think of others. I'm too selfish by half. I've often wished I had more of your humility."

"I'm glad you're not like me. I'm glad you're you."

"Right back at you. Just so you know, if we ever get free, I'll buy you some of that perfume. Or, better yet, I'll take you shopping and we'll pick out your own signature scent."

"That'll go over real well with my mamm," she quipped sarcastically.

"Yes, but think about Jay," Candace teased. "He'd love it."

In spite of their surroundings, Bethanne found herself imagining his reaction. "I don't know if he would even notice my perfume."

"He would."

"Doubt it. Besides, we haven't gotten that close."

"I saw the two of you together at your daed's party. He seemed to notice everything about you. But even if he doesn't, what matters is if it makes *you* feel good."

"I suppose you have a point." Peeking at the covered window again, Bethanne noticed that the light was now brighter. She could see more of their surroundings too. It was a small space they were in. Barely bigger than a walk-in closet. Someone could lie down on the ground, but only just. And if they were over six feet, they probably wouldn't be able to straighten their legs.

The ceiling was a mixture of old metal and tar paper,

and some of the wood walls were so worn and rotted that it seemed a good wind would blow them down. "Where do you suppose we are?"

"I don't know," Candace said. "You've never seen this place? I thought it might be on your property."

"Nee. Our property ends at the woods. Some Englischers lived next door for a while, but they moved away. My daed said they were renting a mobile home or something but then couldn't pay their rent so they had to leave."

"Who owns it, then?"

"I don't know." Bethanne sighed. "Honestly, I've never thought too much about the owners. I don't think I've ever seen them. Lott was the one who liked to go walking through here when we were kids. But last night we didn't walk for all that long, so we can't be too far from my place."

"Maybe it's an old deer blind?"

"Maybe, but aren't those usually higher off the ground?" Once a year, Lott, her daed, and a couple of other men went deer hunting after Thanksgiving. She'd never paid too much attention to the details of their trips.

"Yeah. Maybe it was a spot to get warm or something?"

Bethanne could see that. "That seems possible. Whatever it is, it's obvious no one's been in here for a long time." All her fears and worst doubts rose again. If they were really in an abandoned hunter's shack, would anyone in her family think of that? "What do you think is going to happen now?" she asked.

"I don't know. I guess Scott will come back. I . . . I'm afraid of what he might do."

Tears pricked her eyes. "Don't say that."

"Bethanne, he didn't abduct us just to leave us here. He's going to do something. I'm just sorry that you're involved too."

"We're not going to think about that. We have to get free."

"How? Both of our hands are tied together and we're attached."

She hated how resigned Candace sounded. "Wiggle your elbows. Do you have any leeway at all?"

Candace shifted and moved her elbow an inch. Maybe two.

Bethanne felt the movement pull on her own wrists, but it wasn't painful. "Do you remember when he tied us up?"

"How could I not?"

"Remember how he pushed us on the ground and started to leave but then picked up the rope on the floor?"

"I kind of remember him doing that," Candace said. "Why?"

"What if he just saw this rope on the floor? I mean, what if it's not brand-new? What if it's as old as this shack?"

"Well . . . if it's as old as this shack, then it might not hold."

"Exactly."

Turning her head, Candace muttered, "We need to find something to rub it against. What about the doorframe?"

"Even if we could scooch over to it, I don't know if it would do much. We need something that's at least a little sharp." Bethanne scanned the fairly well-lit interior. "Do you see anything?"

"No. Oh, wait a minute," Candace added with a touch of excitement. "What about that thing on the wall? Is that a nail?"

"What thing?" Even though they were right next to each other, they weren't facing exactly the same direction.

"Let's scooch counterclockwise so you can see it."

Scooching anywhere sounded almost impossible. "Candace. Scooch counterclockwise? Really?"

"Hey, we've got nothing else to do."

"True." There was barely enough slack in between their bodies for them to move. "So, on the count of three?"

"Yeah," Candace said.

"One, two, three."

And they moved—discovering that moving in sync without use of their hands was much harder than they ever would have imagined. Given the fact that Bethanne was in a long dress, it felt even harder. After edging maybe six or seven inches, they stopped.

She was panting. "This is almost impossible."

"Nothing's impossible. Come on."

Fueled by her cousin's encouragement, Bethanne counted off and then they moved a bit again. "Can you see the nail yet?"

"Kind of. But how are we going to reach it?"

"I hadn't thought that far. I mean, until we started trying to move together, I thought we could get up against the wall, then somehow move this rope near the top of the nail and break it."

After a few seconds, Candace said, "Let's try to get over there, then."

The distance was only about three feet, but it might as well have been three yards. Or three miles. It still felt insurmountable. "I don't know, Candace. I don't think we can do it."

"Don't say that. Don't even think that you can't."

"I want to be positive, but I'm scared," Bethanne admitted. "What if no one realizes we're missing? The sun is only just coming up. No one is going to wonder why I'm still in bed. My parents are probably still sleeping in."

"Don't say that. I'm sure people are out looking for us."

"Why would they, if they think I'm asleep? What if they think you are too? Your parents probably thought you left before them. What if they just went inside and went to sleep too? It could take hours for someone to even begin searching for us."

"You're forgetting my car. It was on the street."

"But it was dark. They might not have been looking for it."

"They would have noticed that it wasn't there when they got home," Candace said as they moved some more. Her voice was strained—maybe from pain?

"True."

"I know everyone's worried, Bethanne. My parents would wonder where I was, and when I didn't answer my cell phone, they would've started looking. And, sorry, I know you like to think that you're independent now, but everyone still worries about you. No way would everyone in your family go to sleep without making sure you were in your bed fast sleep."

"But—"

"No. Bethanne, you listen to me." Candace now sounded almost mean. "We are not going to just sit here in this dirty, dark, stupid shack. We are not going to give up hope or start thinking the worst. When that guy gets back, we're going to be ready."

Candace's rah-rah speech was all well and good, but the reality was that they were held captive, and no one had any idea where they were. And they had no idea where Scott, if that really was his name, was. "Candace, lower your voice. He could be standing outside. He's probably laughing at us."

"Let him. I don't care where he is. We are going to get through this, Bethanne. You did *not* survive just to die in some shack. Now, come on. Let's scoot toward that nail."

"I didn't know you could be so mean."

"If we get through this, you can call me mean all day."

Just imagining that made Bethanne smile, and she'd

started to think that she'd never have anything to smile about again. "One, two, three, Meanie. Go."

Bethanne didn't have any idea what was going to happen next, but God did. Until she found out His plan, she was going to fight to survive.

And then fight some more.

"Ready?" Candace said.

Because she had no choice, Bethanne nodded. "Let's do it."

# 25

Candace didn't know if she would ever be able to forgive herself. It was her fault they'd been taken, her fault they were tied up together, and it would be her fault if something unforgiveable happened to Bethanne. Why hadn't she taken Scott's obsession with her more seriously? If she had, she could've stayed away from Bethanne. Stayed in her house.

Complained more to Ryan. Told her parents earlier.

Done anything she could to get Scott arrested and put away.

Instead, she hadn't wanted to give Scott any more of her life than he'd already taken from her. She'd pretended that his fixation on her wasn't as scary as it was.

Sometimes she'd even told herself that Ryan wanted to accompany her mainly because he felt the same attraction that she felt. She'd fooled herself into thinking that they were falling in love.

Now Scott was going to come back any minute, see them attempting to get the stupid rope off their wrists, and freak out. What would he do? She couldn't think about that now. And Bethanne—she knew he'd only taken Bethanne to keep

Candace biddable, but he didn't want her around. Since it wasn't like he could just tell Bethanne to leave, he'd probably kill her.

Even thinking about such a thing made her chest hurt. How would she ever be able to look at Lott and Aunt Martha and Uncle John again? They would probably hate her, and it was no less than she deserved.

If she survived.

"Candace, what are you doing?" Bethanne said. "I just counted to three. Come on."

She shook her head. "Maybe this was a foolish idea, Bethy. Maybe we should go back to where Scott stuck us."

"What? Nee!"

"But he could get really mad."

"He could do a lot of things worse than yell at us, Candace. What's wrong with you?"

"I just don't want you to get hurt."

"It's too late to worry about that, ain't so? You have to know that."

"You're right. I'm—"

"No! Nee! Stop telling me you're sorry. Now, focus."

"Wow, Bethy." Candace could practically feel the anger radiating from her cousin's body.

"Stop thinking negatively and do what I say," Bethanne ordered. Without waiting for Candace to comment, she raised her voice. "On the count of three, move. One. Two. Three."

By now they'd mastered the scooch. They were only inches from the wall. When Bethanne counted again, Candace moved in sync with her. After one more time, they were next to the wall, though both were panting and sweating. She figured Bethy wasn't thinking she smelled all that good now. "Well, we got over here."

"Yes we did. And did you notice something about the rope?"

"Beyond the fact that it's rubbed our wrists so raw that they're bleeding?"

"It's stretched some." Sounding almost triumphant, Beth-anne said, "Look at the space between us, Candace."

If she twisted her body just so and craned her neck, she could get a pretty good look at the section of rope that lay between them. At first she wanted to cry because she had no idea how to tell her cousin that she was seeing things, but then she noticed how frayed the rope had become. "I think a section of it near your hip is a lot thinner. Do you see it, or is it my imagination?"

"I can't bend that much. I noticed that when Scott first tied us up, our backs were almost touching each other. Now we'd both have to bend back an inch or two to touch our heads."

"You're right." It was a small thing, but boy was it good to feel even the tiniest ray of hope. "Bethy, let's get on our feet and try to catch the rope on the nail."

"All right, but I have to warn you, I don't think I'm strong enough to get up without using my hands."

"I'm not either." Glad for the rising sun and how much brighter it was in the space, she said, "Let's brainstorm some ideas."

"Okay. Here's one." For the next couple of minutes, they debated how best to get each other to their feet. At last they decided to simply rest their sides against the wall and use it as leverage.

Their first attempt felt almost impossible.

So did the second.

Candace was exhausted from the exertion. The physical activity, added to her fear that Scott could return at any moment, made her almost break down. She hated feeling so weak.

Beside her, Bethanne sounded as frustrated as she felt. "Maybe this is the worst idea ever. My shoulders hurt so bad."

"Mine too."

"I wish I could think of a better plan."

"I wish I'd done about a hundred more stomach crunches a day," Candace muttered.

Bethanne snorted. "I wish I'd done one a day. When we get out of here, I'm going to exercise more."

Candance was grateful for Bethanne's wishful thinking, but once again her own optimism was plummeting. "Bethy, I love you. No matter what happens, I want you to know that."

"I love you too. And before you apologize again, I want to make sure you hear my words. Don't just listen. Hear what I'm saying. This was not your fault."

"But—"

"Nee, Candace. Stop blaming yourself and listen. No matter what happens, you aren't responsible."

"I would never want you to get hurt because of me. You've been through too much."

"But I survived. And I've been realizing that I'm stronger than people think. I'm stronger than I've even given myself credit for. I got through that, and I'll get through this too. Just like you will, okay?"

Candace's eyes teared up. "Okay."

"Promise that you hear me?"

"I hear you and I believe it," she said around a lump in her throat. "Careful, I'm about to start wiping my face on your clothes again."

"Go for it," Bethanne whispered. After a few moments, she said, "Let's do this."

"I think we should count. It's worked for us so far."

"Fine. One, two, three, go." Together they pushed themselves against the wall and somehow helped each other up. The wall they were leaning on creaked and moaned but didn't break.

But the rope that held them together did.

"We did it!" Candace cried out. "Hallelujah!"

"God is so good. I've been praying nonstop."

"He is good. Now, see if you can kind of twist and get your hands near the nail." As Bethanne contorted, Candace was able to help her reach it. "Can you try to pull it out?"

"I'll try."

Watching Bethanne stretch her arms and then somehow pinch the sides of two of her fingers together to pull on the nail, Candace was in awe. Bethy wasn't giving up, even though the old nail already had her bleeding.

"I think I got—oh!" Bethanne cried out as her fingers slipped and her arms fell.

"Here, I'll take a turn."

"Nee. Let me give it another go. It's just that . . ." Her voice drifted off.

"I know." Candace finished the thought. "Your arms are screaming, your wrists are stinging, and your hand now hurts too."

"Yep. But we're okay, ain't so?"

"Yeah."

Inhaling, Bethanne bent forward and stretched her hands. "Help me, Candace," she said around a groan.

"What can I do?"

"Besides tell me what to do now?"

"Right. You're almost there. A little to the left now. There."

Bethanne grabbed it. "Got it. Now pray."

Of course. "Dear God. Please help Bethanne. Please give

her the strength she needs to . . ." Was she really going to ask God to help her pull out a nail?

"Pull out this nail," Bethanne said through clenched teeth.

"To pull out this nail," Candace repeated, smiling in spite of the situation. Her shy, seemingly weak cousin had more fortitude and grit than anyone had ever expected.

"Candace, help please," Bethanne said with more than a little impatience.

"Sorry. God, please help Bethanne pull this nail. Help her hands and her arms and—"

"And her back!"

"And her back," Candace repeated. "Please give us both Your courage to keep fighting. Your will be done. And please—"

"Amen!" Bethanne cried out as the nail pulled out of the old, worn wood. But it flew out of her hand and onto the floor.

They both gasped. "Oh no," Bethanne moaned. "It slipped out of my fingers."

With how bloody her cousin's fingertips were, Candace wasn't surprised. "Did you see where it landed?"

"No. Did you?"

Candace shook her head. "But we'll find it. Can't be that hard."

Except it wasn't as easy as she'd hoped—even with them both down on their knees looking. The dim light and the dirty floor didn't help, and neither did the tears blurring Candace's vision.

And who knew how much time they had before Scott returned.

She took a deep breath. "Have a seat, Bethanne, I'm going to find it."

"Candace—"

"We can do this. I know we can. My eyes are just fine."

As she fell down to her knees, she hoped and prayed that she was right. *God,* she whispered silently, *Your work with us isn't done yet. It looks like we're going to need You a while longer.*

Fighting back tears, she started searching the floor. One inch at a time.

# 26

Staring at his computer screen at the station, Ryan reminded himself that he'd faced seemingly insurmountable tasks before. Each time, it had taken patience, determination, and a willingness to go above and beyond in order to achieve success. He'd been involved in a number of missing person searches during his seven years in law enforcement. He'd volunteered when he'd been at the police academy during an Amber Alert, spent hours on the phone and computer when a couple had gotten lost in a snowstorm in Waterbury, and had even been at his lieutenant's side when they'd been at the scene of a particularly hairy drug bust.

Each time, he'd worked hard, followed protocol, and been emotionally involved enough to be sweating as each hour passed with little to no results. He'd gotten tears in his eyes when they'd found the couple alive after searching for almost thirty-six hours in a snowstorm.

But none of those situations came close to the emotional turmoil he was currently experiencing. Candace's disappearance was affecting him physically. He felt nauseous and achy. Honestly, he felt like he was about to jump out of his skin.

He was scared and guilt-ridden and angry at himself, her

stalker, and, at times, even Candace. Why had she left the party with just her cousin by her side? Why hadn't she asked Lott or one of the men there to escort her? Any one of them would have done it in a heartbeat. Hadn't she learned anything during the last few weeks?

Of course, just as quickly as he'd thought such things, he'd pushed them out of his mind with a huge sense of remorse. She'd been abducted. Whoever had done it was at fault. Not Candace. Not even a little.

More importantly, all this was on him. He'd made a point of acting as if he were her protector. But what kind of protector was he?

"Any luck going through her high school yearbooks?" Chief Foster asked.

Ryan had been scanning the student pictures, hoping to find a teenager who looked anything like Candace's stalker. It was a last-ditch effort. They'd already asked her friends at the college and even neighbors if they'd spied anyone matching the general description.

"I don't know," he muttered. "I've marked a couple of the guys, but they're just vague possibilities. Boys' bodies can still change after high school."

The chief nodded. "I grew four inches and put on thirty pounds."

"I grew two and put on about that same amount, but I had a buddy whose body hardly changed until the summer of his senior year. When we saw him in September, we all just stared."

"I get it. But I do think, based on the way he's acted possessive of her on social media, that he's known Candace for a while."

"I agree."

"Deputy Ernst from the Crittenden County Sheriff's office

is calling teachers. It's another long shot, but someone in that school had to be aware if a guy was fixating on Candace. Teachers usually see more than students think."

"That's a good idea." Ryan flipped another page. The pictures were of students three grades below Candace. Thinking back to the popular girls at his high school, he remembered one of his buddies saying that a senior girl he was crushing on would never say yes to a sophomore asking her to homecoming. Maybe if Candace had been nice to a junior classman but never gave him a second's thought when he wasn't standing in front of her, the kid might have twisted their interactions in his mind.

Liking that idea, he flipped to the pages of clubs and sports teams. Then he came upon sections for each class that were comprised mainly of candid shots submitted by students.

And there he was.

Ryan's heart seemed to stop as he stared at the image. On the freshman page, a lone student was standing behind a chain-link fence. He was probably a hundred and thirty pounds, maybe five foot seven, and his shoulders looked hunched beneath a hoodie that was probably two sizes too big. An expensive-looking camera hung around his neck. Below longish dark hair, his brooding eyes weren't looking at the photographer.

On this side of the fence, a group of girls in shorts and tank tops were working out together—maybe warming up before some type of sports practice. One of them was blond, hazel-eyed Candace. She was laughing. Even back then she was striking.

The picture's caption read "Scott Conway, the runner-up for the Horizons Photography Contest."

"I've got him!"

The entire room went silent as Ryan stood up.

Chief Foster strode toward him. "What did you find?"

He pointed to the picture. "That's him. And look, there's Candace."

"Are you sure that's our guy? This picture's from a long time ago."

"I know, but I saw him, Chief. I didn't see him up close and he's bigger now, but he has the same kind of slump. And Candace's impressions of him are right on."

"Why didn't she recognize him, then?"

"He never told her that they'd met. And as far as she was concerned, he was just a freshman when she was a senior. Why would she have anything to do with him?"

"But wouldn't she have recognized him? You put two and two together. Why hasn't she?" When Ryan frowned, the chief lifted a hand. "Hear me out. I'm playing devil's advocate here."

"I recognized him because I've been searching for similarities. This guy would've meant nothing to her. There were almost a hundred people in each class at that high school, and she was three years older."

"Still . . ."

"Sir, forgive me, but she would've been eighteen and he would've been fifteen. Now that she's twenty-two and he's nineteen, it doesn't sound like that much of a difference, but at those ages, it's practically a lifetime. The guy's voice probably hadn't even changed. Unless she had a reason to do so, she wouldn't have noticed him." He tapped the camera in the black and white photo. "Plus, this kid has a camera. A good one. We know he's been taking pictures of her."

The chief stared at him for several moments before finally nodding. "All right, then. I agree. He's a good possibility. Let's go see where he's at."

Pure relief surged through Ryan. He knew in his gut that

he'd found Candace and Bethanne's abductor. He knew it. It was all he could do to not throw both of his hands up in the air in relief. "Yes, sir."

As Chief Foster led the way to the computer at his desk, he glanced at Ryan. "Before I forget to tell you this, that was good thinking."

"I agree," Sheriff Johnson from the Crittenden County Sheriff's Department added as he joined them. "I wouldn't have thought to go through high school yearbooks and I sure wouldn't have thought to look so carefully at the underclassmen—or pay special attention to the candid shots. Your detective work is impressive."

Ryan didn't know if it was impressive or not. All that really mattered to him was that they find Candace and her cousin in time. "I just hope I'm right."

"We all do, son. We all do."

Minutes later, they had an address. Scott Conway, age nineteen, had graduated high school in May and had recently moved into a rental unit in a house just off Main Street. And—his mother was Peggy Conway, personal assistant to Walker Burkholder.

Ten minutes later, Sheriff Johnson, Deputy Ernst, Chief Foster, Ryan, and two other officers were putting on bulletproof vests, securing their weapons, and racing out to their vehicles. The lieutenant and sergeant still at the station were on their phones, calling in additional resources. They would be ready to go as soon as they heard plans for the next steps.

The house Ryan pulled up to was as nondescript as any other on the street. White paint, black trim, black front doors. Quaint, older Craftsman style. Likely built in the fifties after the war, it was two stories with an addition and second entrance that looked newer. The landscaping was efficient and easy to maintain. "What's the story on this place, Chief? Do you know?"

"I've never had the occasion to be inside, but when I was growing up, the Hendersons owned it." He scratched his head. "When Mrs. Henderson passed on, her daughter converted it into three rental units." He glanced at his phone. "Scott is listed as a tenant of 1B."

"All right. What's the plan?"

"We're going to knock on the door. Ask some questions. If he's not in, we're going to have to wait until the DA gets done talking with Judge Verona to get that search warrant. He's there now."

"Yes, sir."

They exited the vehicle as the other officers parked their vehicles behind them. As they walked up the front walkway, Ryan noticed several small brass plates with the unit numbers on the black doors. "Chief?" Ryan turned to him for direction.

"Go ahead and knock."

He exhaled, reminding himself to remain calm and steady. Candace needed him to be smart, not barge in half-cocked. He rapped on the door twice, then waited, listening for footsteps.

It was silent.

After about thirty seconds passed, he knocked again.

"May I help you?"

They turned to see a woman in her late forties heading their way. She had on jeans, a matching jean jacket, and a pair of designer tennis shoes. Her hair was cut short in a fashionable pixie cut.

"Hey, KJ," Chief Foster said cordially.

Eyeing their uniforms and obviously feeling the tension in the air, the faint smile on her face faded. "Is there a problem, Blake?"

"We're looking for Scott Conway. Is this his apartment?"

"It is." She glanced at Sheriff Johnson and Deputy Ernst before focusing back on the chief. "What's going on?"

"Do you still own the building?"

"I do. What is going on?"

Ryan stepped in. "Ma'am, what can you tell us about Mr. Conway?"

She looked down at her feet. "Well, first of all, he's hardly a 'mister.' He's just a pup. The guy won't even be able to have a beer for another few years. Is that what you want to know?"

"When was the last time you saw him, ma'am?" Deputy Ernst asked.

She glared. "I'm not a real fan of the way you gentlemen are answering my questions with questions."

"KJ, you know—oh, hold on," Chief Foster blurted before answering his cell phone. "Doug, you got it? Uh-huh. No, I've got someone who can let me in here. Yeah, yeah. Bring it on over. Thanks."

After giving the other law enforcement officers a nod, the chief faced the woman. "KJ, we have reason to suspect that Scott Conway might be involved in a case we're investigating. Doug just obtained a search warrant allowing us to enter his residence. Will you let us in, please?"

Everything in her expression changed. All the hot air and bluster seemed to evaporate. "Blake, what is going on?"

"You know I can't answer that. Do you have the keys?"

She looked him over, then glanced Ryan's way too. "All right, but I have to tell ya, I don't know what he could be involved in," she said as she fished in her jean jacket for her keys. "He keeps to himself most of the time and always calls me ma'am. You can't trust anyone these days, can you?"

"We're still gathering information, ma'am."

She looked at him. "So I see." After stepping forward, she

211

unlocked the door and knocked loudly two times. "Scott, you inside? This is KJ." She moved to one side.

Chief Foster opened the door. "Stay out here." He drew his gun as he followed the sheriff inside.

"Hey," she said to Ryan. "Will you let me know if there's trouble?"

Ryan knew better than to promise anything. "Excuse me, ma'am. Another officer should be here momentarily."

"Yeah, yeah. I'll tell Doug where you're at."

He shut the door and drew his gun. "Chief?"

"We're clear, Ryan," Chief Foster called out. "Come on in the bedroom, son. You've got to see this."

Dread filled his insides as he headed to the bedroom. "Sir?" he said when he spied the expressions on both the sheriff's and chief's faces.

"I'd say you found our guy." Chief Foster's voice was flat.

Shifting his attention to the wall beside him, Ryan felt every muscle in his body tense. Dozens of photos of Candace were taped on the wall. Pictures of her in high school, at a pool in a bikini, around town, in one of her college classes. Even with Bethanne.

But the most disturbing of all were the photos taken most recently. Maybe her getting crowned Miss Crittenden County set him off? These photos were less flattering, taken from awkward angles or when she was frowning or in the middle of speaking.

"Ryan, I'd say he knows who you are," Sheriff Johnson said as he pointed to a pile of cut-up photo scraps. They were all of him. Scott had cut him out of Candace's pictures—and then cut him to pieces.

He felt sick. Why couldn't he have protected her better?

"She's in bad trouble, Blake," the sheriff drawled. "They're obviously not here. Any idea where else he might have taken them?"

"Ryan?" Chief Foster bit out. "Any idea?"

Barely able to do anything but imagine Candace in the grips of this guy, Ryan had a hard time speaking. Only after taking a fortifying breath did he answer. "No, sir."

Chief Foster gripped his arm. "Listen, Mulaney. I know she's special to you, but you've got to hold it together."

"I'm trying. It's just . . . I think I love her."

"Then she really needs you right now. You can go on a guilt trip later. Punch walls. Whatever. Right now, though? We need you to focus."

"Yes, sir."

"You sure you're with us?" the sheriff asked.

"Positive."

"Okay, then. You got gloves?"

"Affirmative." He pulled them out of a pocket and put them on.

"You start taking pictures, then let's go through this place inch by inch. My gut's telling me that Scott's not going to take Candace anyplace open. Not only does he not want to get caught, but he wants her to himself."

"What about Bethanne?" Ryan asked.

"I don't know. The only time she's on this wall is when she's with Candace. I think it's a given that she doesn't mean anything to him. That means she's expendable."

And that thought made everything in their investigation go up another notch. No way could Bethanne's family take something else happening to her.

No way could Candace lose Bethanne.

There was no way *he* could lose Candace either.

"Ryan?"

Pushing his worst fears to one side, he swallowed hard and concentrated on his job. He was going to find them.

No matter what, he was going to find them and finally tell Candace how he felt.

"Officer?" Chief Foster bit out. "You with me?"

"Yes, sir. I've got my phone out. I'll be taking pictures now."

"Good. This is not the time to get emotional, do you understand me?"

"Yes, sir."

"I hope so." His voice softening slightly, he added, "Do your job, son. God gave you some skills and it's obvious that you're putting them to good use. You're doing Him proud. Don't give up."

The reminder eased him in a way few other words could have. His boss was exactly right. He hadn't gotten this stroke of luck in their search by accident. The Lord had to have been working with him. With all of them.

Now it was up to him to do what he needed to do.

He opened the camera app, focused it on the wall, and did his job.

One piece of evidence at a time.

# 27

nch by inch, Bethanne searched the ground of the shack. In a moment of frustration, she stood up, kicked off her shoes, and started using her toes to help push aside the debris on the ground. She still wasn't sure whether her bare toes were making a difference or not.

Candace groaned. "I thought I just found it, but it's only a twig."

"Did it look strong enough to help with these ropes?" Bethanne asked. At this point, she didn't care what they found, as long as it would help get them free.

"Nope. It would just snap."

She swallowed her disappointment. "Oh. Don't worry, though. We'll find it."

"I know. We just have to stay patient."

"Jah. Patience is the key."

And . . . that's what they kept telling each other. They'd find it. They would find that nail, somehow use it to tear through the rope's fibers, and then—with free hands at last—push their way out the locked door and make it to safety.

It was a nice thought, but in reality it was as far-fetched as being sure the police or a forest ranger or one of their fathers would suddenly realize where they were and rescue them.

Searching for the lost nail was harder than Bethanne had thought it would be. And she'd been sure it would be pretty darn hard, given that her hands were still tied behind her back. But they didn't have any other choice. Time was ticking by. The sun was up, and no doubt Scott would return soon.

It was inevitable.

Forcing herself to only concentrate on the task at hand, she grabbed as much of her dress's fabric as she could. Somehow she gathered enough fabric so that her dress no longer brushed against the ground. She was able to move her toe more easily along the floor's surface. She uncovered a gum wrapper and a dead spider. Yet another one. Nothing of use.

She was sure that dirt and grime were embedded in the cuts on her fingers. She felt dirty and sore. Exhausted. Tears pricked her eyes but she ignored them. Crying wouldn't help. All it would do is blur her eyesight and make this herculean task even harder than it was. Turning a few inches to the right, she combed the ground. Shifted and did the same thing. Then did it again.

Five more minutes passed. Or maybe it was ten? She had no idea. All that mattered was finding that nail—or something that would free them.

And then she did.

"I got it," she said quietly. Sure that she now held the piece of metal in her left hand, she waited for some sense of relief or accomplishment.

Nothing came.

All she felt was empty.

"Bethy, you are the best."

"I don't know about that," she said with a small laugh. "Because, to be honest, I have no earthly idea how we're going to use it to loosen our bindings."

Sounding more energized, Candace said, "I do. I'm going to get it from you, then I'll start trying to wear down the rope around your wrists."

"All right."

"Um, I have a feeling I might end up scratching you with it. If I do, I'm sorry."

"It doesn't matter."

"As long as we get free, right?"

"Jah." Bethanne knew she sounded as doubtful as she felt, but what could she do? This idea was a long shot, and that was putting it mildly.

Once again, they shifted so their backs were together. Very carefully she handed over the nail to Candace.

"I got it." Candace sounded elated. Hopeful.

Bethanne's spirits, on the other hand, plummeted. But she kept her mouth shut. She had to. No good would come out of her citing the obvious—that all they were really doing was pretending that things were going to get better and they were going to get free.

"Lift your hands a bit."

After Bethanne did so, she felt Candace's fingers grab at the rope and pull. "That's too hard," she called out.

"I know it's uncomfortable, but it feels like there's an especially weak part," Candace said in a strained tone. "Hold still. I'm going to—" Candace paused again as she poked at the rope. Then poked at it again. "I think that helped. Turn this way a little so I can see."

Doing as she asked, Bethanne held her tongue. But really, she was so tired. And thirsty. She was starting to think they would be better off trying to sleep a little bit and regain their energy instead of poking at each other's ropes. "What do you see?"

"Turn again. I think I've got this."

"Really?"

"Bethanne, it's almost broken. I promise."

She turned, and when Candace told her to tighten the rope between them, she moved her hands as best as she could. Then, she heard a snap. "You broke more."

"I hope so. See if you can pull on it hard. Maybe you can break the rope the rest of the way."

"Okay." She closed her eyes and pulled her wrists apart. But all she felt was the twine dig more deeply into her skin. "Candace, it's not going to help."

"It is. Try one more time. If you can't get it, you can't get it. But just try, okay?"

"Okay." One more time she tried to stretch and break the rope by moving her hands apart. Once again the twine dug into her skin. "I'm trying. It's hopeless."

"It's not. Try again."

She was getting angry. "This isn't easy, Candace!" she snapped. "It hurts! And we're not going to get out of here by ourselves. We need some help."

"That's why you've been praying, right?"

Bethanne was embarrassed to admit it, but she'd stopped praying a while ago. "God doesn't care about my wrists."

"Sure He does. And you would know that too, if you weren't in such a mood."

"Did you just say I was in a mood?"

"You heard me. Now, take a deep breath and come on, Bethy," she coaxed. "Try one more time. If it doesn't break, then I'll try pulling off the twine with the nail again."

"You're making me so frustrated. It's hard enough to do this without you bossing me around," she said as she pulled on her wrists. They stung in protest. She could feel them begin to . . .

And then they were apart.

"It worked." She knew she sounded incredulous—but she was.

"What?"

"Candace, I did it. You did it," she said as she moved her hands. Her arms sent out shrieks of pain. They hurt so badly. But then, she was staring at her two hands in front of her. Her left was now completely free. The right held the vestiges of the rope. It was easy enough to manipulate the rope to get the rest off. "I'm free."

"That's the best news of the day."

Moving to Candace's back, Bethanne retrieved the nail from her hands. After realizing that the knots were tied too tight to loosen, she got to work shredding the rope surrounding Candace's two hands. "I can't believe you were able to hold the nail the way you did. I'm having a hard time not dropping it now."

"Please don't drop it. I don't think I'm up for another nail hunt," Candace joked.

"Don't worry. I've got this."

But of course she was full of bluster. She didn't "have" anything. Not really. It took her another ten minutes to get Candace's ropes separated, and that was with Candace pulling hard on them.

But then her bindings snapped as well and she was doing the same thing Bethanne had done—grimacing with pain as she attempted to move her arms freely again.

When the last of the fiber was on the floor, Candace threw herself at Bethanne. "We did it. Oh, Bethy, I'm so proud of you."

Wrapping her arms around Candace, Bethanne felt her tears begin to fall. "I'm sorry I gave up hope."

"Don't you apologize for anything. We're doing the best we can."

"Are you ready to get out of here?"

"So ready." With each other's help, they got to their feet. It was harder than she'd imagined, mainly because it felt like her limbs had gone to sleep. But at last they were both at the door and trying to get it open.

It suddenly swung out, and Scott was standing in the doorway, his expression a combination of shock and anger. "No!" he yelled and lunged at Candace.

With a cry, she stepped back, tripped, and fell onto the floor.

Scott came into the shed and kicked Candace's leg. As she yelped, Bethanne screamed as loud as she could. Hoping against hope that someone in the woods would hear her and come running.

"Bethanne, run!" Candace shrieked. "Go!"

Instinctively, she backed away from them toward the door. But she couldn't make herself go farther. Getting help was the right choice, but how could she leave Candace alone? "I don't want to leave you."

"You have to. Go!" she cried as Scott kicked her again.

When Candace cried out in pain, Bethanne flinched. Every bit of her wanted to save Candace, but she knew she was no match for Scott.

When Scott lifted Candace like a rag doll and started shaking her, Bethanne froze.

"Bethanne, go!" Candace shrieked at her.

When Scott turned to her, Bethanne knew she was out of choices. She turned and ran. *Please, God! Help me!*

She ran as fast as she could. She had no idea where. All

she knew was that she was running as far away from Scott as she could and abandoning her cousin.

"Help me!" she screamed. "Anyone?"

But all she heard was the rustling of the leaves beneath her feet and the startled screech of a bird.

After all that had happened, she was alone again.

# 28

Jay couldn't sit at the Hostetlers' kitchen table waiting for news a minute longer. Right before the police left, Chief Foster had gotten Jay's—and at least five other people's—contact information. He'd told them that he and Officer Mulaney would be in touch as soon as there was any news. They were supposed to remain calm, keep their phones nearby, and not call the police station unless they had a good, legitimate reason.

"No offense, but you calling one of the officers every ten minutes ain't going to give you much information and it'll make our jobs that much harder," Chief Foster had said.

"I understand," Wayne had replied. Bethanne's parents hadn't looked as if they understood, but they did look too shell-shocked to disagree.

Jay, on the other hand, had been ready to argue, but Lott had placed a hand on his shoulder. "Now ain't the time," he'd said under his breath. "I know how you feel, but you have to think of the big picture—and that's how all of us can help Bethy and Candace."

"It makes sense, but we've been worried sick all night. I can't just sit here."

222

"You can if you have to." Lott looked sympathetic, but it was obvious that he wasn't going to side with Jay.

Then, after the cops left, Lott had taken him outside. "Look, I know what you're feeling. A lot of questions surrounded Peter's death, and my sister was in the thick of it. More than once I flew off the handle, but it didn't do any good."

"You don't know that."

"Looking back, I can assure you that I do. All I did was cost them valuable time. And, ultimately, make Bethanne half afraid to tell me what the sheriff said when he stopped by."

"That was Sheriff Johnson, though. This is the police in Marion."

"That's true, but the sheriff and Chief Foster are working together. Then there's Ryan, of course."

Jay wasn't following. "What about him?"

"Jay, have you seriously forgotten that Ryan has been spending time with Candace? This man is invested in her being found. I daresay almost as much as you are in Bethanne being found."

"She's your sister. I would've thought you would be more anxious to get answers."

"I am anxious, but they can't give answers they don't have. And what I'm trying to tell you is that getting angry isn't going to help anyone. I carried anger inside of me for years. You know that."

"So we should just sit here and wait?"

"Yeah."

Even if it was the right thing to do, Jay couldn't spend another minute staring at the Hostetlers' kitchen phone or Mr. Evans's cell lying in the center of the kitchen table.

After standing up, he put his coffee cup in the sink. He needed to put on his boots and get out of there.

"Jay, what are you doing?" John asked.

He was tempted to lie and tell Bethanne's daed that he was going to go home. Maybe going home would be the right thing to do too. He knew his parents were worried about Bethanne and him. But he wasn't up for playing games. He wanted to be truthful. At the very least, the Hostetlers deserved his honesty. "I'm going to go out to the woods and look around."

John stood up. "I know you're worried and feel at loose ends, but I don't think it's wise for you to do anything but patiently pray. The police told us to stay near the phone. We should all do that."

"I know what they said. And I've been praying. I promise I have. John, I've even tried to be respectful of you and Martha and the Evanses' decision to let the police handle everything. But Bethanne means something to me." He shook his head, mentally correcting himself. "Nee, she means *everything* to me. I've loved her all my life. She's finally my girl. I . . . I can't sit here any longer."

"I'll go with you," Lott said.

Jay turned to him in surprise. "Why?"

"You know why. That's my sister out there." He pulled a cell phone from his back pocket. "I have my work phone too. If something happens, I'll have a way to call for help."

Lott's cell phone was a good idea, but Jay didn't want the guy to start telling him what to do. "Listen, I'm determined to find them. I'm not going to change my mind, even if the police tell us to go home."

"We're on the same page, Jay."

John frowned. "Boys, what are you going to do if you find the girls' abductor?"

"I reckon I'll do whatever I have to in order to get the girls free," Jay said without missing a beat. He knew they weren't supposed to use violence, but he couldn't think of a single man in their community who wouldn't do the same thing.

Bethanne's father didn't flinch. "All right then."

"If we don't see anything in a couple of hours, we'll come back home, Daed," Lott said.

"If the girls return home before then, I'll let you know," John said while he turned around and went back to his chair in the kitchen.

Then they were outside. After mutually deciding to start where Candace's car had been found, they headed toward the small, well-known trail that led into the woods. After walking a bit, Jay glanced at Lott. "Are you surprised that your father didn't argue?"

"Nee. I'm pretty sure he'd be with us if he thought mei mamm would be okay with that. But he's not going to leave her side. Not with Bethanne in trouble again."

"So, do we need a plan?"

"For walking in the woods and trying to find my sister and cousin?"

"Yeah."

"Keep your eyes open, your ears ready, and pray as much as you can."

"I'd say that about covers all the bases," Jay said in a dry tone as they entered the woods.

As they walked along the path, the first thing Jay noticed was that it was far from being unused or abandoned. "Look at some of these patches of grass," he said as they walked. "They've been trampled on recently."

"You're right. Someone's been here."

"Maybe the guy took the girls this way." Sure, he might be jumping to conclusions, but it did make sense. At least, he thought so.

Lott crouched down and ran a hand over the trampled

weeds. "I thought the police thought they left in a car." Looking up at Jay, he added, "Or was that just a rumor?"

"I don't know. But since we can't jump in a car to look, let's figure the girls were definitely taken away on foot."

"Okay. So . . ."

"So, what if the guy forced Candace and Bethanne to go into the woods? If that was the case, they would've had to enter this way," Jay said.

Standing back up, Lott looked down the path. "Jay, everyone looked around in the woods last night. All these bent branches and trampled sections of grass are likely from that. No one was thinking about tracking them down in the light of day."

"I hear you . . ." He let his words drift off. He didn't want to sound ridiculous or make Bethanne's brother more alarmed than he already was. But he honestly felt as if the Lord was nudging him in this direction. Prodding him to imagine what could have happened if a man was desperate and the two women he was taking were so concerned about each other that they'd do whatever he asked so the other wouldn't be hurt.

"Go ahead and say it," Lott bit out.

"All right." He took a deep breath. And with that, he tossed his pride out the window. It didn't matter if he was right or wrong. It didn't matter what Lott thought of his ideas. All that did matter was locating Bethanne and her cousin. "Lott, what if the police are wrong? What if the three of them did go into the woods? If they did go deep . . . where would they go?"

Everything in Lott's posture changed. Now, instead of arguing over what he believed to be true, he was thinking about possibilities. "I couldn't say, Jay. I'm drawing a blank."

"Help me think. Come on, we can do it."

"Jay, it's not that I don't want—"

"Come on. Just think about it. We grew up around here. We tracked deer and wild turkeys in these woods with our daeds. We've fished in the streams and creeks. We even played hide-and-seek in the summers when we were kids. We know this area pretty good. We sure know it a whole lot more than Officer Mulaney. His heart might be Candace's, but he's from up north. The woods here might not make a lot of sense to him."

"You're right," Lott said slowly. "If someone doesn't know this place, they could get lost real easy in the holler."

"There's a lot of places back here that nobody goes to. But there are some places that we've probably seen a hundred times but don't even notice anymore." Thinking about it, Jay added, "Some of those old cabins even have roads leading up to them that are half covered up with vines and bushes."

"Right." Staring into the densest part of the foliage, he lowered his voice. "If this guy took the girls into the woods, he would have to know them well too. It would have to be someone who grew up here just like us. And he wouldn't take them into the woods just to wander around in the dark. He'd have known where to go. He'd have to know of someplace where he could hide them."

"Maybe even keep them there for a while," Jay said. He hated the thought of that, but he couldn't deny the possibility.

Lott's expression darkened. No doubt he was doing the same thing Jay was—imagining how scared Bethanne and Candace would be. With obvious effort, he cleared his throat. "Okay. Let's say that was the guy's plan. He was going to take the two of them to some hidden place out in the woods."

"And . . . ?"

"What I'm wondering is how he got them there."

"It's obvious, don't you think? If the guy knows these woods, he knows where all the paths are."

Lott shook his head. "No. Think about the logistics. Think about actually making someone go where they don't want to go. How do you do that?"

"You force them."

"Or scare them."

"Right," Jay said. "I'm sure the girls were scared to death. But I don't get where you're going with this."

"Okay. Pretend I'm the sick guy abducting Bethanne and Candace. And you? You are Candace."

He folded his arms across his chest. "And?"

"No, come on, Jay. Work with me here." Lott grabbed his wrist. "So, here we are. I'm bad, you're Candace, and you're getting dragged through the woods." Lott yanked on his wrist. Hard enough to make him stumble forward a couple of inches.

"Stop. I get it."

"Fine. Now what about Bethanne?"

"What about her?" He was losing patience. "He took both of them."

"But how, Jay?" Lott pressed. "You know those trails as well as I do. They aren't wide."

At last he got it. "They aren't wide at all. Most of them can barely be called a trail. They're little more than a narrow line of dirt in between a bunch of trampled foliage."

Looking pleased that Jay was finally with him, he added, "Think about it. Pulling one woman along this section is hard enough. But how would he have gotten the both of them willingly?"

"They didn't go willingly. That's the point. They were abducted. They weren't willing."

Lott's voice grew louder. More impatient. "Even if he

had a gun, he couldn't point it at both of them at the same time. If they were on the sidewalk or something, I could see it being possible. But think about the way those old hickory trees grow around Cripple Creek."

At last he caught on. "You're right. Either he had a gun aimed at only one of them . . . or he had the girls tied together."

"And I can't see either girl attempting to escape if the other was trapped. Though they'd probably try to convince the other to go," Lott murmured. "I could see Bethanne telling Candace to run while they're trying to cross the creek."

"No, it would be Candace who was in his grip," Jay said. "If it's Candace's stalker, he would keep her no matter what."

Lott nodded. "Candace feels the same way about Bethanne as the rest of us in the family do. Even though she's come a long way, we all think of her as fragile. Helpless."

"Even though she's not."

"It don't matter if she's as strong as an ox now. We still think of her as weak. Candace would encourage Bethanne to escape—unless—"

"Unless she was tied to Candace," Jay finished. "That must be what happened. He had them secured together in some way. Then he pulled them both along."

Looking back out into the woods, Lott froze.

"What do you see?"

"Nothing new. I was just thinking about that broken bridge on Cripple Creek. Do you recall what's on the other side of it?"

"Yeah. That abandoned shack."

"It blends in, but I went in there once. Did you?"

"Nee. I . . . I'd heard it was haunted. I was too scared when I was little and then didn't care about it when I was older."

"I walked by there sometime last summer. I was with

Melonie. She asked me about it, and so we peeked in." His voice growing excited, Lott said, "Jay, that could be it! When Melonie asked me about the shack, I realized that it had been there so long I hardly even saw it."

"You're right. I've taken it for granted. Like it was an oak or something."

"It's secure in there, Jay." Lott pressed a hand on the tree trunk behind him. "It looked to have a fairly new lock on it. Mel thought that was weird, given that it used to be a deer blind back in the day. I told her that we would likely never know why someone would put a lock on it."

"Unless they had a reason to keep someone out. Or keep someone in." Feeling as if the Lord was guiding them, Jay stepped forward. "Let's go."

"Wait. Do you think we should tell the cops or something?"

"Nee. We don't have the time to waste. And if we call, they're going to tell us to stay put or ask us a bunch of questions."

"That's probably true, but we've got to tell someone. I'll call my parents and tell them. Then at least someone knows. In case something happens."

"Like we get shot?"

"Yeah. Like we get shot. Hurry." As Lott made the call, Jay all of a sudden thought of Seth Zimmerman. He'd always thought that he'd never be like Seth. That no amount of anger or fear could convince him to knowingly hurt another person.

Now he realized that he'd been completely naïve. If their hunch was right and some guy was holding Candace and Bethanne in that old hunting shack, well, he was going to do whatever he could to save them.

Whatever it took.

Even if someone looking at it from the outside might believe it was very, very wrong.

At the moment, he couldn't care about that less.

"I called home. My father thinks it's a stretch . . . but maybe not impossible."

"Did he tell you not to go?"

"Nee. All he did was tell me to be careful . . . and to tell you the same thing. He's going to call the police station now."

"Let's go, then."

Lott glanced back as he walked away. "Already on my way."

# 29

She was running. Bethanne was running so hard and so fast, her lungs felt like they were about to explode. Around her, the woods seemed to have come alive. Noise surrounded her, and all her senses seemed heightened. The trees seemed thicker, more birds were crying out, more rocks and stones were in her path.

Every time she tripped, Bethanne scrambled back to her feet without a care for the scratches on her legs or the cuts on her bare feet. All that mattered was getting help. Getting someone to help her save Candace before Scott killed her.

Tears streamed down her face as she thought of her last seconds in that shack. Scott yelling at her. Hitting and kicking Candace. Her thinking that if her cousin was going to be scarred and hurt for the rest of her life, it would be her fault.

And maybe it would be.

All Bethanne knew for sure was that she probably would've turned back . . . except for one thing. Candace screaming for her to go.

Over and over the scene replayed in her head. The dust and

the smell of sweat on Scott's clothes. The way Candace fell to the floor. The way Candace cried out when Scott first hit her.

The first whiff of fresh air.

The way her legs protested when she first attempted to run. All of it would be permanently etched in her head. All the feelings that accompanied it too. Desperation and helplessness. Even anger that once again she'd been caught at a man's mercy.

But that was it, she thought as she located another break in the woods and sped forward, stumbling over a fallen tree limb. She wasn't just thinking about herself now. She was thinking about Candace. She would do whatever it took to help her.

Just as Seth Zimmerman had done for her all those years ago. He'd risked everything to help her—and had paid for his help by going to prison. If he could do that, then she could do anything to help Candace. Anything.

The pain in her feet lessened when she reached the path. The ground was damp. What wasn't mud was covered with a fine layer of moss and clover. Compared to the leaves, twigs, and rocks she'd been running on, it felt heavenly. She gave thanks to God for this brief respite.

She had no idea where she was. Lott had been the one who'd always pushed the boundaries, dashing into the woods as a little boy, hunting and fishing and sneaking around when he was a teenager. She'd been too good.

Or maybe just too scared. Not of her parents' reactions. No, they might have given her a talking-to, but she'd put the fear in herself. She'd been too afraid to push her own self-made boundaries. Only when she'd been so eager to gain Peter's complete attention and love had she let her guard down.

A woodpecker drilled into a tree nearby, startling her. She

paused, attempted to catch her breath. Saw a pair of sparrows suddenly take flight. Had she scared them? Or was it someone else?

"Is anyone out here?" she called out.

The voice sounded weak and strained. Even to her own ears. Thinking of Candace, of the way she was depending on her, Bethanne cried out again. "Hello! Can anyone hear me? Help! I need help!"

The woods surrounding her rustled again. Afraid and unsure, she started walking, biding her time, slowly building her pace. Gathering her courage. "Hello? Anyone?"

The bushes around her moved again. She felt like a dozen creatures were staring at her. Curious. Unafraid.

"Help me!" she screamed. "We need someone!" *Gott, we need You!* she called out in her mind.

"Bethanne?"

The voice was faint. It sounded like it was coming through an echo chamber. And somewhere far, so far away.

But still, she answered. "Yes! It's me!"

She thought she could feel the ground vibrate. The byproduct of pounding feet on the ground.

"Bethanne, keep yelling! We're coming for ya!"

"I'm here!" Ignoring the pain radiating from her feet, she started running along the path again. "I'm right here!"

"Don't move. Stay where you are. We'll come to you."

Stay? She wasn't that far from Scott. Would he leave Candace behind to stop her from yelling? Or, in retaliation, would he hurt Candace so badly that even if she wanted to get free, she couldn't? Indecision paralyzed her.

No choice seemed right. Nowhere felt safe. She closed her eyes and made herself concentrate on steady, slow breaths. The way she used to breathe when she was having a panic attack while trying to leave her room.

"Don't move, Bethanne!"

She stopped and looked around. The voice had come from another direction. Was it Scott's? She didn't think so, but it didn't sound like the same voice as before.

"Help me!" she yelled again. Even if Scott grabbed her or tried to silence her, she still had Candace to think about.

The noises all around her grew louder. Rougher. More broken. Careless.

"Bethanne?"

"I'm here! I'm not moving!" More softly she added, "I'm right here, God. Please hurry. Please, *please* hurry." No one would hear her but the Lord, but she didn't care.

"Bethanne? Sweetheart, where are you?"

Jay. That was Jay's voice. "Jay? I'm here!"

"We're coming!" His voice sounded wonderful. Relieved. Happy.

Perfect.

"Keep yelling, Bethy! Yell as loud as you can!"

"I'm here!" She screamed it. Realized that she wasn't just yelling to her rescuers. She was yelling to God. Yelling to the world. Yelling to herself.

She was alive and she was worthy and she counted. Never again was she going to hide in a room and convince herself that her own company was better than the love of others.

Never again.

"I'm here!" she called again. So loudly that her voice was already hoarse.

In the woods around her, leaves rustled. Footsteps pounded the ground. And then, practically at the same time, four men appeared. Jay and Lott . . . and Chief Foster and Ryan.

All of them stopped abruptly and stared at her as if she'd appeared out of nowhere.

And then Jay rushed forward and pulled her into his arms.

"Thank God," he whispered as he ran his hand over her hair that was now falling down her back. "Thank You, God."

She clung to him so hard, she was afraid she might be hurting his arms and chest. Keeping her head against his chest for just a moment, where she could hear each beat of his reassuring heartbeat, she whispered, "Jay, I . . . I canna believe it. You found me. But Candace is still there."

Hearing him take a ragged breath, she lifted her head and gazed into his eyes. They were as blue as ever. But they were also filled with tears of relief. Lifting her hand, she swiped her fingers on one of his cheeks, realizing after the fact that she'd left dirt on his skin.

Suddenly, he tensed and kind of thrust her away from him. "I didn't even think. Are you all right? Are you hurt?"

"I don't think so. Not too badly, anyway."

He grabbed one of her hands. "There's blood on your fingers. And your wrists! Oh, Bethy, what did he do to you?"

"We were tied up and then I had to get a nail. It's a long story." Turning to Chief Foster and Ryan, she said, "She's in some sort of building. Scott was kicking her when I left. I didn't want to leave, but I had to get help. She told me to go."

"Do you know where it is?" Ryan asked. "Can you get back there?"

"I think so."

"I know where it is." Jay looked at Chief Foster. "It's that old shack on the other side of the broken bridge on Cripple Creek."

The chief nodded. "I know it. We're close, then. Jay, get Bethanne to the main road. I'll radio for an ambulance. Ryan, you're with me."

But Bethanne couldn't go to the ambulance yet. Candace was still out there. "I want to go with you."

"We need you safe, Bethy," Jay said.

She was about to argue when she noticed her brother walk to her side. "Lott."

"I wanted to give you a moment with Jay, but I can't stay away another second." He held out his arms. When she walked into his embrace, he held her gently and kissed her brow. "I've been so worried about ya."

"I know. I've been worried too. But we have to go get Candace."

Lott held up his phone. "While you've been reuniting with Jay here, I've been texting Sheriff Johnson and telling him where you were. He's heading there now."

"I hope he gets there soon."

"Ryan and Chief will be there soon too. Don't worry."

She couldn't seem to let go of her panic, though. "Nee, I promised Candace I'd help her." Looking back at the path, she added, "Lott, Jay, I need to take you there."

The men exchanged glances. "I don't know if that's the best idea, Bethy," Lott said. "The police will be there soon. I think Mamm and Daed would appreciate it if we took you to the ambulance that's waiting on ya."

"I agree," Jay said as he rubbed her back. "Having you safe will relieve everyone's minds. The policemen won't like you returning to the thick of things."

Turning back to him, she said, "Jay, I canna leave these woods without Candace. I simply can't."

Jay and her brother exchanged glances. "All right, then. Let's go."

"Jay, hold up," Lott said. "She doesn't even have shoes on."

She loved her brother, but he wasn't going to treat her like a child. She really didn't want him speaking about her as if she wasn't standing there. "My feet are going to be okay. Let's go."

"But Bethanne—"

"Lott, Candace is our cousin. I'm not leaving her."

"Fine."

"Let's go." Jay held out his hand, then looked as if he wondered if her fingers were too sore. "Can you hold hands?"

Her fingers *were* sore, but she wouldn't dodge that connection for anything. Slipping her left, slightly less-sore hand into his, she smiled at him. "Always."

"Ach, you two. Enough. Let's go."

Without another word, the three of them headed back in the direction from which she came. Now that she wasn't alone—and she knew that Ryan and the chief were likely already at the shack—some of the frantic energy surrounding her had dissipated. Her heart was still heavy, and she was still scared to death for Candace, but if the Lord could bring Jay and Lott into her path, she felt certain that He would save Candace too.

*Don't lose hope, Candace! Keep strong for just a little while longer. It's almost over.*

Bethanne hoped with all her heart that was the truth.

# 30

There were so many pictures. So many pictures of her. After Scott had tried to grab Bethanne but failed, he'd come back inside the shack, grabbed Candace's hands, and tied them back together. This time they were positioned in front of her. Her shoulders were grateful for the reprieve, but her wrists were stinging something awful. He'd intentionally tied her tight, and the rough rope dug into her already raw skin.

Then, after she was trussed up, he left for a few minutes. Her head felt foggy, and her ribs and side ached terribly from his kicks. But he was gone now, and she could only hope he would leave her alone for a while. For long enough for Bethanne to get help.

Alone in the silence, she prayed with all her might for Bethanne to make it to safety. For Scott to not find her before she could. And for God not to forget her. She knew that by now her family would have notified the authorities. They—along with Ryan—were probably out looking for her.

But how would they know where to go? How many people knew about the old shack not far from her aunt and uncle's property?

Her desolation started to get the best of her. She started thinking about being forgotten. Started dwelling on how thirsty she was. How long she had gone without food. Was she simply going to die in here all alone?

Scott returned, opened a shopping bag and dumped it on the floor. Out fell hundreds of pictures of her. They scattered, kicking up a bit of dirt, and settled in with the grime and decay surrounding them. And then he began to talk. Mumbling. Barely making sense.

Sitting on the dirty floor in the shack, Candace tried to keep herself together, but it was getting harder and harder with every second. Although it had likely only been thirty minutes since Bethanne had escaped, it felt like two days. She was barely hanging on. Now that she was alone with Scott, she didn't know how she was going to survive until help arrived.

And she knew that someone would come, sooner or later. Bethanne would see to that.

She let her mind drift from what was happening to her. Bethanne probably had no idea how much she'd helped Candace. Her cousin had a grit to her that most people overlooked while others had simply forgotten that it was there. Candace had been guilty of doing the same thing.

For so long, she'd thought of Bethanne as "poor Bethy" or perpetually kept her age at sixteen. Even when Bethanne told Candace about her job reviewing books, she hadn't taken it seriously. All she'd ever done was nod and smile and say that her job sounded fun and so good for her. And before her eyes, some of Bethanne's pride and self-esteem had withered.

But Bethanne had been incredible throughout their captivity. It wasn't that she hadn't given up, it was that she'd been strong. And had encouraged Candace to be strong too. Can-

dace really wished that she'd taken the time to tell Bethanne
that she was grateful for her.

Now she wondered if she'd ever get that chance.

"You aren't looking at me, Candace," Scott said in his
angry, nasal voice. "Look at me."

Since she had no choice, she stared into his camera and
did her best not to flinch when the flash blinded her. After
the camera clicked eight, nine, ten times—she really had no
idea how many times he pressed the button—she looked
away.

He was breathing harder now. "I'm not done. And you
weren't smiling. You need to smile."

She swallowed. "I can't."

He let the camera hang from its strap around his neck and
grabbed her shoulder, his long fingernails digging through
the fabric of her T-shirt and pinching her skin. Then, to her
horror, he began to rearrange her hair. It was knotted and
tangled, but he carefully caressed each curl.

He stepped back and lifted the camera again. "It's time
to strike another pose. Move so your legs are laying out flat
in front of you."

No way did she want to start posing for him. "It's hard
to reposition without the use of my hands."

Instantly she regretted saying those words when he
crouched in front of her. After sliding a hand along her
calf, he pulled her leg out. She was hurting so badly from
his beating, even that reposition made her cry out. "You're
hurting me."

"You deserve it. You're not cooperating. Get up."

She wasn't sure if she could.

"Sit up and pose! Do it! I'm taking your pictures."

Somehow she was able to use her elbow to get herself into
a sitting position, but she was in so much pain, she could

hardly bear it. And she was angry. "Stop it!" she yelled. "Stop taking my picture."

"That's why you're here." Picking up another bag he'd brought in and then seemed to have forgotten, he turned it upside down. Even more photographs spilled out. "Don't you see, Candace?" He bent down and spread them out on the floor. "Don't you see what I'm doing for you?"

Every one of the photographs was of her. Some in black and white, some in color. Some had been taken years ago, back when she'd been homecoming queen her senior year in high school. Others were far more recent.

He'd been everywhere. When she was at school, in stores, at the library, with Ryan, driving in her car. With her family. There had to be at least two hundred of them. The sight turned her stomach. "I don't want to see them."

"Of course you do. Look!" He picked up a color photo from the top of the pile. "Look at you here. Do you remember this?"

She stared at it. "Last summer." She was wearing a pair of short shorts, a tank top, and flip-flops. Around her neck, the dark blue straps of her halter bikini top were visible. She didn't have a lick of makeup on, and her hair was a scraggly mess. She'd been with one of her girlfriends on their lake, and for hours they'd lain in the sun, then jumped in the lake to cool off before laying out again.

He smiled as he ran a finger over her body in the picture. "I couldn't believe it when I saw you looking like that, Candace. You looked so bad."

"Bad?"

He nodded. "That's why I took so many pictures of you like this. I had to fix you."

Her skin crawled with horror. If she thought she could, she would've thrown up.

242

But since he was talking and not hurting her, she'd help him keep that up. Bethanne had made it to safety. Maybe Ryan really would soon find her. Maybe God really was listening and going to answer her prayers.

Taking a deep breath, she said, "What did you do?"

His voice and expression softened. "Why, I made you better, Candy. I edited people out of your pictures and fixed your smiles." He held up two pictures. One was how she'd really looked, the other was an almost-cartoonish version of her. "See what I did?" he asked, sounding almost childish. "I put lipstick back on your lips. And I fixed your hair."

He'd somehow cut and pasted another hairstyle onto her head. It was bizarre and scary. "Is that my hair or someone else's?"

"Someone else's," he said with an easy smile. "I once knew another girl who looked like you. She had perfect golden curls." He ran his finger along the hair in the picture. "It was so pretty. It was so soft too." He lowered his voice. "So soft." He glared at her. "Not like yours looks now."

How could he have known that about the other girl's hair? Candace's heart pounded faster. Had he held her captive too and petted it, just like he was petting her hair in the picture? Chill bumps formed on her arms. She needed to keep him talking. "Why did you add her hair to mine?"

He dropped the picture. "Because she always looked pretty. Always, always, always." A muscle in his jaw worked as he visibly tried to control himself. "Unlike you." Still scowling at her, he rose to his feet. "Look at you. You look terrible, Candace. Ugly. I'm going to have to fix all of your pictures."

She wanted to scream at him. She wanted to tell him that he had no business doing such things. Of ever even thinking such things. She wanted to beg him to release her. To untie her and let her go.

243

But she couldn't. There was nothing she could do. She'd never felt more helpless in her entire life.

Scott was breathing hard again. He looked like he was going to hit something—like he was enraged.

"What happened to her?" she asked.

He blinked. "Who?"

Honestly, it was like he wasn't even sure what reality he was in. "The other girl." She pointed to the picture he'd been caressing. "The girl with the pretty hair. What happened to her?"

"Angela?"

She nodded because she had no idea what else to do.

"She's gone."

A chill went through her. "What do you mean by that?"

"I don't understand?"

"What happened to Angela, Scott?"

He blinked again. "I don't know." Looking more agitated, he added, "She ran away." Pointing to the door, he said, "Now I put locks on everything."

When he started pacing back and forth across the pictures of her, talking to himself, Candace finally understood why Bethanne had kept to herself for so long after Peter's death. Even if Ryan and the entire police force burst into the shack that very moment and ended this, she would never be the same. This would haunt her—maybe forever.

Tears pricked her eyes, and she leaned her head back against the wall, closed her eyes, and allowed herself to cry. When she heard the camera click, she didn't move.

"Did you fall asleep?" Scott's yell startled her.

Had she fallen asleep? She didn't know. But she sat up straighter and shook her head.

"You didn't answer me."

"No," she said quickly. "I'm awake."

His eyes narrowed. "Then you were ignoring me again. Just like back in high school. You were pretending I didn't exist."

She had no idea what he was talking about. "When did I do that?"

"You don't remember?" He stared down at her. "You don't remember when I took your picture and they put it in the yearbook because I did such a good job?"

She didn't, but . . . "Of course I remember," she lied.

He clenched his jaw. Then pulled out a knife. "You're lying to me, Candace," he said calmly but coldly. "You're pretending that you remember our conversation, but you don't. I meant nothing to you."

She started shaking. Scott was staring at her, obviously needing her to tell him something, anything about whatever moment he was referring to, but she had no idea what it was.

"I thought you were nice. I thought, all this time, if you and I got alone, you'd love me too. But that's never going to happen, is it?"

She had to bide her time. Had to keep him talking. Say anything to keep him from hurting her. "We can get to know each other now," she said softly.

"You're lying to me." The pain in his eyes was so fierce that it hurt to look at him.

Then she couldn't, because he knelt down, gripped her chin with one hand, and then attacked her with his knife. She cried out as the blade slashed her cheek and bare arm.

Despair hit her hard. Things were going to get much worse, and she had no way to stop him.

She was going to die.

# 31

Ryan had spent his entire career completely focused on whatever job was at hand. He'd been proud of the way he could block out any problems he was having in his personal life. Actually, he was a pro at blocking out just about anything that wasn't directly related to the task at hand. He could ignore concerns about his health, his finances, his partner—everything could be conveniently packaged away while he gave whatever crisis he was involved in his entire attention.

He'd always thought that was a good thing. That he had a gift other officers didn't. And until this moment, he'd also naively imagined that he had a talent for the job. That God had meant for him to be a cop.

Now Ryan realized that he'd never been completely challenged. As he waited in position, listening for the signal, he realized his heart had never been involved before. No, he'd never known Candace before.

Forcing himself to remain still and not triple-check his weapon, his radio, or his surroundings, Ryan asked the Lord to be with him. Asked for His strength and His wisdom. Gave thanks that Bethanne had made it to safety and was essentially unhurt. Then he asked for God to place His protective hand over Candace and give her hope.

Most of all, he asked the Lord to help him accept His will. He needed to believe that the Lord was there with him. Otherwise, it was too much pressure. Too much of his life at risk. If he failed Candace today, he'd never recover. "I can't do this on my own," he whispered.

"Everyone's in position." The chief's low, steady voice came through the radio attached to Ryan's vest. "We'll go in on the count of three."

No one replied. There was no need. He could feel his fellow officers' bodies tense as they waited for the count.

"One. Two. Three."

Sheriff Johnson shot the lock, took two steps forward, and kicked open the door. Deputy Ernst and Ryan followed him in.

"Drop your weapon, Scott!" the sheriff ordered.

Scott barely spared any of them a glance. He was fixated on Candace. "You're ruined," he said, shaking his head. "You're going to have to go away now."

She flinched.

The scene would no doubt be Ryan's worst nightmare for the rest of his life. Candace was propped against the weatherbeaten wall of the shack with her ankles and wrists bound. Her hair was matted, her jeans and T-shirt were dirty, and her feet were bare. With tear tracks running through dirt and blood on her face, she looked petrified.

Blood! Scott had cut her face. And her arm.

That gutted him.

But almost worse was the look of resignation in Candace's eyes.

She'd almost given up hope.

Maybe she already had?

247

His beautiful, vibrant, caring Candace had had her light taken out. Scott Conway had not only hurt Candace's body, he'd hurt her whole being.

Pain washed over him. Why had he not been able to find her sooner?

"Mulaney," Chief Foster murmured.

He nodded. There would be plenty of time for guilt and recrimination later.

Candace hadn't even flinched. Ryan wasn't even sure if she was aware of what was going on around them. Her attention was on Scott and the knife in his hand. Her eyes were open, but it seemed like she could barely breathe. Remembering that Bethanne had said Scott had kicked Candace, he wondered if the guy had broken one of her ribs.

"Scott Conway, drop your weapon!" Sheriff Johnson repeated. He and the chief had their guns trained on him.

But they might as well have been pointed at the ceiling. Scott continued to stare at Candace with a mixture of hunger and horror. "I don't think I can fix this," he said.

Only then did Ryan notice the images of Candace littering the floor. Drops of blood dotted the ones at Candace's feet. Ryan had seen a lot of bad things over the years, but this had to be one of the most chilling.

"Drop the knife, Scott," the chief said. "Candace needs medical attention."

Slowly, Scott turned to face them. "She's ruined. She'll have scars." He grimaced. "I don't know if I can fix them."

"She's going to be pretty as a picture again, Scott." Sheriff Johnson's voice was as cool and even as if they were discussing the weather. "All she needs to do is see the doctor. He'll fix her up."

Glancing toward Ryan, the chief nodded. Giving him the signal to approach her.

Ryan eased closer. He couldn't wait to lift her into his arms and carry her out of this place.

Sheriff Johnson kept speaking in that low, relaxed way. "You need to drop your knife so we can get her the help she needs."

When tears started falling down Candace's cheeks, Ryan couldn't help but close the gap. He was done standing to one side while she was bleeding and scared to death. "I'm here, Candace."

With a look of horror, Scott veered toward him. "No! You stay away! She's mine."

Ryan so wanted to draw his weapon and shoot him. Anything that would stop Scott and get Candace in his arms. But his training and experience had served him well. He lifted his hands. "I won't take another step. Not yet. But she's bleeding, Scott. She's bleeding bad."

Scott shook his head as if denying the obvious would change Candace's injuries. "This is your fault. Yours! You were everywhere she was. You were too close to her. I saw you kiss her. I saw it!"

That had to have been what set him off. Feeling Chief Foster's eyes on him, Ryan flushed. He should've known better. Should've never given in to desire that night.

But he knew that he never would've been able to deny Candace anything. Or maybe he had been the one who couldn't deny his feelings.

Feeling the other officers' eyes on him, Ryan guessed that they were hoping he would distract Scott's attention long enough for one of them to tackle Scott and knock the knife out of his hands. "What did you want me to do, Scott?" he asked, adding a thread of disdain to his tone. "Ignore her?"

"You should've left her alone."

"How could I?" Noticing how Sheriff Johnson and Deputy

Ernst looked ready to move, Ryan spoke louder. More boldly. Anything to keep the guy focused on him. "Can you really blame me? She's beautiful. And she smells so good, like vanilla and fresh flowers." He lowered his voice. "She's so sweet too. I knew she was special."

Scott glared at him like he'd forgotten anyone else was in the shack. "You don't get to talk about her."

"How can I not? Look at her! Even lying there on the ground, it's easy to see she's got an amazing figure. No wonder she's Miss Crittenden County."

"No." Scott shook his head. "No. You can't. You're sullying her image. I took pictures of her. I kept pictures of her being perfect. I made her pretty. I made her better. I loved her even when no one else was around!" Tears formed in his eyes as his voice rose. "I didn't want her to be—"

Deputy Ernst tackled him to the ground. As Candace screamed, Chief Foster and Sheriff Johnson rushed to immobilize Scott and cuff him.

Ryan dropped to his knees beside her. "Candace. Candace, honey, it's over."

Behind him the chief was barking orders into his radio. Deputy Ernst knelt down and used a knife to gently slice through the rope around her wrists and ankles. Outside, they could hear the blare of sirens and emergency vehicles. Ryan realized they'd been parked on a long-neglected stretch of road, waiting for the opportunity to arrive.

Kneeling close, he pressed his fingers to her neck and felt her pulse. It was sluggish but steady. Pure relief coursed through him as he realized that she was going to be okay. Unable to help himself, he kissed her uninjured cheek and carefully moved closer.

"Ryan," she whispered. "You didn't forget me."

He felt like collapsing on the ground. At last, she was

with him. "Never," he replied as he wiped her cheek with his thumb. "You are always with me. Always. Whenever you need me, wherever you need me, I'll be there. No matter what. I promise."

Smiling weakly, she closed her eyes.

# 32

Everything smelled clean. Clean and sterile. Candace loved it. Almost as much as she loved feeling safe. As minutes passed and she became more aware of her surroundings, another scent filled her senses. It was one that she'd become fond of—the scent of woodsy cologne mixed with shampoo, soap, and mint. She'd recognize it anywhere. Even in the middle of a hospital, it seemed.

Ryan.

"I think she's waking up."

Keeping her eyes closed, she registered the voice. Her mother.

"I hope so," her father whispered. "The doctors said it would be anytime now. Come on, Candace," he coaxed in a louder voice. "Come back to us."

Did she want to? She wasn't sure. Here in her self-made cocoon, nothing could hurt her. She was safe and clean and didn't hurt. She didn't want to face reality.

"Ryan, what do you think is wrong?"

"I don't think anything is," he said in a soft, sure voice. One of his hands caressed her arm. His touch was warm and solid and sure. He wasn't touching her as if she was fragile. Only as if she mattered to him.

"I think she just needs a little bit longer," he said in a low voice. She sensed him lean forward, just as one of his fingers lightly caressed her cheekbone. "I know it's hard, darling girl, but you can do this," he whispered.

"The doctors did say that might happen." Her father sounded so worried.

She knew it was time to open her eyes and face them all. She just hoped she wouldn't see recriminations in their eyes.

"Candace, it's okay," Ryan whispered in her ear. "If you want me to stay with you, I will. I'll protect you from anything you want me to." He paused. "And if you want me to leave . . ." He paused again. "If . . . if you want all of us to leave, I'll make that happen as well."

She knew he was telling the truth. She didn't know how he could make all her wishes happen, but she realized now that Ryan would do whatever it took. That was the kind of man he was. Capable. True.

She had no idea what their future entailed, but she did know that right at this moment, she wanted him by her side. Maybe that was enough? She wasn't sure.

As his fingers curved around her hand, she gripped them. An unspoken response for him to remain.

She could feel some of the tension emanating from him dissipate. "Thank you, sweetheart," he said.

"Did she just say something, Ryan?" her mother asked, her voice anxious. "Candace, can you hear us?"

Taking a deep breath, she found her voice again. "Yes, Mom."

Hearing her mother release a ragged breath, Candace knew it was time to pull out of her cozy cocoon. She owed her parents that. She opened her eyes.

"Oh, Candace. Thank the Lord." Her mother's eyes filled with tears.

"It's okay," she whispered.

"Oh, honey. It's okay now that I know you're with us again."

Her father came over and kissed her brow. "Candace."

"Hi, Daddy."

"You gave us a scare."

She smiled weakly. "I know." She'd been scared too. "I'm going to be okay, though."

"I know you will," Ryan said.

To her surprise, both of her parents stepped a little bit away, allowing Ryan to get close again. When he ran his fingers along her arm, warming each inch with his touch, she relaxed. "How is Bethanne?"

"Bethanne? She's doing okay," her mom said. Swiping her wet cheeks, she gathered herself together. "Like the rest of us, she's been worried about you."

"The last I saw her, she was running away." Still feeling in a fog, Candace cleared her throat. "So, she found someone? She's really okay?"

"Yes, honey. Bethy's okay," her mother soothed. "Bethanne found Jay and Lott, believe it or not." She paused as Ryan helped Candace take a sip of water through a straw. "Jay and Lott got tired of waiting and decided to search for you. They remembered that old shack on the Lerners' property."

"Actually, I think it was Jay who came up with that idea," her father said as he approached the other side of her hospital bed. "He's the reason we realized you and Bethy were gone. He'd been trying to find her to say good night and knew she'd been with you. When he couldn't find you, he knew something was wrong."

She looked at Ryan.

He nodded. "There are a lot of heroes involved—including you and Bethanne. You girls were so brave and tough."

"I was scared."

Sympathy shone in his eyes. "I know, but you didn't give up. I'm so proud of you." Rubbing his thumb over her knuckles, he added, "I promise, Bethanne is okay. Like your mother said, she's been worried about you."

"Is she here in the hospital too?"

"No, honey," her mother said. "She . . . she wasn't as badly hurt as you. She's resting at home. Do you want her to come see you? Dad or I can go get her."

"Or I can send someone from the station," Ryan added. "It's no problem."

"No. It's okay."

"You sure?" Her mother brushed back her hair. "We'll do whatever you need, Candace."

"I'm sure. And you're right, it's best for Bethanne to be at home. It . . ." She ran out of words. How could she convey just how scared they'd been?

How desolate she'd become?

To her surprise, her mother's expression crumbled just as her father pulled her into his arms. "Honey, we're going to get your mother a soda," he whispered. "You know how a Diet Coke can pretty much solve all her problems."

For some reason, that was what Candace needed to hear. Not the Diet Coke cure-all, but the reminder that life went on. Even as hurt and sore as she was, she was grateful to be alive and to have her parents. "I love you both."

"And we love you back," her father said. "Now, um, you, ah, take a moment with your man here. He's been a wreck. We'll be back in about a half hour." He paused. "That good with you, Ryan?"

"Yes, sir. I'll watch over her." He looked down at his hand on her arm as her parents closed the door behind them.

Now they were alone. Candace hurt all over, but nothing was unbearable. She supposed one of the tubes attached to her arms was responsible for that.

When Ryan said nothing for a few seconds, she began to get worried. Peeking, she noticed that he was barely looking at her in the eye. Was he uncomfortable? Was he only staying because she needed him so much? "If you'd like to leave too, you can."

Leaning down, he carefully brushed a strand of her hair away from her face. "I don't want to leave, honey. I don't want to leave you ever again."

What did he mean by that? She swallowed and stared at him.

"Candace, I need to tell you something, but I don't know how."

What was wrong? She closed her eyes so she wouldn't have to see his expression. "You can say whatever you want."

"All right." He took a deep breath. "Sweetheart, I . . . I'm sorry. I'm having such a hard time coming to terms with the fact that I let you down so badly."

Stunned, her eyes popped open. "You didn't."

"Yeah, I did. We knew someone was stalking you. I should've tried harder to figure out who it was."

"Scott wasn't at every appearance, and I didn't even know his name."

"Still."

"Ryan, Scott knew me. He remembered me from high school." Her cheeks heated. "It was so awful. He was acting like I should've remembered him too. If I had, I think things sure would've been different."

"No, don't put the blame on yourself. When we were hunting him down, we talked a lot about how people's appearances change, especially between ages fourteen and eighteen or nineteen. It's also true that Scott went out of his way to look different, what with his scruffy face and longer hair."

"I don't know. Maybe some of the blame is mine. How could I not even remember talking to him? Was I just that self-centered?"

"Don't you do that to yourself. His fixation wasn't healthy. It wasn't normal. This isn't on you."

She heard his words. She just wished she believed them completely. Realizing that she didn't even know what had happened to Scott, she looked at Ryan warily. "Where is he now?"

"He's at the station in holding. Once he's had psychological testing, he'll be sent to the county jail or a psychiatric facility."

"So . . . he's not about to get out?"

"Sweetheart, he kidnapped you and Bethanne, has been stalking and terrorizing you for months, and assaulted you. In addition, we've figured out that he was the one who set the fire near the dumpster at Burke's and stole those cards." His gaze darkened. "We think he's been planning to kidnap you for a while. Scott Conway will not be getting released anytime soon." Picking up one of her bandaged hands, he pressed his lips to her fingers. "You're safe. It's over."

She liked that idea. She wanted it to be over.

A knock on the door interrupted them.

"I heard you were awake," a nurse in light blue scrubs said as she walked in, pulling a cart. "It's time to check your vitals."

Ryan let go of her hand. "I'll wait out in the hall."

She didn't want him to leave. She wanted to hold his hand and close her eyes again and pretend that everything was going to be just fine. But that wasn't how she was supposed to act. "Okay."

"Your young man has been worried sick about you, dear," the nurse murmured as she put a blood pressure cuff on her arm. "You are blessed to have him in your life."

Candace didn't dare correct the nurse, but the fact was that she didn't know if Ryan actually was hers. Sure, he'd been her escort and he'd been affectionate and caring, but they had never made a relationship more than friendship official.

The nurse didn't seem to need a reply as she chattered on, discussing the weather, lightning bugs, her beagle, and a sale at the market. All the while, she checked Candace's pulse, temperature, and IV site and bag. When she paused for a breath, she was looking carefully at the stitches on her face. "How's your pain, dear?"

"I don't know."

She frowned. "On a scale of one to ten, with ten being the worst, what do you think?"

"I don't know. Maybe a five?"

"The doctor said to go ahead and adjust your pain medication if needed. It might make you sleepy, though."

"That's fine." No, it was better than fine. She had no desire to do anything but sleep and exist.

And try to forget what it felt like to sit in the middle of several hundred altered pictures of herself while a madman sliced open her face.

But she wasn't sure if forgetting that would ever be possible.

# 33

She was safe in his arms at last. Holding Bethanne close on the couch in her living room, Jay tried to come up with the right words to convey everything he was feeling. But how was that even possible? Too many emotions kept running through his head. Love. Relief. Fear. Anger. All of it tangled together.

Then he realized that Bethanne didn't expect him to spout any words of wisdom. All she needed was his arms around her.

He could do that.

"You still okay?" he whispered.

He, Lott, and Bethanne had arrived at the shack just as all the commotion was finished. When Chief Foster saw them, he radioed for another ambulance. In seemingly no time at all, Bethanne had been on a stretcher, and he'd been sitting by her side as the ambulance rushed toward the hospital. Lott was riding with one of the police officers. After she'd been bandaged and seen at the hospital, her parents had taken her home. But beforehand, she'd asked Jay to visit soon.

That was why he was now sipping hot tea next to her. She wore a faded gray dress, a clean kapp, and fluffy socks. She was also curled up under a blanket with her own cup of tea. At first, he'd been worried about her being chilled, but her mamm said Bethanne simply wanted to feel cozy.

Jay could understand that.

Bethanne suddenly looked at him. "Did you say something?"

"I asked if you were okay, then I realized it was kind of a dumb question. Of course you aren't." Her cousin was in the hospital, and they'd both been through a traumatic experience. Her feet were covered in bandages, and her hands and wrists had to be so sore.

Moving to rest against him, Bethanne murmured, "Why do you think I'm not?"

"You know why."

"Are you sure about that?"

Something in her voice made him pull back far enough to see her face. "What are you trying to say?"

"That I'm okay, Jay."

Her voice was softly reassuring. Humbling him. Was she actually trying to make him feel better? Running a hand down her side, he gave thanks for about the hundredth time that she was unharmed and safe. "I'm glad, Bethy. I was so worried about you."

"I know. I was too." Looking more troubled, she added, "And Candace. I thought he was going to kill her."

He shuddered at the memory. When he'd seen Candace getting loaded into the ambulance, he'd thought Scott had killed her. He reckoned Ryan had thought the same thing. The police officer looked like he was going to expire there on the spot.

"He didn't, though." Turning so she could sit up a little, he said, "Do you remember what the officers said when they found you?"

260

"Kind of."

"They said you girls were strong and brave. You two were amazing and you should be proud of yourselves."

"I'm glad we survived. I'm glad I found you too."

"You did find me and Lott. You told us where she was, Bethy. You helped save her."

"Jay. There was so much blood."

"I know. But she's going to be fine. And Scott's behind bars. You're both safe now, and you'll get through this together."

"That's what Candace and I kept telling each other. That we were going to get through it together." Releasing a ragged laugh, she added, "Once, we even promised to be in each other's wedding."

"I like that idea." Kissing her brow, he whispered, "I cannot wait to make you mine forever."

His words were dreamy. Sweet. Made sweeter by the fact the ordeal was over and she was going to be able to spend many, many days with him for the rest of her life. "I can't wait to be yours," she admitted.

A look of complete satisfaction slid into his expression. "It's settled, then. As soon as Candace is healed, we'll marry."

"Jay Byler, are we seriously planning our wedding on this living room sofa?"

"Yep."

"With my hands all bandaged up?"

"Yep." He grinned. "You know I love you." Caressing her cheek, he continued, "Bethanne, I've waited for you for years. Don't make me wait much longer."

"I won't."

He leaned back to see her expression. "Do you mean it?"

She nodded. "Jay, I've wasted so much time. I let myself descend into such a dark place after Peter died. I don't want to live in the past anymore. I don't want to wait another day to do the things that I want to do."

"It's settled then. We'll marry in a couple of weeks."

"Jay."

"I'm serious. I want to know that you'll be there every day when I get home. I want to know that you'll be the first thing I see every morning and the last thing I see every evening." He knew he was likely sounding too determined, but he didn't care. After all, not long ago, he'd thought he'd lost her forever. How would he have survived that? "Please don't be scared. I won't push you, though."

"I'm not scared."

Jay was about to say something more when both Chief Foster and her parents approached. All three of them wore looks of concern.

Chief Foster crouched down so he was at eye level with them. "Bethanne, I know you're exhausted, but I wanted to stop by to check on you before I head on home. Is there anything else I can do for you?"

"Nee. I mean, no, thank you."

"We have a counselor who specializes in trauma response therapy. Isabel is excellent. If you'd like me to have her come over, I can call her for you."

"Thank you, but I don't need more counseling."

Her parents exchanged looks. Both of their expressions looked ravaged, and there were tear marks on her mother's face.

"Maybe just to be on the safe side?" her mother asked.

Deciding it was time to get her point across, she pulled off her blanket. "Jay, I need to stand up," she said.

"Of course." He got to his feet and then grasped her arms, gently helping her to stand.

It was soon obvious to all four of them, though, that Bethanne didn't need any help standing on her own two feet. She was standing tall and straight.

"Look at me. Yes, I'm hurt and tired. I'm also rattled and worried about Candace, but I'm all right."

"You really are, aren't you?" her father said. "I guess I was worried because . . ."

"Because I wasn't okay for such a long time. But I am now. I promise."

"And you, Jay?" Chief Foster asked. "You are doing well too?"

"I'd say so." He grinned at Bethanne.

"Jay and I were just discussing our wedding."

Her mother gaped. "Your wedding?"

"Jah. Jay asked me to marry him, and I said yes. We just want a simple wedding too," she added.

"Bethanne is taking pity on me and allowing us to have a short engagement," Jay added.

"We'd like to be married as soon as Candace can attend."

Her parents exchanged glances. Her mother said, "Bethanne, I think perhaps you should consider—"

"Nee. I'm not waiting any longer than we have to. I've been putting my life on hold long enough."

"All right, then."

Chief Foster chuckled. "Bethanne, we're going to need a statement from you, but given the time and the fact that there are so many other things to attend to, I reckon tomorrow morning will be soon enough." Turning to her parents, he said, "Martha and John, I'll plan on stopping by sometime in midmorning. Say, sometime between nine and eleven?"

John inclined his head. "Of course."

"Yes, thank you, Chief Foster," Martha added. "Thank you for everything."

"You're welcome, but to tell you the truth, it's Officer

263

Mulaney and Lott and Jay Byler here who are the true heroes. They worked their tails off trying to get to you girls as quickly as they did. I'm very glad you're all right, Bethanne." He winked. "And let me be one of the first to offer my best wishes for a long life together."

"Danke," Bethanne said softly.

After shaking Jay's hand, the chief headed toward the door.

Her father exhaled. "Bethanne, I think it's time you got some rest. Your aunt Dora promised to keep us updated on Candace."

Bethanne knew that made sense, but she didn't want Candace to feel forgotten. "I'm still worried about her."

"Of course you are. We all are, but she's in good hands. The doctors and nurses will take care of her, and Dora and Wayne will look after her too."

"And I daresay Officer Ryan," her mother added in a loud whisper. "The looks he was giving her at the hospital showed how much he cares."

"I know he likes her a lot."

"It's more than that, Bethy. Trust me, it's love," Jay said.

Looking into his eyes, she felt a surge of warmth coat her insides. Yes, she was physically exhausted and emotionally wrung out. But the Lord was so good. In the midst of the hardest twenty-four hours of her life, He'd reminded her about how much she had to be thankful for. She had no doubt she and Candace would be even closer now.

She would also never take her family's love for granted again.

Just as importantly, she realized that her hardened heart had softened enough to start beating again. She'd discovered what real love felt like, and it was the love she felt for Jay. That was love. That was everything.

Reaching out a hand to him, she said, "I'm so thankful you're in my life. I'm so glad that you didn't give up on me. That you waited for me."

"Of course I waited. Giving up was never an option. My heart, you see, was never going to allow anything else." Right in front of everyone, he gently wrapped his arms around her and kissed her brow.

# 34

After spending the night in the hospital, Candace had been released the following morning. The doctors said that resting at home would be the best medicine.

She had been looking forward to being home too—though she knew she was going to miss Ryan. Except for when he went to the station to write his report and then home to take a shower, he'd stayed by her side. He'd even gotten the nurse to let him spend the night in the chair by her bed. Every time she'd tried to convince him to leave, he'd taken a look at her face, seemed to understand that she was afraid to be alone, and said he was good.

It was because of him that she got any rest at all.

She knew her parents were a little taken aback by the way he'd hovered and the way she'd leaned on him for support. Actually, they seemed to be a little unsure about their relationship, but Candace didn't let that bother her too much.

She'd kept them in the dark about just how bad Scott had been. She also hadn't been very forthcoming about how close she and Ryan had become. Candace had assumed there would be a time and place for explanations, and she knew she'd have lots of time while she recovered.

In addition, those last moments in Scott's presence had been particularly frightening. She'd realized that her time on earth was fleeting and that anything could happen. If the police hadn't arrived when they did, she didn't know what else Scott would have done. He'd seemed to be getting increasingly unhinged with each passing moment.

When she got home from the hospital, her mother had helped her draw a bath. When Candace first sank into the steaming water filled with bubbles, she'd begun crying. In the privacy of the bathroom, she allowed herself to admit just how petrified she'd been. She'd been sure she was about to die. Or, at the very least, would be covered in cuts by the time Scott finished with her. She'd had no way to save herself—and worse, she'd just about run out of hope.

Her mother had found her sitting on the floor wrapped in a towel and shaking uncontrollably. To her surprise, all her mother had done was pull out another towel, wrap it around her, and then sit on the bathroom floor with her arms around her. Eventually she'd gotten dressed and fallen asleep in her bed.

Now that another day had passed, Candace was sitting on the couch and wrapped up in her favorite blanket. She'd eaten her favorite breakfast of pancakes and was half playing on her phone and half dozing.

In her best moments, the entire experience felt like a bad dream. It was surreal that such a short amount of time could transform the entire way she viewed both herself and her family.

At her request, she'd asked that her parents keep any visitors away. They'd agreed, especially since Ryan and Chief Foster were expected to come over between one and two and ask her more questions.

When the doorbell rang, she knew she should be ready for

anything. But seeing Chief Foster and Ryan brought back everything in a flash. Her eyes filled with tears, and she began to shake. Next thing she knew, she launched herself into Ryan's arms.

He held her close. Whether he didn't care about the chief and her parents standing there or he'd simply forgotten about them, she didn't know. All that did matter to her was that he was holding her close and that some of the nerves and fears seemed to be held at bay whenever she was in his arms. "I'm so glad to see you."

He rubbed her back. "Hey," he said in the sweetest, softest voice ever. "Sweetheart, how are you doing? Still shaken up?"

"Kind of."

When he looked down to meet her eyes, she said, "I mean, yes I am."

He pressed his lips to her brow. "There's nothing wrong with that, is there, Chief?"

"Honestly, I'd be surprised if you weren't still shaken up," the chief said in a kind tone. "You've been through quite a traumatic experience, Candace."

Wearing a determined expression, her mother said, "Perhaps we should wait until tomorrow for this questioning."

"I'm sorry, but I'm afraid we can't do that, Dora," the chief said. "We need to have Candace's statement to make sure our case against Scott Conway is solid."

"I can't imagine there are any questions about what that man did to my daughter and her cousin," her father said.

Walking Candace to the couch, Ryan said, "Let's sit down."

Candace sat next to Ryan, of course, but she knew for everyone's sakes that she was going to need to pull herself together. "I'll be fine." Looking at her parents, she said, "I can do this."

"Do you want them in here while we get your statement?" the chief asked Candace.

Candace felt she could go either way. Part of her wanted to tell her story only once. If her parents were here, then she wouldn't have to go over it in detail once again. Plus, the chief's presence would probably help them from getting too emotional. If her mother dissolved into tears or her father burst out into anger, she didn't know if she could handle that.

"Mom, Dad, I'd love for you to stay . . . unless you think it's going to be too hard to hear."

Her father shook his head. "We just went through twelve-plus hours of not knowing if we'd ever see you again. We can handle the truth."

"All right then," Chief Foster said. "Candace, even though I know you already shared bits and pieces of your ordeal with Ryan and some of the other officers on the scene, I'd like you to answer each question as completely as possible."

"I understand."

"I'm also going to be recording your answers. Is that all right?"

"Yes, sir."

After getting out a small recording device, Chief Foster set it up. In addition, Ryan took out a notepad and pen.

"Ready?" he asked.

"I'm ready."

"All right. Please state your name for the record."

"Candace Evans."

"Candace, tell us what happened from the very beginning."

"I was at the Hostetlers' house for my uncle's fiftieth birthday party. There were almost a hundred people there. It was crowded."

"Okay. And when did you leave?"

"It was almost eleven at night. I was tired, and Bethanne felt the same way. When I told her I was going to go, she offered to walk me. I suggested she just go half the way to my car."

"Why only halfway?"

"It sounds foolish now, but I thought that was good enough. I also didn't want her to have to walk the entire way home in the dark."

"You were worried that something could happen?"

"No. I mean, not really. Nothing any different than most women feel when they're walking alone at night. You know, you don't want to do something stupid." Feeling like that was exactly what she had done, she felt her bottom lip tremble.

Ryan reached for her hand, squeezed slightly in support, and let go, then resumed writing on the notepad.

"So the two of you were walking. Did you notice anything unusual?"

"I didn't. But it wasn't my street. I guess I would say the whole evening was unusual. It's not like the Hostetlers throw big parties all the time."

"Understood."

Knowing she needed to continue, Candace wracked her brain. "Everything feels like a blur now, but I remember hearing noises in the woods. I figured it was an animal or something." She gulped. "And then he was there."

"Scott."

"Yes, but I didn't know his name then. I just"—she started breathing harder as she forced herself to relive the moment— "I was in shock. One second I was thinking about driving home and the next Scott was there and he was dragging us into the woods."

When she started having a difficult time catching her breath, Chief Foster said that he was stopping the tape.

Ryan pulled her into his arms. "I've got you," he whispered. "You are safe, understand?"

She was still struggling for air. Ryan held her close and rubbed her back. "Come on, Candace. Listen to me," he whispered. "Big, deep breaths. Slow."

Little by little, she was able to do what he asked. Eventually, she calmed down. She felt so weak and tired. All she wanted to do was roll into a ball.

"My daughter's exhausted. We need to stop for now," her father said.

"I agree," Chief Foster said. "Ryan, come out to the hall when you're ready."

"Yes, sir." When Candace turned to him, practically biting her lip so she wouldn't beg him to stay, he reached for her hand again.

"I'm not going anywhere just yet, you brave, brave girl. Chief Foster is just going to have to wait."

"You sure?"

"Positive. Close your eyes and try to relax." Kissing her brow, he whispered. "You need your sleep."

His calm reassurances rang in her ears as she fell into an exhausted slumber once again.

# 35

Two weeks had passed since Ryan first visited Candace. A lot had happened since then. Bethanne and Jay Byler were now engaged to be married; Scott Conway had been formally charged with kidnapping, attempted murder, and a host of other charges; and Ryan had been given a commendation for his work during the investigation. The chief had pulled him aside on more than one occasion to say that he was glad Ryan was there.

Ryan couldn't lie to himself. To have so many positive things happen after leaving Connecticut in embarrassment felt good. He'd taken getting passed on for promotion hard. He'd taken the breakup with Chloe harder.

Now, he felt like maybe he was getting to be a good cop. In addition, his brothers and sisters were pleased for him, and his father had almost burst into tears when Ryan had told him about Candace's and Bethanne's rescue.

And now it looked like he'd soon be hired on a full-time, permanent basis, and given a nice raise. Life was good. He was thankful for it all too.

But the only thing that was going to make him happy was Candace. So far, every time he'd visited her, she'd seemed pleased to see him but withdrawn. She wasn't the same. Not even close. It was like all the spark had vanished from her personality. He supposed it was understandable—given the trauma she'd been through—but he didn't know how to help her.

Especially since the last thing he wanted to do was be stalker-like.

But as he approached her house again, he knew that his heart was involved. He was in so deep, he knew that he would never be able to recover if she broke things off with him.

Dora opened the door before he'd even had time to knock.

"Good evening, Ryan," she said, as welcoming as ever. Her faded blond hair was in a short ponytail, and her jeans and cotton sweater were fashionable and looked comfortable too. Every time he looked at Candace's mother, he had an idea of what Candace would look like one day. Imagining her in a pair of jeans while she greeted one of their children's friends always made him smile.

"Dora," he said as he gave her a gentle hug. "How are you?"

"We're hanging in there." Glancing over her shoulder, she said, "She's had a bad day. Wayne and I know that she just needs time, but it's hard to watch her suffer. I'm glad you're here."

"I am too." The evening had been a little crisp. He'd worn a thick barn jacket. Pulling it off, he said, "Where is she?"

"In her father's office." She pointed down the hall. "Last door on the right."

Every other time he'd visited, he'd sat with her in the kitchen or in their family room. "Is there a reason she's in there?"

"There's a pair of chairs, a fireplace, and a TV in the back of the room. Sometimes she likes to go in there and nap."

"Maybe I should come back another time?" The last thing he wanted to do was wake her up from a much-needed nap.

"Oh no. Candace knows you're coming." Her bottom lip trembled. "I think she wants to talk to you about something."

"Yes, ma'am." After handing Dora his coat, he walked down the hall. He wondered if Candace was getting ready to break things off with him.

When he got to Wayne's office, he saw that the door wasn't all the way closed. Candace was curled up on one of the chairs just the way her mother had described. The television was on, a fire was in the fireplace, and a candle was burning. She looked a little drowsy but definitely awake. "Knock, knock," he said.

Immediately, she shifted. "Hi. Come on in."

"When your mother told me where you were, I was surprised. I didn't even realize this room was here."

"It's one of my favorite spots in the house. It's private, you know?"

He nodded as he took a seat in the other chair. "So, what are we watching?"

"Hmm?" She looked at the TV like she'd forgotten it was even on. "Oh. Nothing." Picking up the remote, she clicked it off. "So, how was your day?"

"Fine."

"Get any bad guys?"

He chuckled. "I'm afraid my only claim to fame today was stopping five speeders."

"At least you're keeping the streets of Marion safe."

"At least." Leaning forward, he winked. "I told Chief Foster that I'm looking forward to escorting Miss Crittenden County around again. She makes me feel useful."

Her hazel eyes widened before they shuttered. "Oh. I . . .

I've been thinking about giving up my crown. Lacy was the runner-up. She'd do a good job."

Boy, he hated to hear that. He'd loved watching her with all the little girls. Interacting with them made her happy. Getting out and about again would be a good thing for her too.

But he sure didn't want to push too hard. Keeping his voice light, he murmured, "Any reason why you don't want to continue?"

"Nothing specific." She darted a glance his way before looking down at her clenched hands. "It just doesn't feel the same."

"I'm sure the folks at the chamber will understand if you want to wait a little longer to resume your appearances."

"Yeah, they said that."

"You talked to them?"

"Well, someone from the chamber called. My mom talked to them."

"I see." Still choosing his words with care, he added, "If the chamber is good with you waiting, maybe you should consider that. Everywhere we went, people were happy to see you. You were good at being Miss Crittenden County."

"It didn't mean anything."

"It meant something to the community members you visited. It meant something to all the little girls you met."

Hurt shone in her eyes before she looked away. "Ryan, I . . . sometimes when I sleep, all I do is dream about being in that shack."

"I know. That's why you need to talk to Isabel. She's a good therapist, Candace."

"I've talked to her some. She said to give myself time." Meeting his gaze again, Candace flushed. "I might need lots of time."

Hating that he couldn't have her in his arms and hold her

protectively, he tried to give her what she needed in words. "You're right. I shouldn't have pushed. If you don't want to do appearances, you don't have to."

"I was thinking about us too."

"Okay . . ."

"Ryan, maybe I should give you a break too."

He knew if she pulled away, he might never get her back. That wasn't an option. Not without a fight, at least. "No."

Obviously shocked, she gasped. "What?"

Needing to be closer to her, he knelt in front of her chair. "Candace Evans, you are a pretty amazing woman. You are brave and determined and you love hard. I love how much you love your cousin. I love how you smiled at all those little girls who wanted to touch your dresses and your sash and your crown. I love how you have goals and could practically live on vanilla ice cream. I think you're just about the prettiest thing I've ever seen in my life. But most of all, I love that you're my girl. I need you, Candace. Don't leave me."

Her bottom lip trembled. "But I'm not the same, Ryan. I don't know if I'll ever be the same Candace you first met."

"Then be different. I'll love the new Candace too."

His words startled a laugh. "You can't mean that."

"I mean every word. I want you forever, Candace . . . if you think you can one day love me too."

"I do. I love you too. But—"

No. He was not going to let her put up another obstacle. Not after everything she'd been through. *They'd* been through. Pulling her close, he said, "Then, still be mine."

"Do you really think love is that easy?"

"With you, yes." Brushing his lips along her cheekbone, against her temple, he said, "Do you want to hear my dream?" When she nodded, he whispered, "One day you and I are going to be older. We're going to have a bunch of kids and a bunch of grandkids, and we're going to be sitting in a room like this on Monday nights, watching TV." He leaned forward and kissed her lightly on the lips before leaning back again. "And then, at the end of the night, when we're both yawning and tired, we're going to walk to our bedroom."

Her eyes lit up. "And then?"

"And then, on one of those evenings, you're going to stop in the middle of the hallway. You're going to look up at me with those beautiful eyes of yours that I love so much and ask if I remember this moment." He lowered his voice as he got down on one knee. "You're going to ask if I remember kneeling in front of you just like this. If I remember baring my heart and begging you to give us a chance."

Her eyes luminous, Candace whispered, "And what will you say?"

"That of course I remember. I'm going to tell you that I remember every detail of this room, every word, every feeling. I'm going to tell you that I haven't forgotten a single thing."

Candace's lips parted. She seemed to catch her breath. And then she said the one thing he needed to hear.

"Good."

Turn the page for a *sneak peek* at

**SHELLEY
SHEPARD GRAY'S**

next Amish suspense, *Unshaken*

She had twenty minutes. Twenty minutes to get off the bus, locate her bag, and navigate her way through the throng of people until she found the escalator. Twenty minutes to then step onto the thing without breaking her neck and go to the parking lot outside. Twenty minutes to drag her bag outside, pull out her cell phone and call Hardy, the man who was supposedly going to drive her to Crittenden County. Take her to her new home in the center of Marion, Kentucky.

Bev, the counselor at the clinic she'd visited in Cincinnati, had made navigating so many things sound easy. Nee, she'd called it a piece of cake.

Stephanie was pretty sure it was going to be anything but that. She liked cake. She liked it a lot. Never had she had to go through so many obstacles to have that first bite.

Instead, she was pretty sure that anything that could go wrong was going to. There were too many variables involved to mess up each step. Especially given that every bit of it was out of her comfort zone. Something so hard could never be easy.

She'd learned the hard way that nothing ever was.

"Miss? Are you getting up or heading down to Nashville?"

"Hmm?" She looked to her right. Realized the quiet woman she'd been sitting beside during the bus ride was waiting on her to move. The tightening of the woman's jaw practically screamed that she was seconds away from losing patience.

"Sorry," Stephanie mumbled as she grabbed her purse and got to her feet. Aware that the clock was ticking, she scooted out to the bus's aisle and stepped forward.

"Wait!"

Fear prickling at the base of her neck, she turned.

"Don't you need this?"

Her brother's old backpack hung from the woman's hand.

"Danke," she whispered as she quickly grabbed it. Right as she realized that she'd forgotten to speak English.

When the woman frowned, no doubt trying to connect the woman dressed in jeans and a ponytail with Pennsylvania Dutch, Stephanie felt her hands begin to shake.

She was not going to make it. She was not going to be okay.

*Gott, help me*, she silently prayed over and over as she followed the rest of the passengers down the aisle and eventually made her way down the steps of the bus. *Please help me*, she continued. *It's real obvious I'm not going to be able to do this on my own.*

Of course she heard no reply. But maybe He had been listening, because she easily found her suitcase. It also wasn't difficult to locate the escalator leading upstairs to the main exit.

Now all she had to do was follow everyone else onto the thing. Quickly.

Everything inside herself protested. She'd never been a rusher. She would do her chores well but never all that fast. She often had the highest marks on her tests in school, but she was usually the last to turn them in.

She was slow and methodical. It was like her head needed more time than most to understand things.

It was almost painful to push a lifetime of carefully tended wariness aside like it was day-old trash.

*Nee*, it *was* painful.

Biting the inside of her lip, Stephanie watched carefully as the three people directly in front of her stepped onto the moving stairs, then after adjusting her backpack's straps on her shoulders, she stepped forward. Her right hand gripped the rail while the other pulled her bag behind her. Amazingly—or maybe it really was God's grace—she didn't fall and was even able to step off the contraption without knocking into anyone.

If she ever made it to her new apartment in Marion, Stephanie decided to give herself a little cheer about that. She'd done real good on that moving staircase, especially since this was only the second time in her life that she'd been on one.

Her momentary burst of happiness fled as she spied the electronic screen on the wall. She had less than ten minutes to follow the last of Bev's directions.

She needed to get to the exit, stand on the sidewalk, pull out her cell phone, and call Hardy. At least Bev had already programed the number in her phone. All she had to do was push the button. She'd practiced that at the clinic too.

Swallowing hard, she ran a hand along the seam of her new jeans. The soft fabric gave her courage to ignore the continuous stream of doubts running through her head and to walk through the automatic sliding glass doors.

Immediately, she was pulled into chaos. Cars lined the street. Other vehicles honked impatiently. Travelers dragged suitcases much like hers while staring at their phones. Children darted among anyone stopped for too long. A pair of homeless men were sitting against the terminal's concrete wall holding signs. When she paused to read one, someone knocked into her back. She stumbled.

At least another two minutes had passed.

Her breath caught as she scanned the area, looking for a

safe place to stand and place her phone call. Bev had told her that Hardy was honest and kind but punctual. He wasn't going to wait too long if she dallied.

Stephanie hadn't had the nerve to ask why.

Was this Hardy man really so busy that he didn't believe in giving anyone the benefit of extra time? Even someone who was completely out of her element?

Maybe he was or maybe he wasn't. It didn't matter.

After carefully moving to a recently vacated spot next to the curb, Stephanie pulled her phone out of her purse, tapped the name on the screen, and held it up to her ear. Just like she'd practiced. It rang once.

"Stephanie, you ready?"

"Jah. I mean, yes." Hating that she'd once again forgot herself, the taste of blood hit her tongue. She'd bitten her lip. "Sorry. I mean, is this Hardy?"

"Nobody else going to answer my phone, sugar. So, you ready?"

"Yes. I'm standing outside. I mean, I'm standing near the curb and some sliding glass doors." Remembering what Bev had said, she added, "I have on a pair of blue jeans, a long-sleeved white T-shirt, and black tennis shoes. Oh, and I have long blond hair."

"I see you. I couldn't miss you if I tried. I'll be right there. I'm driving a black pickup truck and have on a black baseball cap."

He was here. She'd done it. "Okay," she said before she realized he'd already disconnected.

Quickly stuffing her phone in the back pocket of her jeans, she took a deep breath. Noticed the sky was cloudy and the air was thick with humidity. A storm was coming. A fierce one, she reckoned.

She wondered if she knew that because she'd grown up on a farm or if people in all walks of life thought such things.

All thought of rain and humidity fled as the biggest black truck she'd ever seen in her life pulled up and a man who looked like he could easily wrestle a bull and come out the winner hopped out and strode toward her.

When he held out his hand, she froze.

"I'm Hardy and you're okay," he said in a low drawl. "Come on now. Don't shut down. Not yet."

Not yet.

Impatience flared in his eyes before he tamped it down. "Hand me your suitcase."

She didn't want to touch him. Didn't want to trust him. Saliva was forming in the back of her throat. She was going to either throw up, choke, or pass out.

Somehow, he managed to pull the bag from her grip. "Breathe, sugar, and get in." He pointed to a silver step on the side of his vehicle. "That's a running board. Use it to get yourself up. But do it now, okay?"

At last, she inhaled. "Okay," she whispered.

He didn't hear her. He was securing her suitcase in the back of his truck.

After opening up the passenger door, she grasped the seat with one hand and a little gray bar with the other, stepped on the running board, and pulled herself in. Then, of course, she had to slide off the backpack from her shoulders.

"Put it back there and close your door," Hardy said as he closed his. "We've got to go."

There was the reminder about time again. Forcing herself to stop thinking so much, she followed his directions. The backpack was now sitting on the floor behind her seat and the passenger door was closed. She'd done it.

"Seat belt. Come on now, pull it out and strap yourself in."

She'd forgotten! Pulling on the black belt, she fastened the buckle just as he pulled out of the parking lot.

Hardy didn't say a word as he switched lanes, switched again, and then turned left at a light.

She gripped the sides of her leather seat as he turned, picked up speed, and then merged with traffic on the highway. Only then did she realize she was sitting on her phone. After darting a glance at Hardy and debating a couple of minutes, Stephanie shifted, pulled the phone out of her pocket, and held it on her lap.

He glanced her way. "Don't call anyone. Not yet."

"I won't." Swallowing again, she added, "I mean, I'm going to put it in my purse."

"Why haven't you?"

Because she didn't know how to act. Because she'd never had a phone before. Because she was used to always being told what to do. Because no matter how much Bev had told her that Hardy was a man she could trust, Stephanie didn't completely believe it.

But none of that sounded like a good excuse. It wasn't any of his business, anyway.

"I don't know," she said at last.

"Put it away if you want," he said in a gentler tone. "We've got a little bit of a drive ahead of us."

She bent down, unzipped her purse, and slipped the cell phone inside. Just as she was about to zip it back up, she spied the light blue slip of paper the policeman had given her before he'd left the examining room. It had his name and phone number on it. He'd handed it to her just as the nurse practitioner had finished cleaning and sewing up her wound.

The policeman had seemed to think she might need to contact him again, on account that a stray bullet had hit her arm and all.

Hating to remember the way she'd been shaking, she quickly pulled the zipper back up and sat up again.

Hardy glanced her way. "You doing all right? You look like you just saw a ghost or something."

"I'm fine. I, uh, just saw something that sparked a memory I wanted to forget."

"Hmm. You think zipping it away is going to do the trick?"

"No," she said honestly. "I don't think it's going to help me much at all."

To her surprise, he laughed, the sound deep and rough. "Yeah, I didn't think so. Hiding my bad doesn't help me much either. Lord knows I've tried."

Stephanie folded her arms across her chest. Thought about that. She figured Hardy was right. Zipping away the evidence of the crime she'd seen wasn't going to help her much at all.

No matter what she did, she was never going to forget that she used to be Amish, she was now on the run, and she was currently heading toward the southwest corner of Kentucky in the care of a very large man in a very large truck.

She really hoped he was as trustworthy as Bev had claimed he was.

It might have been easier if she could forget the other piece of sage advice the older woman had given her—that hoping and wishing didn't help much. Sometimes all it did was make the wait for relief seem like a whole lot longer.

# ACKNOWLEDGMENTS

Even though writing is a rather solitary career, I'm blessed to have a great many people who enrich both my life and my books in a variety of ways. First and foremost, I'm indebted to the team at Revell for their tireless efforts to make my stories shine. I'm grateful for the talents and patience of my editors Andrea Doering and Kristin Kornoelje. I don't think there's ever been a timeline that I couldn't mess up! I'm grateful that readers won't have to worry about that—or many of the other fumbles and foibles that seem to happen in all of my manuscripts.

Working hand in hand with these fine editors are Brianne Dekker and Karen Steele. These ladies go above and beyond to promote my books and get them into readers' hands. I continue to be amazed by their gifts and creativity.

Closer to home, I'm grateful for Lynne Stroup for always reading my second drafts—sometimes a chapter at a time. To Jean Volk, for working with my Facebook group and organizing street teams. Also to my lovely, very kind Amish friend who never fails to give me advice.

In addition, I'm so blessed to have been championed by

the Seymour Literary Agency for over twenty years. Nicole Resciniti works miracles, and Lesley Sabga inspires me every day. Each works so hard for their authors. I'm indebted to them for their tireless support.

As always, I'm grateful for my husband, Tom, who very kindly treats my characters like I do—like our new next-door neighbors. I can't imagine any other person on earth who would patiently listen to me talk so much about made-up people. It's just one of the many reasons he's the best guy I know.

Finally, I'm so grateful for the glory of God, who guided me to write "chapter 1" during a lunch break at work almost thirty years ago. I owe Him everything.

**SHELLEY SHEPARD GRAY** is the *New York Times* and *USA Today* bestselling author of more than 100 books, including *Unforgiven* and the A Season in Pinecraft series. Two-time winner of the HOLT Medallion and a Carol Award finalist, Gray lives in Ohio, where she writes full-time, bakes too much, and can often be found walking her dogs on her town's bike trail. Learn more at ShelleyShepardGray.com.

# THEY'RE EACH OTHER'S BEST HOPE FOR REDEMPTION—AND LOVE

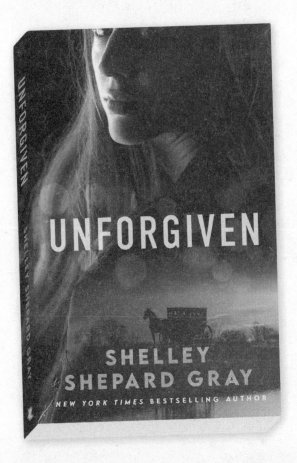

Ex-con Seth Zimmerman has spent the last three years making amends by helping the vulnerable in his former Amish community. This mission includes calling on Tabitha Yoder, whose divorce from her abusive husband has isolated her from the community. An uneasy friendship is just starting to take hold between them when Tabitha finds she may be in danger once again—and Seth might be her only hope at maintaining her hard-won freedom.

# TRAVEL TO PINECRAFT FOR FRIENDSHIP AND NEW BEGINNINGS WITH SHELLEY SHEPARD GRAY

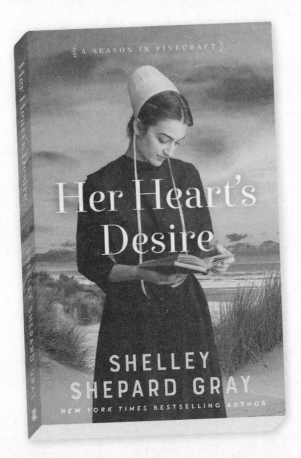

"*Her Heart's Desire* is a tender journey that explores friendship, heartbreak, second chances, forgiveness, and finding true love. Shelley Shepard Gray highlights that God's grace and mercy are with us even when we're certain we're alone and don't fit in with our community."

—**AMY CLIPSTON**, bestselling author of *Building a Future*

Find more sweet romance in the rest of the
# A SEASON IN
# PINECRAFT SERIES

# Meet Shelley